NOT QUITE SUPER

**FORMERLY
MEMORY FOAM**

By: RICHARD GRIFFITH

Inspired by: Fleur Lind
(Author of: NO TIME FOR RULES)

For Kelly, Kara, and Matt

TJ, Joey, Melinda

Chris, RJ, Ashley, and Eric

"Dreams are worth attempting"

Self-Published

This book is the work of fiction. Any use of real places, organizations, or departments is done in a wholly fictitious manner and should not be taken literally.

All characters written herein are the works of fiction and completely imaginary. Any resemblance to any persons living or dead is purely coincidental.

Copyright 2018 Richard Griffith

All rights reserved. Except as permitted under the U.S. Copyright Act of 1976, no part of this publication may be reproduced, distributed, or transmitted in any form or by any means, or stored in a database or retrieval system, without the prior written permission of the author/publisher.

Richard Griffith 1968-

NOT QUITE SUPER/Richard Griffith 1st Edition.

COVER ILLUSTRATION BY: RICHARD GRIFFITH

COVER PHOTOGRAPHY BY: RICHARD GRIFFITH

COVER MODEL: **RICHARD GRIFFITH**

Other Titles by this author:

Lady Excalibur, Beginnings

Lady Excalibur, Bane of Wolves

Lady Excalibur, Wind of Witches

Lady Excalibur, Mist of Dragons

Lady Excalibur, Mission of Magic

Levi Garret/Space Detective, Engines of Deception

Levi Garret/Space Detective, Stage of Desire

Levi Garret/Space Detective, Ruffled Wing Feathers

Levi Garret/Space Detective, Euphoria Epiphany

Levi Garret/Space Detective, Artificial Vengeance

Levi Garret/Space Detective, Wings for Clipping

Staker, Monster Enthusiast

Janitor 51

Janitor 52

Mirror of Spies

The Ten Millennium Millennial

The Marshal of Samurai Moon

Mix and Match Murder

Pieces of Murder

Not Quite Super

Co-Author: The Terran Conservatory

MEMORY FOAM

CHAPTER 1

For eons, the duo of Blikzak and Raknid had watched humans. They had been in their disguised base, the moon, for longer than either of them cared to remember. Studying the primitive primates of Earth was their mission and they had been doing it since before the last ice age turned a pretty blue planet into a mostly white sphere. It was, in a word, boring.

The only bright spots the two had were the monthly supply runs to pick up necessities, and the occasional instructions to go down to Earth and collect a lifeform or two to study. There were tests that would reveal how far the primitive apes had come and gauge how much of a threat they were to the rest of the universe.

Blikzak and Raknid scarcely saw the point, as it was obvious that humankind would blow themselves up long before they were a threat to anyone else. Still, the two 'Roswell Greys' did their duty, obeyed their orders, and watched the humans.

When the mission started, there were a lot more of them, hundreds of personnel in fact. That was before budget cuts, reassignments without replacement, and the fact that nobody really cared about humans that much anymore, took their toll. Now it was just the two of them. Alone on the massive space station, covered in camouflaging dust, posing as the Earth's moon.

There had been a real moon, once upon a time, sitting where the space station was now. But the comet that had taken out the dinosaurs had slammed into it, splitting it in two before continuing on and careening into Earth. Most of the debris that was left over, spread out around the Earth and formed a beautiful ring that lasted for millions of years. Later, it was that ring that was harvested to build the space station that they now lived in. It produced an evolutionary anomaly for the Earth, as the history of the planet's oceans was to have tides for millions of years, then no tides for millions of years, then tides again as the space station was completed. It was a unique altering of the planetary ecosystem, and the main reason the place warranted study. The aliens in charge of protecting this sector of the galaxy, wanted to see if the introduction of the ocean's tidal forces, would have an effect on the development of humankind.

To the two lone beings doing the observing, the assignment was stupid. There was simply no way to know how mankind would have proceeded without the tides, so what good could come of studying them with the tides? Still, it kept them employed and as long as paychecks and rations kept flowing, they would do their jobs.

"I'm bored." Blikzak groaned for the millionth time this month. "This watching Earth stuff is really getting old."

Raknid spun in his overly comfortable chair to look at his comrade as he walked into the command and control center. He sympathized with his friend.

"We got in some new vids in our last supply shipment." Raknid pointed out. "Why don't you see if there is anything worth watching?"

"There never is. Besides, I'd rather watch that Earth movie again." Blikzak plopped down in one of the several chairs at a vacant console. "You know that one with the magic kid and his friends? I really like those films. So creative."

For some reason Blikzak had really taken to stories of magic and superheroes. It was things like that, science couldn't explain. Even though the math, physics and science that mankind studied was primitive and creatively incorrect. The level of imagination humans displayed was something that the Earth people had that no one else did. The imagination of humans when it came to stories, especially stories about magic and superheroes, was incredible. No other race in the universe wasted so much time on make-believe as these humans did.

That was not to say that other species didn't have high levels of creativity. But other races seemed to focus on science, math and physics. Whereas humans spent their creative juices on made up things.

"Hey." Blikzak called out from his station as he read through the changes in operating procedures that never seemed to change. "We've been authorized to conduct a social experiment."

"What kind?" Raknid inquired as he turned to his own messaging board.

"It doesn't say." Blikzak scowled at the screen in front of him. "It just authorizes us to conduct the experiment and says for us to use our discretion."

"That could get interesting." Raknid was now reading the same orders and thoughtfully trying to put them to good use.

"What kind of experiment should we run?"

"Well," Raknid rubbed his almost non-existent chin in thought. "We've done global warming, earthquakes, nuclear meltdowns and a significant number of flybys in the past. Do you want to do one of those?"

"Not really." The enthusiasm of the past few seconds quickly deflated out of Blikzak. "We've done all those. How about we do something new?"

"Like what?" Raknid challenged.

"I don't know, but I'm sure something will come to me."

Later the dynamic duo were immersed in watching another one of Raknid's favorite movies from Earth. They had run the movie through their intuitive computer programs and used it to create a three-dimensional and fully immersive product, now it was as though they were part of the movie instead of just watching it.

"I've got it." Raknid shouted, interrupting Blikzak's enjoyment of the viewing.

"You've got what?"

"I know what kind of social experiment to run on Earth." Raknid shut down the projection and was up and pacing now.

"I'm afraid to ask." Blikzak was already shaking his head but was interested in finding out what epiphany his coworker had stumbled upon.

"We make a suit that gives the user super-powers." He replied, a little over enthusiastically. "We then monitor him and study how it changes society."

Blikzak didn't want to sound too enthusiastic of this plan, in fact he had already come up with a million reasons as to why this was a bad idea. The problem was, that he was just as bored as his cohort. Besides, if they messed up and caused all kinds of problems, it wasn't their planet.

"I suppose we do have all that micro-circuitry gear down in storage." Blikzak was thinking now. Giving serious consideration to Raknid's proposal. In fact, he was downright excited about it. "The human body isn't genetically modified to accept the nanite clothing we wear, but if we infused that circuitry into the memory nanite bonding material we have, we could come up with a nanite bonded suit with a host of powers to give the user. Very much like our own nanite clothing when put into industrial mode. Flight, super speed, invulnerability and super-strength would all be easy. Laser eyes and ice breath would be more problematic."

"He wouldn't be super-dude, but he would be close." Raknid was getting excited now. Something that had not happened in centuries.

"Alright, so there are some obvious problems." Blikzak was up and pacing now as well. The logical part of his mind still wanted to say no to this insane idea, but the curious side of him really wanted to see what would happen. "How do we choose a human for the experiment? Then, how do we monitor him in a way that he doesn't know that we are watching?"

"We've been studying humans long enough to know how to pick someone with a...what's the term they use...good moral compass." Raknid was already pulling files on humans to search for a candidate. "As for the monitoring, we can use the satellites the humans have for some of it, street cameras for more, but we need an independent way check on him that doesn't depend on an outside view."

"What about that memory foam download experiment?" Blikzak thoughtful now, trying to come up with a way to make this the best experiment he could muster. He didn't like things being done halfway.

"You mean when we started that pillow business in Minnesota and got people to sleep on the micro-circuitry pillows?"

"Yes." Blikzak confirmed. "We downloaded thousands of people's experiences and dreams. Some of them quite disturbing." A shudder ran through his alien body as he recalled the dreams and nightmares of millions of people that he had sat through and watched. It was stuff that made horror novels look like children's stories.

"Not exactly the brightest bit of computer wizardry there." Raknid pointed out. "I mean the system worked, but since everything we learned was being filtered through the point of view of a pillow, it wasn't the most educational. It also took time to figure out what were real experiences and what were dreams."

"I think it would still be accurate enough to fill in the blanks." Blikzak defended his idea. "Besides, the pillows got smarter as they learned, and we did get a lot of useful information."

"I can agree with that." Raknid nodded enthusiastically. Which was a gesture he had picked up from watching humans, but he liked it. "Back to our first problem; who do we choose?"

Both of them were silent and thoughtful on that point for a long time.

CHAPTER 2

Walter Scrum was not much of a man to look at. He wasn't horrible looking or anything like that. It was just that there was nothing special about him. Average height, average build, brown hair, brown eyes and a face that was…well…average. He lived in an average neighborhood in the suburbs, drove an average car, owned a cookie cutter house and kept it looking like it blended right in. He did nothing to stand out. His car had no bumper-stickers or vinyl clings, his house had no bright paint or flowers, and he only hung out his flag on holidays. His work consisted of a mid-level management position for a large company, his hobbies were unexciting things such as writing fiction books and collecting coins and stamps, and his days off were spent on typical vacations and mowing the lawn.

As for his social life, he really didn't have one. He had a few lady friends over the years and had even tried online dating once or twice, but he really wasn't looking that hard. He liked his life simple and other people tended to complicate things. Best to stick to his questionable internet search history and the occasional trips to local massage parlors. He was not a saintly man by any stretch of the imagination, but neither was he a kidnapper, murderer, or one who cheated on his taxes.

That day, like so many others before, he pulled into his garage, walked down the driveway to his mailbox, and waved to a couple of neighbors that were out. He had no idea that his simple life was about to come to a spectacular end.

It was to be his simple life's averageness that was to be its undoing. For high above, in a secret moon base, two aliens had decided that Walter Scrum was just average enough and moral enough to fit their needs.

Predictably Walter spent his time after work taking care of household chores. After that came a somewhat healthy dinner consisting of a small steak, some broccoli, and an ear of corn. Since it was a work night and six in the morning came all too quickly, there would be no heavy drinking or going out tonight. Instead it was a documentary or two on the television, catching up on the news, a little wasted time on the internet, and an evening glass of whiskey.

When the appointed hour came it would then be the usual before bed rituals and off to bed itself, to be wrapped up in its warm blankets and welcoming pillows. Little did he know that those pillows had a hidden agenda, all their own.

It wouldn't be accurate to call the pillows he was sleeping on alive, but they were aware, at least in their own right, to what was going on. They had instructions to follow and would obey orders, that was not to say that they were the sharpest chips in the game of information collection. This day, however, their job was incredibly simple. Produce the required tone to place the human into a deep sleep. It was something the pillow had done a thousand times and would do a thousand more. It seemed, at least almost, that the pillow took its job as a sleep aid very seriously and therefore was committed to giving its owner the best sleep possible. Little did anyone know that it wasn't the *magical* stuffing that enabled these pillows to give their user such a good night's sleep, but the computer micro-circuitry that did it.

When sleep did come to Walter Scrum, it was a deep and relaxing kind. The kind of sleep where a cannon could go off in your bedroom and you wouldn't move a muscle. It was exactly the kind that Blikzak and Raknid were waiting for.

Walter Scrum never saw the bright light that flashed over his bed, he didn't feel the sensation of being lifted out from his covers or the motion of traveling through space at insane speeds, and he didn't even flinch when set on the cold examination table deep within the celestial body he knew as the moon.

"Hurry." Raknid voiced unnecessarily. "We don't have unlimited time."

"Don't nag." Blikzak shot back. "I know the timetable. We are exactly four minutes ahead of schedule."

Raknid then pointed a gun-like looking instrument at the human on the table and pressed the firing stud. A light shot from the gun and enveloped the man, dissolving his clothes and leaving him naked on the table.

A fluid then flowed out from the corners of the table and began to flow over the human. It was dark, cool and not liquid at all. In fact, the 'fluid' was made up of millions of tiny, interconnected robots, known as nanites. These nanites would bond together and form a power suit that would give the wearer a myriad of superpowers.

"How long until the bonding is complete?" Blikzak inquired, as he watched the nanites encompass the human.

"Four minutes." Raknid replied. "The very four minutes we are ahead of schedule."

Both of them then watched as the human on the table suddenly began to buck and fight. He strained against the energy restraints holding him there and attempted to claw at his face.

"What is he doing?" Blikzak wondered aloud as he watched with intense interest.

"I am uncertain." Raknid replied as he checked the health readings. "He shouldn't be fighting like this. He should be out."

A look of worry, surprise and shock then covered Blikzak's face.

"Did you remember holes for his airways when you designed the suit?" Blikzak asked, hoping the answer was yes.

"So that's what I forgot." Raknid thumped his head with the palm of his hand. "Here, I'll make some adjustments."

Raknid punched commands into the pad he carried and waited to see the response. In seconds nanites around Walter's mouth and nose parted and allowed air to flow in. His struggling subsided and he relaxed, at first. The problem now was that Walter, fueled by the sensation of drowning and adrenaline, was now wide awake.

"What the hell is going on?" He shouted as he struggled against the bed restraints.

"I told you we would wake him up." Raknid sighed. "Now pay up."

"I'm not paying you." Blikzak countered. "You were the one who woke him up."

"Not on purpose."

"Hey!" Walter shouted. "Down here! What the hell is going on? Where am I?"

"You are on the moon. To be more precise you are in the moon. We monitor your species from here, have for centuries, actually eons. As for why you are here, you are being given a gift." Raknid informed him as he looked down at him.

Walter looked at the small, grey, naked alien that was looking down at him and promptly fainted. His brain simply couldn't process what it was seeing, overloaded, and shut down. One would argue that it was a perfectly human response.

"Do we wake him up again?" Blikzak asked, looking over at his boss.

"Not yet." Raknid replied. "We'll let him sleep until we have to do the preliminary tests. Then we'll rouse him and put him through the paces."

"Sounds good." Blikzak then looked around until his eyes finally settled back on his coworker. "Lunch?"

"I could eat." Raknid replied, and the two made their way down toward their dining facility. Leaving the sleeping human strapped to the table quietly snoring.

Walter awoke to a whole lot of nothingness. He had to squint in the bright, white, light of the room that seemed to come from everywhere. He was strapped to a white table in the center of said room. To add insult to injury he was naked, with no visible signs that anything had happened to him. There was the vague memory of the grey alien looking at him and the feeling of drowning, but it wasn't clear, and he wasn't sure if it had happened or not.

"Ah, sleeping beauty wakes." Blikzak called out as he and Raknid entered the room.

"What's happening to me?" Walter demanded to know. "What are you doing to me? Why am I naked?"

"Technically speaking," Raknid began. "You are not naked. You are wearing a nano-suit which mimics your body so perfectly that you appear naked."

"What?" Walter's grasp of the technical was not as smooth as it should have been. Waking up with aliens staring down at you tends to throw off one's sense of reasoning.

"You're wearing a nano-suit." Raknid repeated. "It can change in accordance to your wishes." To demonstrate, Raknid blinked and his naked body was replaced by a silvery suit. Much like the clothing aliens wore in many science fiction classics. "Just try it. Think about any article of clothing you desire."

Walter closed his eyes and concentrated. His face turning a slight bit of red from the effort.

"Nothing is happening." He finally sighed.

"Oh wait," Blikzak voiced almost embarrassed. "I forgot to turn them on. Hold on a second." He then punched a series of commands into his pad. "Try it now."

In a few seconds the nanites made his body appear as if he were wearing the same pajamas he had on when this nightmare started.

"Cool." Walter confessed. "Now who the hell are you two?" He demanded as the nano-suit faded back to a naked appearance. He didn't have the mental focus to maintain the appearance. Yet.

"I am Commander Raknid and this is First Officer Blikzak." Raknid hadn't used their formal titles in centuries. It sounded most odd to him as it rolled off his tongue. "We are of the interplanetary defense force. We are charged with finding heroes to fight for the galaxy. You have been selected."

"What kind of crap is that." Blikzak whispered in his commander's ear. "Interplanetary defense force?"

"I can't tell him it's an experiment." Raknid whispered back. "It would ruin it if he knew he was under constant observation."

"He's not going to remember any of this anyway." Blikzak reminded his friend with a whisper. "We are going to wipe his memory of most of this night."

"Oh yeah." Raknid hit his forehead with the palm of his hand, just as he had seen the humans do. "I forgot."

"You've been watching humans too long." Blikzak shook his head. "I can't believe that the council put you in charge."

"I think it had less to do with wanting me in charge than it did about wanting me as far away from the Grand Leader as possible." Raknid replied with a longing sigh.

"You mean the Grand Leader's daughter." Blikzak rolled his eyes, which was undetectable with his black, almond shaped eyes.

"Her too." Raknid agreed.

"Uh Hello," Walter then interrupted. "Naked human on the table here!"

"You're not naked." Raknid re-informed the confused and slightly agitated human a little more sternly. "You're wearing a nano-suit. Actually, to be more precise, you are bonded to a nano-suit. Much like we are." He indicated his cohort and himself.

"All we have to do is think about how we want to look and concentrate." Blikzak jumped in. "Observe."

A silvery jumpsuit then replaced his nakedness as he stood in front of the human on the table. He then made it change to green, then white, then purple with pink spots. He even threw in a little fashion twirl for emphasis.

"Try it? Just picture what you want to look like and it will appear." Blikzak suggested. "It is just one of the many super powers it possesses."

"I don't know what to do?" Walter stammered. "I've never thought of myself as the superhero type."

"Most superheroes in your Earth culture are either born special or get powers through some kind of accident." Raknid pressed. "You have been chosen for your role. Like that Green Headlamp guy."

"Lantern." Blikzak whispered to him. "It's a lantern."

"Whatever."

"You mean I could be like that spider guy?" Walter was now getting excited and was spurred on when his suit changed to be blue and red with a large spider on the front, just like his childhood hero wore.

"Hardly original, but effective." Blikzak then looked down at the human. "Uh…we might want to do something about that."

Raknid followed his cohorts gaze down toward Walter's more manly bits and pieces. It would appear that the bonding of the suit worked so well that Walter's manhood was plainly visible, as if he were wearing a thin coat of paint.

"Well that's different." Raknid mused. "I accounted for our muted bodies, ones where the sexual organs remain internal until needed, not one where reproductive organs are so…pronounced."

"The boy's got game." Blikzak observed.

"This could possibly be the reason all those comic book superheroes wore their underwear outside of their pants." Walter threw in.

"Try going invisible." Blikzak suggested. "The suit can match its surroundings and render the wearer virtually invisible."

Walter thought for a moment then closed his eyes. He concentrated on his surroundings and the white walls, white table and white ceiling above him. Both Blikzak and Raknid gasped as he faded away to nothing.

"Well that's impressive." Raknid observed. "I didn't think he would get the hang of everything so quickly."

"I guess years of indoctrination into the superhero genre has paid off."

"Too bad we didn't think of that." Raknid griped. "Still, the creativity of this species should put us in good stead."

"Just out of curiosity?" Blikzak wondered aloud. "How much are we going to show him, if we are just going to blank his memory anyway?"

"Not too much more." Raknid informed him. "I just want him to remember enough not to go out and kill someone on accident. At least not right away."

"We could leave him an instruction book." Blikzak suggested.

"Oh I'm not falling for that worn out gag." Raknid protested. "We're not giving him something that he can lose and have to laughably figure out how to do everything on his own."

"It was just an idea." Blikzak was being pouty now.

"It was a laughably unoriginal idea. I'm not recycling old television shows for you."

"Fine." Blikzak was disappointed, but he still had a job to do and would be about it. "I'll start downloading the basic information he needs to use the suit into his mind. But I'm warning you, there is no way of knowing how much of this is going to take. Not to mention we still have to blank parts of his memory. I'm not being held responsible for blanking anything important."

"Your disclaimer is noted." Raknid replied with a certain level of disgust and sarcasm.

CHAPTER 3

Walter awoke from the strangest dream he had ever had. The problem was, that he could remember none of it. He knew it was weird and involved aliens, but nothing else stood out in his mind. He made a decision right there, that he would consume no more day-old pizza before bed.

Walter fought the urge to hit the snooze and lost the battle. Instead he slammed his hand down on his alarm clock and crushed it into a million pieces. The problem was, he didn't even notice.

Unfortunately for Walter it was only Friday and his work beckoned. If it were Saturday it would not be a problem as he happened to have weekends off. His job was the typical nine-to-five workday, five days a week. When he finally did rouse from his bed and make the decision to get up he was going to be late. Lucky for him there was not anything at his work today that was incredibly pressing.

Drowsy and droopy-eyed, he stumbled past the ruin of his alarm-clock without noticing its destruction. He then proceeded to the bathroom for his normal morning rituals. Using the toilet seemed straightforward enough and went without incident. The same could not be said of brushing his teeth. Upon grabbing the tube and squeezing it in the middle, Walter proceeded to empty the entire contents of the container, splattering it spectacularly against the bathroom mirror.

Dumbfounded, Walter simply stood there, staring at the mirror and wondering what had just happened. He then shook his head, dismissing it as a fluke, and proceeded to begin cleaning up the mess.

The rest of his day would only get stranger.

****

Memory foam informational download, day one:

First item of the day. Human experienced a sonic attack from the time keeping device on the nightstand. Attack was quickly foiled and offending time keeping device was destroyed. It is quite possible that this outcome was unintentional. Human appeared to be in much distress over the condition of his time keeping device upon retiring to recharge.

Second item of interest: Although this unit is unsure what transpired between the human and the mouth soap contained in its tube, the human must have decided it was a threat. Upon judging the mouth soap to be hostile, the subject crushed the tube and expelled the offending soap. Although this caused considerable time to be expended in cleaning, the offending agent was defeated easily.

Third item of interest: Upon returning to his domicile after completing his occupational duties, the subject seemed to express interest in an activity known as camping. This unit believes that this is a necessary retreat required to destress after fighting evil. Much like a fortress of seclusion. To prepare for this activity, the subject engaged in an activity known as chopping wood. First few logs were split easily with a single swing. This seemed to please the subject, until his tool's handle was rendered inoperable due to catastrophic failure. Subject's enhanced strength caused the handle of the ax to break on the third swing.

Once the tool was rendered unusable, the subject decided to attempt to chop the logs in half with his bare hand in a blade hand strike. It is this unit's opinion that this was done in jest, as the subject was exhibiting laughter at the time of the attempt. Nevertheless, the subject succeeded in cutting several logs in half with his bare hands. No damage was sustained by the subject.

Fourth item of interest: Subject was invited to participate in an activity known as bowling. It would appear that the subject believed that the pin setting machine was a threat, as he destroyed it with his first throw. He was then forced to leave the bowling alley and return home. No other items of interest occurred before downtime.

****

Blikzak and Raknid poured over the report from the micro circuitry pillow and looked at each other with a combination of shock, surprise and disbelief.

"It would appear that the memory wipe removed all information about the suit." Raknid gave his coworker a dubious look. "Almost as if you had planned it that way."

"Hey, I warned you that this very thing might happen." Blikzak protested, his hands up and shoulders shrugged in defense.

"Yes you did." Raknid agreed, still doubting his friend's sincerity. "And since I have absolutely no way to prove you did this on purpose, I guess I'll just have to believe you."

Raknid then tossed his electronic reader on his console and put his feet up. It was something he had learned from humans. It was amazing that such a primitive species should stumble upon the most comfortable sitting position ever invented. Now if he could just get his hands on one of their recliners. It wasn't as if he didn't have tons of room for a couple of them.

"So what do you want to do now?" Blikzak inquired.

"I don't believe we have much of a choice." Raknid sighed. "I think we are just going to continue on with the experiment and hope that nobody gets too badly hurt."

"This should be interesting."

CHAPTER 4

Walter Scrum woke up on Saturday morning still thinking about the events of the past day. He also considered the vague, dream-like memories, he was experiencing. Ordinarily he would dismiss such fanciful dreams as an overactive imagination, but now with the evidence of the previous day staring him in the face, he was forced to lend credence to his dreams.

"They said, think about what you want to look like." Walter mumbled to himself as he looked down at his nearly middle-aged body. He then concentrated on what he believed a superhero should look like.

His body seemed to ripple and change colors. He was having a difficult time keeping it looking like one thing. Too many images of different heroes were flashing though his mind and his nano-suit was struggling to keep up. Despite his success on the moon base, it was not coming as easy now. Before his mind was preoccupied with everything else that was going on around him, and now he was overthinking the process. What was especially disturbing to him was when he stumbled upon the invisibility feature and watched the lower half of his body disappear.

For a moment he was going to yell out when his legs disappeared, but fortunately logic prevailed. He was then able to reason that since he still felt his legs, that they were still there. This calmed him considerably.

"Ok Walter," He huffed to himself. "You've got this, just think it through."

It took several hours of practice, but eventually he was able to produce a black covering with a hood and mask that covered him completely. Unfortunately, the problem of his nano-suit wearing like a coat of paint returned.

"Well ain't that a fine mess." He chuckled as he looked down at himself. "I'll save the day, only to get arrested for indecent exposure."

Over the next several hours Walter practiced with his nano-suit and finally got his desired design to come on immediately on command.

The next day consisted of much of the same. Practicing his appearance seemed to take up an inordinate amount of time. This was understandable, as Walter wasn't aware of the fact that the suit still worked, even when he couldn't see it. He mistakenly believed that it had to be visible in order for it to function. This was a cause of great concern for the new superhero.

Walter then decided to call in sick to work the next day and spend the day doing research and practicing with his newfound powers. He wasn't even sure what they all were yet.

****

Memory foam informational download: Day four.

Items of interest: Subject spent day practicing and learning how to use the powers granted by the nano-suit. Research into activating abilities seems to involve watching recordings of every superhero entertainment video ever produced. Indications are that this type of research will continue for several days.

This unit does not comprehend why superheroes use a deep throaty voice that is difficult to understand. Requesting clarifying information from programmers on this subject.

Item of interest: Subject has discovered super strength, x-ray vision, and has experimented with heat vision. Since these abilities are granted only when the nano-suit is in masking configuration success has been limited. Subject has not yet attempted to experiment with flight.

****

"I thought we agreed not to give him the optic powers?" Raknid glanced over to his companion as they both sat at their consoles.

"No," Blikzak defended. "We only agreed it would be difficult. I believe the word you used was problematic. I found a work around by equipping the nano-suit with a mask that would cover the eyes of the user, thus giving him powers he could use through the lenses."

"Ah yes." Raknid nodded as he went back to reviewing the data. "I recall the conversation more clearly now. You are correct. We never specifically agreed not to do the optic powers."

"I can't wait to see how he does experimenting with flight." Blikzak was both excited and apprehensive. If it worked out the way he believed it would, it would be highly entertaining. But if it caused too much damage, they would not be allowed to conduct this kind of social experiment ever again. Something he was looking forward to. "Do you think we should introduce a supervillain?"

"Let's see how this goes first." Raknid sighed. "We are not even sure if this power is going to corrupt him. And even if it doesn't and he chooses to use his powers only for good, he's outnumbered by the criminal element by a million to one. Not to mention that it seems once a hero rises a villain usually follows suit. At least that has been our experience from watching all those superhero vids."

"You're right, you're right." Blikzak agreed. "I guess after all these years of watching the same old cycles of activity, I'm eager to see something new."

"Humans do tend to go in circles." Raknid shook his head.

Over the millenniums that they had watched humans they witnessed the progression of the species from stone tools to the modern age and had each come to the same conclusion, mankind's problems were the same today as yesterday and probably forever.

Teenagers had always been rebellious, marriages had always had the same arguments, and governments had always tried to rule their populace in the exact same ways. If one were to even take a moment to look at the graffiti written on the walls of ancient Roman bath houses, they would see that mankind's mental attitude hadn't changed that much in thousands of years. What had changed was the ability to let everyone know about the problems, faster and with reckless abandon. Information systems and social media had simply allowed information to spread farther and faster, making modern man feel bombarded by problems that were sometimes not even real. The new term for it was 'fake news' when in fact that kind of deceit had existed since one person could talk to another.

History was replete with travelers spreading gossip, bards making up tales to get free meals and knights going around with huge bones and skulls that had been dug up, regaling young maidens with tales of their bravery in slaying a huge beast in order to score points or earn political favor. In short, people in ancient times were just as unsure what to believe as the modern man was watching the news or reading a meme.

Still there was a lot of truth out there, if one could sort through it all. Wars were still being fought for the same reasons, people still died from disease and famine, and some sought to do good noble work while others were self-serving and selfish. In short, mankind had not changed in attitude or personality, they simply changed in abundance.

The cyclic nature of human beings was one of the things that they sought to disrupt. If only in a small way. Introducing a super-human into their mix, might just shake up the status quo. Then again, it was always possible that human nature would prevail, and someone would find a way to exploit Walter, or he could become corrupted by his power and swing toward darker goals all on his own.

There were a lot of unknowns in this little venture, but that was part of the point.

"Well I guess we'll just have to see where this goes." Raknid finally sighed as he shook himself out of his musings.

"I'll get the popcorn!" Blikzak agreed heartily.

"If you make one more run to Earth for popcorn…" Raknid didn't finish the threat. There was, after all, not much he could do to his cohort.

"I still have some left." Blikzak defended, holding his hands palm up in defense. "I keep my jaunts to Earth down to the regular schedule."

"Oh you think I don't know about all the times you've snuck down there to conventions or on Halloween?"

"I was hoping you didn't." Blikzak confessed.

CHAPTER 5

Memory foam download, day four: Subject once again was deceitful to his employer in regard to his health status. Instead of going to his place of employment, subject once again spent most of his time watching superhero videos. Time was taken to practice his abilities and work through the minor difficulty of covering his reproductive parts when in a superhero configuration. This problem has been temporarily alleviated by changing to a type of undergarments known as boxer briefs. As these come tight fitting and in a variety of colors, subject will be able to maintain discretion in several different color schemes. What the subject will do when activating invisibility mode is unknown.

Item of interest: Subject spent several hours online attempting to pursue information on copyright law and trademarks. The purpose of this query is unknown, however each search concluded with the removal of a fanciful title from a notebook. Notebook paper was then crushed with ease and disposed of.

****

"Every good name is taken." Walter mumbled to himself as he readied himself for work that morning. "How am I going to be a great hero, without a great name?"

This time he carefully squeezed his toothpaste tube and let it slowly crawl across his brush. He wondered again, for the hundredth time, just how long he was going to have to focus on simple tasks like this before it became second nature again.

It did strike him as odd that for every benefit he had discovered about his new abilities, there was at least one drawback. For instance, he was sleeping better than he had in years. The suit seemed to make him feel like he was floating, and the rest was blissful. On the other hand, his appetite had increased to make up for his increased metabolic rate. He surmised that he was going to go broke on food if this kept up. Buying as many groceries as he was going to need might just tip his hand as to who he really was.

His new attributes were becoming as much nightmare as they were dream come true. Like most people he had dreamed of having super strength, x-ray vision, and the yet untested power of flight. The quandary now was that it had evidently really happened, what should he do with his new-found power? Could he really be the hero he believed he could be when this was all just hypothetical?

****

"Blikzak, get up here!" Raknid called into his communication station. "He's finally going to do it."

Blikzak was excited, a feeling he hadn't really experienced in a long time, as he flew toward his monitoring station. Immediately he put his live satellite feed up on the main viewer, so they could both bear witness to Walter Scrum's triumphant attempt at flight.

"Where is he?" Blikzak asked as he searched the screen for the identification number on the screen. The number that would indicate exactly which satellite was watching Walter at this very moment.

"He refers to this area as the desert, but it's really more of a grassland area." Raknid explained. "There is no one around for miles and it's wide open enough for him to practice without hitting anything. I hope."

Walter stripped himself down to his undergarment and configured the suit into the all black configuration he was growing to prefer. His black underwear blended in nicely and his face was hidden by the mask-like covering. No one that knew him would ever recognize him in this configuration.

They both watched as Walter's first attempt at flight was more of a jump. A leap, straight up, that took him from a crouching start to over a hundred feet straight up. It was doubtful that he had even given it full power. Still, his less than graceful return to Earth testified as to the prudence of his caution.

"Well that was less than impressive." Blikzak murmured between mouthfuls of popcorn.

"I disagree." Raknid countered. "He made quite an impressive jump. Given his lack of knowledge about his abilities, his caution is understandable."

"You're the boss." Blikzak shrugged.

****

Walter got up and dusted himself off. He then checked himself over for injuries and sighed a great sigh of relief when he found none. He then spent several minutes jumping up and down, at ever increasing heights in order to practice his landings. It was true, he learned, that the superhero landing was hard on the knees. A squatting landing was much easier to accomplish, and the tuck and roll was painless.

"Now let's try sustained flight." Walter mumbled as he crouched slightly. He then took off on a three-step run and launched himself into the sky.

To say his flight was less than smooth would be an understatement. He dipped and dived, swooped and fell, and twice plowed long, deep, furrows into the ground.

Crawling out of the ground, Walter shook himself off and returned to his starting point. He then spit out a mouthful of dirt and prepared to go again.

****

Memory foam update: Item of interest. This unit does not comprehend the offenses that the water tower had committed against the subject, however the dispatching of the opponent was quite thorough. It would appear that the subject suffered from considerable remorse from his actions, however, and rectified the situation by patching the offending tower by welding scrap material to it with his laser vision.

Although subject's flight would not be considered to be proficient, his ability to move from one point to another at super speeds, on the ground and in the air, is well established.

Item of interest: Subject's metabolic rate has increased to the point that caloric intake is shockingly high. Subject has taken to liberating some basic fruits and vegetables from their source plants, rather than purchase them at the local produce distributor. Meat, however, has still been procured in this societies traditional fashion, just in greater quantities.

Query; this unit requires explanation as to the meaning of B-B-Q.

****

Walter had finally come to the full realization that his powers were real and that his dreamed alien encounter was no dream. That still, however, left a lot of questions for him to have answered. Those would have to wait though, as he was now determined to go out and do some good. The question was, how to do that?

When he concentrated, he found that he could hear the minutest detail from a great distance, but even that was too limited to really catch bad guys in the act. For that, he would have to be more proactive. The problem with the old police scanner trick was that if it came over the scanner the crime in question was usually over or the cops were already on the way. No, Walter needed something different. He needed an inside man.

An insider was not something he had a great deal of knowledge about and didn't want to take the time to search for. He concluded that such a relationship was going to have to wait. For this night was going to be his first night of trying out his powers in a real-world environment.

Walter knew where some of the bad areas of town were. The news was replete with stories of muggings, robberies and assaults in certain neighborhoods. Gangs were prevalent in other areas and there were simply places that one didn't go at night unless they were looking for trouble. This night, Walter was looking for trouble.

Walter decided that flying into one of those neighborhoods, especially with his inability to stick a landing, might not be the best approach. Driving into those areas was out of the question as well. He might well be invulnerable, but his car certainly wasn't. A sudden thought then raced through Walter's mind. Was he bulletproof? He knew from his attempts at landing and jumping that he could hit things incredibly hard and not get hurt, including the ground, but did that extend to bullets, explosions, and the like? He also knew of no way in which to find out. He did not own a gun and even if he did, he sincerely doubted he had the courage to shoot himself. Likewise asking a friend to shoot him would probably result in getting the police called on him and a short trip to the looney bin.

Running finally became the preferred mode of transportation into the city from the burbs. He was fast enough to pass traffic with ease, even at the fastest highway speeds, but more than that he could follow the railroad tracks into town and avoid being seen by most people. Even those who did catch a glimpse of him would see nothing more than a blur.

With that obstacle overcome, Walter simply waited for darkness to envelope the land and started making his way toward the city.

His suit was all black, including a hooded area that left only two white spots where his eyes should be. In place of his chosen boxer briefs were a pair of black bicycle shorts. He figured that would be the best balance between modesty and durability. He was nearly invisible as he traversed the railroad tracks and made his way toward the more crime ridden neighborhoods of his beloved city.

"My first night of saving the day." He muttered to himself as he moved at superspeed.

Finally, Walter arrived at his destination. Now, all he had to do was listen and wait.

****

Memory Foam download: Subject attempted his first night of crime fighting. He was heroic in his actions of moving from place to place to check on victims and reassure the masses. Unfortunately, his encounters with criminals was non-existent. His ability to travel at superspeed was negated by the speed at which the criminal element tends to operate. He arrived too late to stop the mugging of a senior citizen, a robbery at the convenience store, and an assault in an alleyway. Assisted with cleanup and did so at super speeds. He also transported assault victims to the hospital much faster than ordinarily possible by local EMS.

Undaunted, the subject intends to attempt his 'daring do' tomorrow in a different area of the metropolis.

****

"Well, at least the pillow circuitry seems to be getting smarter." Raknid sighed as he reviewed the footage of Walter in action and the report downloaded by the memory foam pillow. "I'm just not sure this guy is getting the full benefit of the superpowers we have bestowed upon him."

"Give him a chance." Blikzak defended. "It was his first night out and he had to work the next day. That's pretty brave all by itself."

"I suppose it will be more entertaining on the weekend." Raknid was forced to concede. "I just hope he doesn't get it in his head that stealing what he wants and not working would be better suited to himself."

"A supervillain is just as good as a hero." Blikzak was thoughtful now. He was well aware of his superior's orders not to introduce a supervillain, yet. But that wouldn't stop him from at least considering the possibility.

"Hero first." His commander reiterated a little more forcefully than he had intended. "We'll see about adding a villain to this story later. For now, let's let him get his feet under him."

"Personally, I think he's going to stay a pretty good guy." Blikzak was pacing now, waving his arms for a little emphasis. "I think if he were going to rob a bank and quit his job he would have done it already. This guy is way too into his superhero comics to not want to be the good guy."

"I hope you're right."

CHAPTER 6

Walter could scarcely concentrate the next day at work. His mind wandered, his focus was elsewhere, and he was still tired from the activities of the previous night. Still, he managed a passable workload even though there were several people in his office that commented that he was acting like a clock watcher this particular Friday. Fortunately, Walter was not known as a man who took a lot of sick days, so having missed two days this week with a 'cold' meant a lot of people were willing to cut him a little slack for still feeling a little off.

At five o'clock, Walter was out the door like he had been shot out of a cannon. He took particular care to avoid his boss on his way to the exit, lest his employer suggest that Walter work Saturday to try and catch up on his work that had piled up from his missing two days earlier in the week.

It wasn't until he was sitting in his car, pulling out of the parking lot that it occurred to him to attempt to use his powers at work to try and accomplish his assigned tasks faster. His office wasn't completely private, but if he was careful he could limit what others could see inside his glass box. It was something that he would file away in the back of his mind to try on Monday. If he could get far enough ahead on his work, perhaps he could argue to his boss to let him work from home several days a week. That would certainly aid in freeing up time for hero work.

Walter swung by two grocery stores and three fast food places on his way home in order to stoke his increased appetite. He was ravenous as his lunch was normal sized lest he draw attention to himself with how much he was eating. It had been less than a week since gaining his new powers and he could already see transformations in his body and noticeable weight loss. Evidently the suit worked to tone and condition his body along with its other functions. Even if nothing else came about from his hero work, the health benefits alone would make all this worthwhile.

After devouring his food and disposing of the garbage, Walter decided a nap was in order. It was going to be a long night, just as the previous one had been. A little sleep would go a long way toward keeping him sharp and focused.

****

Memory foam download: Subject again attempted a night of crime fighting. First attempt was that of thwarting an armed felon in the repeated robbing of a convenience store. Suspect was apprehended, his weapon destroyed, and turned over to the proper authorities. Suspect received several broken bones and other injuries from single punch from subject. Store suffered damage believed to be in high amounts as suspect crashed through refrigeration unit and destroyed a large amount of merchandise.

Query: Meaning of the phrase 'law suit'. Term was liberally branded about by both criminal and victim.

Second item of note: Subject attempted to break up a gang shooting on a street corner. Positioning himself between the two warring groups, the subject soon became the concentrated target for both waring groups. Conflict was then resolved when subject used super speed to confiscate and destroy all weapons.

Query: This unit requires information on the superhero chant, 'ouch'. It would seem that the subject has an affinity for this mantra while performing his duties.

****

"Well," Blikzak sighed as he read the report downloaded from the memory foam pillow. "It would seem that he is getting the hang of this hero stuff."

"I would not call his performance last night, stellar." Raknid countered as he finished the same report his friend was reading. "Still, he has sought to do good things, so I guess we could quantify him as a success. Now the question is, how long do we let him have these powers?"

"Oh you're not thinking about taking the suit away from him so soon are you?" Blikzak was shocked and disheartened at the mere thought of having his favorite pet project and the only thing interesting they had done in years, taken away.

"No." Raknid consoled his friend. "I'm not thinking that way yet. I just was wondering if and when we should. I'm sure the council will want to pull the plug on this sooner or later."

"What have you told them?" Blikzak was curious as to the reports his superior was sending home.

"Nothing yet." Raknid shrugged. "All my downloads are ready for the next supply shuttle return though. It's too expensive to send this minor experiment faster than light. They'll have to decide if this is something worth keeping or if they want something different."

"Well that's going to take some time. Unless they FTL a message to us, telling us to stop, it's going to be months before we hear from them again." Blikzak seemed quite relieved about that. "Maybe Walter Scrum will be confident enough with his powers by then that he can really clean up this rock."

"Judging by the bruising he took against simple gunfire, that's asking a lot." Raknid mused.

"We could turn up the power."

"What?"

35

"We could turn up the power on the nanites." Blikzak explained. "I purposely left them at a lower power setting. If we want to, we can always ramp it up."

"Could be dangerous." Raknid cautioned.

"Could be fun too."

"Alright." Raknid nodded. "As soon as we see he's getting comfortable with using his powers, we'll turn them up."

"Hot dog?" Blikzak slapped his hands together.

"Why would you want a hot canine?"

"It's just an Earther expression."

"You've been watching humans too long." Raknid shook his head.

****

Walter sighed for the hundredth time as he sat in his tub full of water, as cold as he could stand it, and looked over the dozen or so small bruises that were pocked all over his body. He must have been hit by bullets over a dozen times, which in his mind, put to bed the rumor that gang members can't shoot straight.

He would still count the night as a success as no innocent bystanders got shot, no gang members either for that matter. The convenience store robbery was foiled, although he would hold back on his punches next time. He even stopped a bridge suicide, although that only involved super hearing and the ability to talk to a young man who thought the world was better off without him.

"Ok," Walter voiced to no one as he splashed in his tub. "Bullet-resistant, not bulletproof. Good to know."

In his mind he was already going over the changes he would make for Saturday night. His plan involved practicing his flight most of the day, a large dinner, a short nap, and a night of crime fighting. He was still confident he needed an inside man, cop, CIA or one of those other three letter organizations, to assist him in his crime fighting efforts.

"Where to recruit some help?" He asked himself as he sat there pondering his next move.

As it would happen, the night of excitement was a bit much for poor Walter. As he sat around on Saturday morning he couldn't help but replay the events in his mind. He was aided in looking at the bright side as his bruises were gone. Completely healed by the suit he was bonded to. This left him excited and more than a little amorous. There was a proven and time-honored link between sex and violence, not so much a link as a correlation. Exposure to violence often led to a heightened sex drive. A desire to feel alive as one had cheated death and defied the odds. Walter was experiencing that at the moment. He was, in a word, horny.

"I guess a trip to one of my professionals wouldn't be out of order at the moment." He reasoned to himself.

With that decision made he oriented his car toward one of his frequented massage parlors and headed that direction.

In no time at all he was naked on a table, while a woman with remarkable hands rubbed all over his body. She was familiar to him as he had been there before, but this time she seemed to be having trouble with his changing body.

"You've been working out." The woman he knew as Lidia observed as she worked to make a dent in his now superpowered body. "I've never seen you this tense or difficult to work."

She had barely worked fifteen minutes on him before she called in another girl to assist her. Five minutes after that, woman number three was recruited to help out.

Walter did not speak Chinese, but even his lack of language skills didn't stop him from figuring out that the women working on him were frustrated by the lack of progress they were making in trying to relax his tense muscles.

"You know what Lidia?" Walter began, turning over on his own. "We're all adults here, why don't we just skip to the end?"

"You want oral?" She asked, hoping the answer was no, but intensely desiring the extra money that it would bring.

"No Lidia." Walter replied honestly. "I think we will just stick with the simple things for now."

Lidia nodded and began to massage his more personal regions. Even that required much more effort than it should have. In moments the two other women were back and assisting her in finishing Walter off.

Walter, to his credit, said nothing about the women's lack of being able to bring him to climax. Instead he focused on every erotic image he could think of to help speed along his happy ending.

Finally, after much sweat was produced by the women working on him, he was at a point where he was feeling like he was going to burst. A cacophony of sensations rushed through him at the moment of climax. His control was gone, and animal instinct was the order of the day.

With a tremendous grunt he let loose. The women jumping to the side as Walter's ferocity in that moment frightened them.

Moments later plaster, wood and dust fell from above him. Several people coughed on the dust and shook off the debris, including Walter himself. Walter found himself at a loss as how to explain the hole he had just shot through the ceiling and roof from the sheer power of his release. Everyone was dumbfounded and speechless. At a loss as to what to say. Walter took advantage of that confusion and shock and quietly got dressed, left a large tip on the table, and exited out the front.

As he drove home he felt the oddest combination of humor and regret as he knew he could never show his face there again but couldn't help but laugh at how he had managed to damage the place. Still, there was an underlying sense of nervousness as he didn't want the cops called on him for destroying the place, nor did he want anyone to find out that he was the night stalking superhero, that he had yet to decide a name for. He was, however, very grateful that he had not chosen the oral option for his release. He shuddered to think that he might have killed his masseuse had he released anywhere near her head.

****

Memory foam download: Subject suffered a night of extreme agitation. A much higher level of power was needed to put the subject to sleep. Dreams were frequent and fitful. Subject seems to be experiencing a great deal of anxiety in regard to his super powers, although his nervousness is not limited to what might happen to him. He seems to be genuinely concerned about accidently hurting an innocent in the course of his duties. This unit believes that this level of concern is typical of one imbued with great power. This unit believes that this is an indicator that the subject represents a suitable candidate.

Query: This unit requires clarification about the term 'rub and tug'.

CHAPTER 6

Walter blew through his workload for the week in a matter of hours on Monday morning. His focus was keen and pure as he threw himself into the distraction of his nine-to-five job. It was true that his job was less than exciting, but the pay was good, and he was getting enough excitement doing his crime fighting. He just needed to find ways to do it better.

Walter returned to his thought that he needed an inside man. Police, FBI, CIA or possibly NSA to guide him on his adventures. He had the ability and the skills, he just needed the targets mapped out for him. The question was, who?

****

Thomas Cantrell was a lifer. At least he would have been if the police force had turned out to be anything remotely like he had thought it would be. Instead, he had transformed from an idealist that wanted to change the world, to a clock puncher who only wanted to survive his current shift.

"Car 54, where are you? Please give your current location." The radio crackled as the dispatcher inquired for the third time the whereabouts of Thomas' squad car.

Cantrell, and his partner Rebecca Simone, had been ignoring dispatch for the better part of an hour now. Instead of going on their assigned patrol, they had simply parked near one of the notoriously violent gang neighborhoods and watched as the locals played basketball.

To say that they weren't doing anything would be a trifle unfair, as their very presence had put drug deals on hold, smash and grabs were delayed, and gang violence victims could walk around breathing for one more day. It would seem that no one wanted to commit a crime in front of the two lethargic police patrolmen.

"So, Thomas," Rebecca began, getting her partner's attention. "You want to answer that?"

"No, but I guess I will." Thomas replied picking up the mic. He then gave his position and requested further instructions. None, however, were forthcoming as his position was visible enough with the neighborhood to please his superiors.

"Tell me," She continued after he hung the mic back up. "What do you think about these reports we've been getting in about this new vigilante?"

"Today's hero, tomorrow's body we'll have to fish out of the river." Thomas replied. "But at least that will make him some detective's problem, not ours."

"Amen to that." Rebecca replied, hearing exactly what she wanted to hear. "Another bat-guy-wanna-be without the training, skills, or money."

"Oh he has some skills." Thomas defended. "At least the skills to build a bullet proof suit of amazing flexibility. At least according to the juveniles, the gang unit brought in Saturday night. He just doesn't have the training to really put it to use."

"What has led you to that conclusion?"

"The fact that they claimed he yelled in pain with each hit, but the hospitals have no gunshot victims registered." Thomas answered, explaining his reasoning. "I doubt that a professional hero would be so…pronounced in his discomfort."

"In other words," Rebecca began. "A pro wouldn't yell out in pain and let the enemy know that they were hurting him."

"That about sums it up." Thomas concurred. "Still, he didn't need to go to the hospital, so he wasn't badly hurt. That tells me his suit works, it's just painful."

"Well look who's the junior detective." Rebecca taunted.

"I was a detective remember?" Thomas defended.

"Car 54 are you still at your previously reported location?" The radio inquired. Prompting Thomas to pick up the receiver.

"This is car 54." He spoke calmly into the mic, expecting a berating by the shift supervisor for not being active on their patrol and just sitting parked. "We are still at Oak and Harmon."

"We have report of a robbery suspect at McLean Park." The dispatcher continued, ignoring the length of time it took them to respond. "Description is being forwarded to you."

"T-man Johnson." Thomas sighed as he read the suspect identification and description.

"You know him?" Rebecca inquired as she shoved the remains of her lunch back into the fast food bag it had emerged from and tucked it away on the floor.

"I've busted him before." Thomas sighed. "He won't go down easy. And if he's in the park that means he's over by the courts and might have friends with him. It could get messy."

"Call for backup?" His partner reached for the mic, not waiting for his reply.

"Call for backup." He agreed.

Minutes later they arrived at the park and had the suspect, T-man, in sight.

"Where the hell is our backup?" Thomas demanded, of his partner who could only shrug. "Never mind, he's seen us. He's running."

T-man looked over and saw the squad car pull up and stop. He knew that he had done some questionable things in the very recent past, therefore it was logical to conclude that one of those things was coming back to haunt him at this very moment. The problem was, he had no idea what action had provoked today's response. Was it the convenience store he had robbed, the man on the street he had mugged, the drugs he was running or the rival gang member he had shot in his garage?

Any one of his actions could have gotten him jail time, but it was the drugs and the murder that concerned him most. Those were serious time, the kind he would kill to avoid.

Rebecca and Thomas bailed from their car and began to pursue their suspect. Thomas was in great shape as he had never let himself go from his football days back in college. Tall, lean and quick, he was confident he could run down T-man.

Rebecca was no slouch in the physical fitness category either. At least not usually. She had just returned from maternity leave and was not at the top of her game yet. Still trying to lose baby weight and not having the time she used to at the gym was conspiring against her. There was no doubt that she was still in better shape than most of her colleagues, but she was not back to her old self yet. That being the case, both Thomas and T-man began to pull away from her.

T-man looked back to see the police officer gaining on him. For a moment he chastised himself for not staying with his friends and taking the cops on or making them back off. Then again, just because he played ball with the guys on the court, didn't mean that they would be willing to risk jail time for him. He had his own crew of guys for things like that, but they weren't the people he liked to hang out with.

As he ran he let his hand brush over the pistol he had tucked in his pants. He considered himself lucky that he had not shed them down to his shorts yet. Had the police arrived just a few minutes later, they would have caught him unstrapped.

His gun was not an ideal option. Not only did he not want to get into a shootout with the police, but his gun had been used in several illegal endeavors and was most probably in the system somewhere. It wasn't registered to him, so if he could find a place to ditch it, chucking it might just be the most prudent option.

"Dammit T-man it's too hot to be doing this." Thomas yelled at the fleeing suspect. Which would have made him laugh had it not been so close to the truth. The temperature was in the mid-nineties and humid.

Thomas looked back at his lagging behind partner and seriously considered ending the pursuit. Up ahead lay several twisting alleyways that would be perfect for an ambush. There was no possibility of backup and he really didn't feel like shooting someone today. To that end, he began to slow down as well. There would always be another day to bring in someone like T-man.

****

Walter was not one to spend a lot of time in the area of town he was currently in. But he was off to see an elderly client who refused to move to a better neighborhood and wasn't as mobile as they once were. It was not as if it was a crime ridden cesspool, but it verged on the edge of a high crime area. At one time it had been a great, family friendly neighborhood. As the years passed, however, it had gone downhill and was now verging on major decline. The client Walter was on his way to see was one of the last old school holdouts. She had been born there, lived most of her life there, and was damn well going to die there.

Walter had just rounded the corner near the park when he saw the police take off chasing after, what he assumed to be, a criminal. After all, he seriously doubted the police would be running off after someone who wasn't a suspect of some kind.

"Well this looks like a job for…whoever I am." Walter mused as he quickly found a place to pull over.

Walter considered stripping down to his underwear, which were his favorite bicycle shorts, and going full hero, but it was daylight, there were people around, and he had no place to change. Instead he simply threw his suit coat in the backseat, yanked off his tie and activated the mask feature on his nano-suit.

He then leaped to the rooftops and started moving in the direction that the he had witnessed the chase heading.

****

Thomas had all but given up on the chase. He had let T-man get too far out ahead of him to be able to safely keep up the pursuit. Instead, he decided to lightly jog for another block or so as to keep up appearances, but he had no delusions about catching his foe. It was then that he heard the muffled pop. Less than a gunshot, more than a car backfiring. It was something that he had heard before but couldn't place. It nagged at him and made him curious. He was driven to find out what had just happened.

As he turned the corner into an alley and saw something he would never have thought he would see. There, hanging upside down from a fire escape, wrapped in a chain-link fence, was T-man. He was unconscious and bleeding from the lip, but otherwise seemed to be fine. His weapon, which had been recently fired, lay on the ground beneath him. The barrel twisted by an incredible force. As to who had managed to put him there in the thirty seconds he was out of sight, now that was a mystery.

Thomas was then able to place the muffled pop he had heard. T-man had attempted to fire his weapon and it either misfired or he had the muzzle up against something solid when he pulled the trigger. As a result, the bullet never cleared the barrel making the explosive force backfire out the slide and ejection port of the weapon.

Thomas was still standing there, staring at the criminal before him, looking around for any evidence as to who put him there, when Rebecca caught up with him.

"What the hell?" She stammered as she took in the sight before her. Just like Thomas she looked around searching for whoever had done this to their suspect. She knew, logically, that there was no way possible for her partner to have done all this in the few moments he was out of her sight.

"Now what?" She inquired of Thomas as she waved her hand at T-man for emphasis.

"I guess we call the fire department." Thomas replied, wiping sweat from his brow. "I sure as heck ain't getting him down from there."

"I'll call it in." She nodded. "Who the hell did this anyway?"

"I didn't see." Thomas sighed, wondering how he was going to explain this to his captain. "He was like this when I got here."

"Our superhero?"

"I have no idea." Thomas reached up and gave T-man a little spin, mostly for fun, but also to get a better look at how he was attached and bound. "But someone would have to be awful skilled and strong to do this in the few seconds he was out of my line of sight."

"Our very own Bat-guy." Rebecca mused as she started her radio call.

"Probably not a good thing."

****

Walter put his tie and suit coat back on and looked around. It was a hot day and a guy removing his outerwear wasn't likely to garner much attention. He fumbled a little with his hand, as it was still sore from grabbing the barrel of T-man's weapon as he squeezed the trigger. His hand had stopped the bullet from leaving the weapon, but he bruised his hand doing it. Out of anger, Walter had crushed the weapon and been a little more violent in his apprehension of the suspect than he needed to be. He would have to govern his emotions better in the future. Control was going to be key in regard to his powers. Especially if he ever wanted to have a girlfriend again.

Satisfied that he looked presentable, Walter got back in his car and headed back in the direction of his awaiting client. He still had a job to do and wouldn't let a little thing like criminals slow him down.

****

Memory foam download: Subject appeared to apprehend one of the males of the human species who was running, for reasons neither the subject or this unit comprehend. As a result, the running man attempted to respond to his forced cessation of jogging with lethal force. Subject then disarmed the forceful jogger and wrapped him in metal wire to prevent his resumption of his physical fitness activity.

Query: Meaning of the term fencing? This unit's internet research does not correspond with the subject's use of fence material.

****

Blikzak read through the report from the micro circuitry pillow and sighed. Just when he thought it was getting smarter, it sends a report like this. It would seem, that for every two steps forward there would be a step back.

He was encouraged by the actions of the human subject. His moral compass was keeping him solidly in good guy territory. One just wondered if he would stay that way as he got more comfortable with his powers. The human phrase 'Absolute power, corrupts absolutely' had been a time-proven axiom.

"I think it's time that we turn up the power." Blikzak informed his friend as he put down the reader he was holding.

"Already?" Raknid was surprised he was proposing the increasing of power so soon after they already had an exchange about it.

"I'm worried that he's going to get hurt if he attempts to do too much." Blikzak was up and pacing now. Waving his hands like he had seen so many humans do. "I think we need to go up to fifty percent. That will keep the bullets from bruising him, but he won't be able to withstand things like heavy missile fire."

Raknid was quiet for several moments. He was considering his cohorts proposal. He really didn't want the experiment to come to an end soon and if the bad guys figured out that an armor piercing round would penetrate at this power level, the experiment would come to a halt in a single spectacularly bloody moment.

"Alright." He finally agreed. "I can go with that. Increase his power level to half. Send a message about the power increase to the micro circuitry pillow to have it implanted in a dream."

"Will do."

"I just hope he masters flight before too long." Raknid sighed. "If he doesn't, his higher power level will cause an interesting amount of damage."

"Should be entertaining." Blikzak shrugged. "Beer?"

"Beer." Raknid nodded enthusiastically. His greatest human weakness was his affinity for alcohol. He was still amazed that humans had stumbled onto it so early in their development. It nearly defined them as a civilization. He also wondered why his culture had never embraced it. Nor had any other he had read about. It might just be mankind's greatest contribution to the universe, and it made him a jolly good fellow.

CHAPTER 7

Walter woke early the following day. He was more than a little excited and a little apprehensive, for today was the day he was going to request to start working from home. Something that was not guaranteed to happen. But Walter's work was more than caught up, he was a senior employee, and he had never missed a deadline. He figured that if that didn't earn him the right to try and work from home, then nothing would.

He did have a nagging feeling. A sensation, or feeling, that something had changed during the night. He had dreams again involving his powers but couldn't remember them. He wasn't sure if that was all that it was either. He just felt different. A little tingly and slightly off kilter.

He was about to chalk up his morning unease to the excitement about his job, until he once again shot the toothpaste all over the mirror.

"Oh no." He sighed. It was about at that moment that he realized how ravenously hungry he was. He was certain, at that moment, that something had changed.

Walter decided to take a moment to make sure that he was feeling what he believed he was. To that end, he walked out into his garage and looked at his car. Carefully he grabbed the area where he knew the jack went and slowly and effortlessly he lifted the car. Something he had been able to do before, but with a great deal of effort.

"Well ain't that something?" Walter mumbled as the ramifications of his increased power began to sink in. "I'll bet I'm bullet proof now."

It was now more important than ever that he get permission to work from home. He needed more time to concentrate and learn how to use his powers proficiently. That being the case, he needed to get moving to make sure he got to work on time. It would not be a good thing to have the day you were asking for special favors from your boss to be the one day this year you were late.

This was one of the moments where having superpowers was of a great advantage. He was showered, dressed and in the kitchen making breakfast in moments instead of tens of minutes. If the water came out of the shower faster, he would have been even quicker.

One of the things he couldn't change was the basic laws of thermodynamics. His breakfast still cooked at the same speed. The difference was, that he could now wolf it down hot and not feel like he was being burned. Evidently the suit's powers extended to inside his body, just as easily as it did his exterior.

As he left for work that day, he took special care with all of his actions. The last thing he needed was to accidently rip his car door off or put his foot through the floorboards of his car while hitting the gas. One thing that did concern him was other drivers. Should he have to hit the brakes hard out of reflex, he wasn't positive he would be able to avoid punching his feet down into the street. He was certain that would bring his vehicle to a sudden stop, but he really didn't want his car to look like a Flintstone-mobile. Perhaps he would consider taking the bus from now on. The thought made him chuckle. Riding to the rescue via public transportation. Not the sexiest look for a superhero.

Four hours later Walter walked out of his office with a new spring in his step. He was not only granted permission to work from home, but he was actually given more time than he asked for. He wanted Monday, Wednesday, and Friday to work from home and only come in on Tuesdays and Thursdays, instead, his boss was so impressed by how caught up Walter had been, he offered him a work week that consisted of working eight hours a day, four days a week from home and only having to come into the office on Wednesdays. That gave him four days a week to work on or recover from crime fighting.

****

Thomas Cantrell and Rebecca Simone were both being grilled by Internal Affairs as to their conduct in the apprehending of the thug known as T-man. It would seem that wrapping a suspect in a chain-link fence and hanging him upside down, was a frowned upon method of apprehending a suspect. No one wanted to admit to believing their story that he was like that when they found him.

As it was, there was not enough evidence to punish the two patrolmen as both of their stories were similar enough to back each other up. Even the fireman IA questioned seemed to confirm that there was no way two people could have hung T-man up like he was in the short amount of time that they had.

As T-man was still unconscious, but not quite comatose, he was not available for questioning. Days later, when finally questioned, he would describe his assailant as a shadow, wearing dress shirt and slacks. He had two piercing white spots for eyes and was incredibly fast and strong. T-man was so rattled by what he had experienced that he confessed to shooting his attacker, which had no effect. This landed him enough charges that going to jail for a long stretch seemed like a done deal.

"Well that was sufficiently brutal." Rebecca sighed as the two met up after their debriefing. "I don't think IA likes us very much at the moment."

"I don't think IA likes anyone." Thomas agreed. "But they didn't recommend we get pulled from patrol so we're clear on that front."

"Well we're not going to get out there today." She checked her watch and noted the time. "We just don't have the time. What do you say we grab some lunch and use what's left of our day to catch up on some paperwork?"

"Sounds like a plan." Thomas agreed.

Thirty minutes later, the partners were in a small Asian restaurant having lunch. It was one of Rebecca's favorite places. Thomas always was amused by the fact that his Latino partner, who was married to a French immigrant, loved Asian food so much. It just didn't get any more American to him than that. Not that Rebecca wasn't proud of her native roots, but it just didn't seem to extend to her food choices.

Thomas was likewise proud of his African American roots. He had even traced his family line back to their voluntary immigration from Liberia so many years ago. Coming to America in the twenties, his family changed their name to something that sounded American to them and made their way westward from New York. Their trip was short lived as they came to a halt and settled halfway through the state. There the family established a dry goods store, a small farm and several other odd jobs to provide for themselves. Most of his family was still there, spreading out only a few miles from where they settled. Thomas, however, didn't want small town life. Instead he joined up with a police force in the big city, which was a bit of a culture shock for him.

Thomas had never experienced the blatant racism that so many others with his skin color had in the city. Small towns, where everybody knew each other, racism was too much work. People didn't want to invest the time in it. He had never been followed through a store, had someone refuse to serve him, or been oppressed by "the man". But in the big city, racism seemed to come second nature to people of all colors, not just white. He had seen the same no reason hatred coming from both sides. There were accusations, mistrust, and anger everywhere. Thomas didn't know if it was more prevalent, if it was just because there were more people, or if it was just in his face more because of his job. Personally, he couldn't see wasting his time or energy hating people he didn't even know, just because they had a different skin color.

That was not to say that Thomas did not have his little prejudices. In his eyes, if you were a criminal or someone that took advantage of others, you were scum and would be treated like scum. He would move heaven and earth to take you down hard and fast.

"Are you finished?" Rebecca asked of her partner, a hopeful look upon her face.

"You mean, 'am I going to eat that last dumpling' or something like that?" Thomas gave her the eye then relented. "You can have it."

Thomas then watched with amusement as his partner snatched the last bit of food. It would not be a stretch to say that a praying mantis has slower reflexes than Rebecca Simone going after the last dumpling.

The two had finally finished and were contemplating getting up when things took a dramatic turn.

Thomas wasn't sure exactly what tipped him off. Perhaps it was an instinct that police get after so many years on the force, maybe he recognized one of the men coming in and didn't realize it, maybe it was the obvious fact that they were wearing heavy trench-coats in July, but whatever it was it alerted him to trouble.

The four men in long coats that came into the restaurant went straight toward the elderly man behind the counter. In their haste, they hadn't even bothered to look around at who else might have been there. Instead they all focused on securing the man at the counter and any access to a phone. Each one produced a weapon of some kind. Two with shotguns and one with a pistol.

The one that seemed to be in charge, simply pulled out a butterfly knife then elegantly and with much flourish, produced the blade.

"You haven't paid up old man." Knife guy, the guy who seemed in charge of the group, announced to the proprietor.

"I will not pay." The man countered. "I already pay taxes for the police to protect me. I do not need help from you and your ilk."

"Wrong answer." Thug number one replied.

"Shall we make our presence known?" Thomas inquired of his partner.

"It would be rude not to." She smiled a shark's smile in reply.

The two then drew their weapons and started making their way toward the front of the restaurant. They were trying to creep low and stay around what cover was available, but there wasn't much to hide them.

"Shit!" One of the shotgun wielders yelled out as he noticed the two blue suits creeping up on them. "It's five-oh."

Thomas jumped forward and yelled at the men to drop their weapons. The response he got was less than cordial. The buckshot that came his way flew past close enough for him to feel the heat from the blast.

Thomas had never been an advocate of the police policy to move and shoot. It was drilled into guys from the academy. Move then shoot, move then shoot. The theory was that a moving target was harder to hit. Thomas was of the mindset that if you are lined up on the shot, take it. Don't move first, just shoot. So that is exactly what he did.

Adrenaline caused Thomas to squeeze the trigger harder than he did in training, which caused his shot to go high. Which was fortunate, as the short distance caused his shot to go above center mass and strike his opponent in the face. Bad guy number one, then toppled backward and hit the floor with considerable force.

Another shotgun blast and several pistol rounds came back his direction in response to his clean kill.

Thomas felt the impact just to the right of his stomach but couldn't tell if it went through his vest. The buckshot in his left arm was a little more problematic. It felt as though someone had just hit is arm with a baseball bat, but he didn't have time to check it. His neck also felt distinctly wet.

Shots rang out behind him as he heard Rebecca join in on the fight. One more bad guy went down as he switched up targets. That left only the loud mouth guy and the other shotgun wielder.

It was then that the talkative guy switched his knife for a weapon with greater range. The machine pistol he produced threw lead at an insane rate and every bullet was headed toward the two police officers. It took only seconds for both cops to go down and both remaining bad guys to make a quick exit.

****

Walter was in a celebratory mood. His boss had given him more than he had asked for, he was able to complete a whole week's worth of work in hours, and he was a superhero. All of these things were combining to give him a sense of euphoria that he was going to capitalize on. That being the case, he decided to celebrate by trying out an Asian cuisine place that he had driven by several times, but never stopped at.

Walter had barely gotten his car parked when he heard the gunfire. It only took him a second to realize where it was originating from. Instantly he activated the nano-suit's masking capability and exited his vehicle. A blur was all that anyone could have seen as he ran toward the sound of violence determined to protect innocent lives.

Just outside of the restaurant was a newspaper machine that Walter took cover behind in order to assess the situation. Running in and throwing around some guys with guns that turned out to be undercover cops would not be something he would classify as a good thing. That was when he saw the two thugs exiting.

Now Walter might not be the most experienced person when it came to weapons and what law enforcement used, but he was pretty certain that a machine gun was not authorized in the local police departments' inventory. Therefore, he succeeded in identifying the two as perpetrators and not victims.

"Gentlemen," Walter called out stepping to a location where he was clearly visible. "Put down your weapons and surrender."

His call to do what was right, was answered with a hail of bullets from the duo. This time, however, instead of dancing around yelling ouch, Walter absorbed every shot, barely registering the impacts. It was then that he looked down at the great flaw in his approach as his work suit was shredded by the gunfire. Even his cellphone was broken. Now he was mad.

He shot forward and grabbed thug number one, picking him up and throwing him directly into thug number two. Both of them then continued back into the restaurant, smashing into the counter and coming to rest on the floor.

Thomas knew he had seen the two leave the restaurant, he then watched as they both came flying back in through the door and smacked into the counter. He was able to muster a small smile as he imagined the two had just run out to get hit by a car. Knocking them back from whence they came.

57

His vision began to fade as he consoled himself with the fact that the bad guys had been stopped. It was then that he saw the man in the shot-up suit and black mask enter through the front door. Thomas willed himself not to pass out as he observed the masked man check the two thugs and then quickly make his way.

"Stay with me officer." Walter begged, his voice being modulated by the mask to sound deeper and more ominous.

"Check her." Thomas croaked, trying to point but not being able to raise his hand.

Obediently Walter moved to the other police officer and checked her. He was no doctor but using his x-ray vision he was able to tell that all of her internal organs seemed intact. Her lack of consciousness seemed to be from a graze to the head. Fortunately, the bullet didn't penetrate her skull.

"Looks like she'll be ok." Walter informed the downed officer. "Let's get your bleeding under control."

Using his super speed, it took only seconds for him to bind the wounds of the two fallen police officers. He only wished that he could do more. It was only when he was finishing that he noticed that Thomas had stopped breathing.

"No, no, no!" Walter chanted as he examined Thomas with his enhanced vision. He paled as he saw that Thomas' heart had stopped.

Walter was no expert in CPR, but he had taken a few classes for work. Making sure to be careful about his strength he started chest compressions and worked feverishly. It was then that an idea occurred to him. He placed his hands on each side of Thomas' heart and concentrated. It wasn't even something he knew if the suit could do, but it was worth a shot. Sure enough, Walter's hands glowed slightly, and a jolt was sent through the officer's chest. He convulsed, just as Walter had seen on TV, and his heart regained a quiet, but steady rhythm.

Sirens were getting louder, and Walter realized he would have to vacate quickly. His work as a superhero wasn't done yet and he wouldn't take the chance that the police would take him in. Instead, he checked each officer one more time and bolted out the front door. In less than a second, he was out of sight, and safely back at his vehicle.

Not hearing any noise and feeling safe for the first time since the shooting began, Mister Woo, the restaurant owner, proprietor and chief cook, tentatively looked out from his hiding spot behind the counter. He wasn't sure what had just happened, but he knew he had a mess to clean up.

CHAPTER 8

Walter was both furious with himself and ecstatic as he pulled into his garage. He had just saved the lives of two police officers and taken out two heavily armed thugs. This made him euphoric. Then he looked down at his suit and felt the crushed remnants of the phone in his pocket. Of course, it was the latest model.

****

Memory foam download: Subject was successful in thwarting an unspecified illegal activity. Although the subject failed to ascertain the original crime being committed, he was quite sure that the uniformed peace officers were on the side of law and order and the people that had shot them were not.

Both suspects were incapacitated, and the lives of the officers were saved. The subject was even successful at restarting the officer's heart through the giving of an electric shock.

****

Raknid looked up from the report from the circuitry pillow in shock. He had to read the message three times to be sure.

"Blikzak!" He yelled out to his comrade. "Have you read the latest?"

"Yes I have." Blikzak confessed. "And I'm at a loss to explain it."

"The suit shouldn't be able to do that." Raknid pointed out needlessly. "At least, it is not in its programming."

"It would seem to be evolving." Blikzak replied as he punched in some calculations on his e-reader. "It's changing to fit what it believes its user needs or desires."

"It shouldn't *believe* anything." Raknid sounded exasperated and maybe a little nervous in his reply. "It's a machine. It's not even equipped with anything more than basic AI."

"It does have highly sophisticated programming." Blikzak defended. "Also, there are a lot of them. It is possible that the nanites are acting much like individual brain cells. Individually they do not represent much, but in mass they become able to think or function much like a living entity. I will remind you that the nanites we used to create the nano-suit are several generations more advanced than the ones we have in our bodies."

"Perhaps we should end this experiment." Raknid didn't like making the suggestion. This was the most interesting thing they had watched in decades. But if the suit was truly growing beyond its programming, then it might just be time to call it a day.

"We can't do that." Blikzak protested. "The suit is exhibiting behavior that could affect our species. We can't simply shut it off and walk away. What we are seeing here could affect us."

"But we might not be able to control it."

"That is exactly why we need to study it further." Blikzak was now digging through the computer files to call up some of their mission parameters. "According to regulations, any behavior that could be interpreted as a threat to us, must be carefully studied, documented and reported. I would say that our nanites growing beyond what they were designed to do, qualifies."

Raknid read the regulations that Blikzak called up and went quiet in thought. They might be splitting some mighty fine hairs if they continued with a situation that they had created. However, the fact was that the nanites they had used were common in their society. If they truly were capable of independent evolution, then they needed to be studied to determine their threat potential. It was quite possible that in the end, his people might have to take a step back from relying on nanites. If he were even to suggest such a thing, he would need mountains of evidence to back that assertion up.

There was also a small part of him that needed to reconcile part of his mission. The charter for this expedition seemed to indicate that observing Earth was part of learning as much about themselves as it was learning about humans. Parts of the human's evolutionary patterns mirrored what they believed their own society to be like eons ago. In fact, there was a time when one of Raknid's species could have walked the Earth and fit right in.

Hundreds of thousands of years had passed since that point and many of his home world had forgotten about their past. It was probably true that more information about their past had been lost than most civilizations would ever learn.

The hiccup in the evolutionary pattern of humans had been the eons Earth had spent with no tidal forces. If most scientist's theories were correct, humans should evolve on a line parallel with Raknid's species. However, that could have changed with the destruction and rebuilding of Earth's moon.

Raknid thought the theory was based on too many assumptions. Who was to say that Earth's humans would have followed the same evolutionary path. They could branch off at one of a thousand points or more. But his was not to reason why, his was to do and get paid for it.

Raknid snorted at some of the pictures of the future that Earth's science fiction liked to paint. They envisioned a society with no money, no material needs, a virtual utopia. The fact was, that the utopian societies still used systems of value, barter and trade just as they always had. Oh they called it something else instead of money. Years of service to the community to get housing, education and medical treatment. There were still poor, rich and those in between. Society might eventually get rid of the money, but there would still be value attached to everything. Always was, always will be.

That brought him back to his own dilemma. One of the reasons he agreed to this assignment was the promise of the things he would receive when he returned home. He had been offered more and more as the time went by and he had now been on the station for over ten-thousand-years. At what point was it going to be enough? At what point would he have enough to earn the protectorate's daughter? If she was even still available. He had not heard from her in centuries.

"Moon to Raknid." Blikzak interrupted the musings of his superior. He had been trying to get his attention for several minutes now, but Raknid had been too lost in thought.

"I apologize," Raknid turned to face his companion. "What did you say?"

"I asked what you wanted to do."

"For the moment, nothing." Raknid replied, getting up and starting to pace. "I believe this requires further study and, as you said, it's in our regulations to identify threats. If the nanites really can grow beyond their purpose, I concur that it qualifies as a potential threat."

"Good." Blikzak thought for a moment. "Say can I upgrade my nanites too…."

"NO!" Raknid replied forcefully, before Blikzak could even finish.

****

Thomas felt like he had just ridden a washer through a complete wash and rinse cycle and then been tumble dried for six hours. There wasn't a single area on his body that didn't hurt. He wasn't even sure if his eyes were open or closed as he began to regain some of his cognizance. He took notice of the immobility of his arm, the soft rhythmic beeping of a machine and the foot traffic sounds emanating from the hall. Finally, convinced that his eyes were indeed closed, he forced them open only to slam them shut when the much too bright lights of the sterile hospital room burned into them.

"What the hell was I drinking last night?" He groaned to himself as he again attempted to peek out through the blinding glare.

Eventually his eyes adjusted, and he was able to look around and survey the damage he had sustained. Tubes, wires and other assorted medical equipment seemed to be everywhere. His left arm was in traction and most of his left side was immobilized.

"Well, well." A familiar voice announced itself from the doorway of his room. "Sleeping beauty wakes."

"You know, I was having such a good day until I saw you." Thomas groaned at his precinct captain. "I'm sorry, but my paperwork on this is going to be a little late."

"Well I think I can let you slide this time." Captain Culpepper conceded. "I think you've earned a break."

"How's Rebecca?" Thomas mustered the courage to ask. He was hoping for the best but fearing the worst.

"She's not good." Culpepper shook his head. "The bullet she took to the head didn't penetrate, but fragments of her skull did. Her brain swelled but they were able to keep it from getting too big. They have high hopes, but the doctors are certain she will have some forms of minor brain damage. How severe is impossible to say. It could be debilitating, or it could be barely noticeable. They just don't know.

"So for now, they are keeping her in a chemically induced coma. Which means she is still more productive than you."

"Ha ha." Thomas barked sarcastically. "Don't make me laugh so hard, it hurts when I laugh."

"I don't doubt it." Culpepper chuckled. "You have broken ribs, a pretty badly shot up and broken left arm, and you took a pellet to the neck. That's where you lost the most blood."

"I didn't even feel that one." Thomas reached up with his right hand out of reflex and located the bandage on his neck.

"Clinically you were dead."

"Good." Thomas replied flatly. "Now pay me my life insurance and let me go lay on a beach somewhere."

"Not that easy, I'm afraid." The captain then pulled a video up on his phone and showed it to Thomas. "They caught the guy that saved you on the security cameras. It looks like he used some kind of electric pulse, maybe a built in taser, to restart your heart."

"Not much to go on for ID though." Thomas observed.

"To be honest we're not really looking for him." Culpepper confessed. "He saved your life, I would think that would earn him the right for us to leave him alone. It sure scored points with me."

"He's going to get himself killed." Thomas grumbled in reply.

"Maybe." Culpepper agreed. "But there is no law against stupidity. I would have to lock up every cop on the force if there were."

"But this guy isn't a cop!" Thomas was a little more forceful in his protest than he meant to be, which hurt his ribs greatly.

65

"We're not so sure about that." Culpepper replied, ignoring the disrespect that others might have interpreted. "I mean the guy doesn't move like a cop, but he might just be doing that to throw us off. Regardless he shows a great deal of concern for the police and a similar dislike for the criminal element. Odds are he either is a cop or wanted to be one at one time in his life. Maybe a cadet that failed out."

"Could be someone that was forced out or retired out too soon." Thomas's gears were turning now. There were some people in his recent past that might just fit that bill. One of them might even have the money and knowhow to pull it off as well. "I mean, how many active cops do you know that would have the energy to be doing something like this during their off hours?"

"And trying to do it on the clock would be too easy to notice." Culpepper finished his thought for him. "It's a good theory, but like I said, we're not looking too hard at him. For now, that is."

"And what if he hurts or kills somebody?" Thomas pressed. "What if he does some major damage?"

"Then we'll reevaluate." He captain admitted. "Honestly I don't know why you've got such a hard on for this guy. He did save your life, you know."

"Maybe I'm just angry about the fact that he couldn't help Rebecca." Thomas was honestly trying to work out the reasons for his distaste of this superhero himself. He just couldn't put his finger on why he disliked the guy so much. Was it jealousy? He really had some in depth soul searching to do.

"Well it doesn't really matter at the moment." Culpepper set a bag full of books and magazines on the nightstand. "You're out of the game until you get better. Which had better be quick. We're shorthanded enough at the moment."

"I'll work on it Captain." Thomas then watched as his boss waved and exited the room.

****

Walter scoured through the internet and local news reports for any mention of the incident at the restaurant in the newsfeeds. Most of the local stuff was buried on back pages or not even mentioned at all. It took him a while, but finally he managed to find some information on one of the news message boards.

Earlier today, Henry Woo's restaurant, The Lonely Dumpling, was the victim of an apparent robbery. Unfortunately for the men determined to commit the crime, two police officers happened to be on scene eating lunch.

A firefight soon ensued which resulted in all four robbers getting shot, two fatally and two brave police officers receiving serious gunshot wounds of their own. All the victims were transported to St. Mary's hospital for treatment where two of the suspects were declared dead. Both officers are listed in serious, but stable condition, as are the two remaining suspects.

According to one witness a good Samaritan applied first aid to the wounded police officers but did not remain on scene to be identified. Police do not suspect that the good Samaritan was involved in the shooting and are not looking for him at this time. They do wish, however, to extend their thanks and hope other members of the community will get involved.

Mister Woo intends on reopening as soon as the damage is repaired. There are no reports of any innocent bystanders being injured.

Walter breathed a sigh of relief for many reasons. The police officers seemed to be doing alright and weren't in any danger. His identity had not been compromised, and it would seem that the authorities were sending a message that they were not looking for him. He even got the bad guys without killing anyone.

Now if he could only get these things to happen while he was in full superhero configuration and wouldn't have to sacrifice his best business suit to get the job done. He counted no less than twelve holes in his suit coat and shirt. Even his tie was ruined, as a bullet ripped right through the center of it. Then there was his phone, which he would have to replace in the morning. Another expense he hadn't counted on.

This superhero gig was getting expensive. For a moment he considered ways to make a small profit from his powers. Each option for honest work he could come up with had reasons to dismiss it. All of them were legitimate work, but it always had a downside.

For instance, he knew of several drain tunnels being built to control flooding and store water. It was taking months to complete even one tunnel and there were at least eight that needed to be dug. Walter was quite confident that he could complete the work in a fraction of the time, thus bringing in the project well under budget and ahead of time. The problem was that it would put hundreds of people out of work if he did it.

The possibility of moving very large loads great distances also came to mind. Something that shouldn't put a dent in the big shipping and moving company's profits. Especially if he limited himself to things that were too large to be traditionally transported. Of course, that would mean getting a lot better at flying and very quickly.

Most solutions he came up with, had the same kinds of problems. Then there was the problem of getting paid, filing his taxes, and still maintaining his anonymity. How could he fill out the proper W-4 forms if he wasn't willing to give out his real name and address? It simply would not do for a superhero to cheat the United States government.

A thought occurred to him about putting items into space for the government. Certainly, it would be alright to save the taxpayers and NASA a boatload of money by putting a couple of satellites up for a minor fee. He then remembered that not only was he not the best flyer, he had absolutely no idea if he could even operate in space.

Space flight was something worth investigating. As he was a huge fan of those movies where a meteor was about to strike Earth. Being able to save the planet was definitely something he would put into the 'good thing' category.

A new idea then popped into his head. If he couldn't think of ways to use his powers to make a little money, then perhaps there were others that could. Someone who might know who could be relieved of a little cash without any innocents feeling the pinch. Someone who might know some underworld, illegal operators, who carried lots of cash, and the world would be all the better if they were removed. Someone, like the police officer he had just saved.

Walter made a decision right then and there to sneak into the hospital and pay the police officer he had saved a visit. He was not only genuinely curious about the man's condition, but also wanted to prod the man's memory and make sure he wouldn't forget about him. There was something to be said about making friends in new places.

CHAPTER 9

Jimmy Fang was furious. He threw things around his Chinatown office, smashed expensive vases, and yelled at anyone within earshot. All this display of emotion made the men in his crew that had known him the longest, extremely nervous. Jimmy Fang was not a man known for loud outbursts or losing his cool. He was known for cool, calculated, and exceedingly successful ventures. Criminal ventures to be sure, but still successful ones.

Jimmy had been known as the Mayor of Chinatown for nearly a decade now. The unelected position usually went to the person who controlled the crime in the area. For now, that was Jimmy Fang. No one was sure how many bosses had died at Jimmy's hands for him to earn his title, but one thing was certain, there wasn't a gambling hall, brothel, opium den or bookie that wasn't in Jimmy's pocket. He even had a long reach within certain political arenas and the police department.

His rule over Chinatown was brutal, efficient, and just low key enough to not draw the attention of the major crime's unit. At least not for anything that would stick.

"My son!" He spat as he smashed his hands down on his desk and flopped, exhausted, into his chair. "My only son! In the hospital in intensive care, may never walk again, and most certainly headed to jail. How could he be so stupid?"

The man standing there, Jimmy's number one, who went by the name Mister Koi, had no answer and knew better than to try and offer one. Instead he simply shrugged at the rhetorical question and stood silently in the same place he had for over an hour.

"Stupid, arrogant, little snot!" Jimmy continued, his temper beginning to cool. "How could he have been so foolish as to not check the building for cops before confronting Woo? It's such a simple thing to do. Look around. Are the police there? If they are, then don't do anything illegal. Simple.

"How are we on my son's legal status?"

"It will be difficult." His aide admitted. "We can't even claim police brutality to gain sympathy because he was roughed up by a passerby."

"And who was this passerby?" Fang was showing his fangs now. He was looking to vent his anger at someone, and this good Samaritan might just be the best target for it.

"Unknown." Mister Koi admitted, then he quickly put a disk into the DVD player and called up the images. "Our usual contact in the police department provided us with this." Both of them looked intently at the footage from Woo's security cameras. "As you can see, the man has a mask on. He obviously didn't want anyone either thanking him or coming after him."

"I want him." Jimmy slammed his hand down on his desk. "He broke my son's back. Put him in intensive care. No one does that to my family. I want him, and I want him now!"

"We are working on it." Koi assured his boss. "But we have little to go on. The outside camera must have malfunctioned at the time of the incident. The man is just a blur leaving the restaurant."

"I care not for excuses." Jimmy growled. "This man is going to pay. He is going to die at my hand, I swear it."

Mister Koi did not dare contradict him.

****

Thomas was bored out of his tree and he had only been in the hospital for two days. Already he was tired of television and had read through all of the magazines his captain had brought. He considered calling the nurse, just to have someone to talk to, but thought better of it. It was late, they had been working hard all day, and the last thing they wanted to do was to have to entertain a frustrated cop.

Thomas liked and respected nurses. Almost more than he respected doctors. He knew how hard they worked and how little they were thanked. The hours were long, the pay wasn't great, and they had to listen to people who were having the worst experiences of their lives. It was a lot like being a cop, but nobody shot at you.

After heaving a mournful and self-pitying sigh, he decided to take one last shot at the news and then try to get some more fitful sleep. It was then, that the loud crash of something hitting the window, made him jump painfully.

He stared at the window for several moments, contemplating the size of the bird that must have just smashed itself against the glass. It didn't break, but whatever hit it, hit it hard.

Thomas was just about to return his attention to the television, when he noticed the window begin to open slowly. He found himself caught between curiosity and fear as he knew he was several floors up and shouldn't be getting any traffic through the window, yet he was unarmed and anyone coming through his window at this hour, might just be a threat. It was then that he took in the all black, almost shadow looking figure, creeping in through the open window.

He found himself struggling with the bed control/TV remote/nurse call button unit when a black hand covered his and quietly took it away.

"Please don't call for help." The black covered man whispered quietly. "I mean you no harm."

"You!" Thomas' brain began to kick into gear. "You were the one that saved me and took down the gunmen."

"Correct." Walter replied, making a little bow. "I'm sorry I couldn't do more. I was only in that area by chance and came as fast as I could."

"I thought you'd be bigger." Thomas observed. "The way you knocked those two guys around, I figured you'd be built like a linebacker."

"My size is not how you should judge me." Thomas replied, varying his speech patterns. His voice was already modulated, but he believed in being prudent. Changing how one talked and used certain phrases was just as likely to keep them off his track. "I have certain strengths of which you are not privy."

"I suppose I should thank you." Thomas grumbled. "But I don't like vigilantes. Especially ones that are likely to become homicide investigations later on."

"At least any death of mine would be a choice." Walter countered. "I have no illusions of where this hero business may take me. Sooner or later I will probably run into something I can't handle and get myself killed. Until then, I intend on doing as much good as I can. I believe that you can help me with that."

"What can I do?" Thomas was genuinely curious. He wasn't sure how much help an injured patrolman could be.

"You can direct me to crimes. Feed me inside information on bad guys. Maybe even tell me who to take down and break up drug deals or things like that." Walter came in close to Thomas. "I can do some of the jobs you police can't. You can even help me when it comes to doing it legally. Gather evidence and stuff like that."

"I won't feed you targets for execution." Thomas was still curious, but cautious about what this man was asking.

"An assassin, not, am I"

"Ok Yoda." Thomas shook his head. He could tell the man was talking like this on purpose, but that didn't help him with an identity. Just because he was aware of the man's tactics didn't mean they weren't effective.

"That being said, I am not morally opposed to taking down some fat cats and keeping a little bit of their stash."

"I'm not going to help you line your pockets either." Thomas protested.

"Look friend." Walter sighed, dropping some of his act. "If I wanted to, I could break into Fort Knox and make off with all the gold and sit happy the rest of my life. But I don't want to be that kind of guy. I like being the good guy.

"But I have to be honest with you. I'm going broke here trying to keep this hero thing going. I need massive amounts of food and I'm going to need some equipment. Maybe even a hideout of some kind. I'm going to need money.

"Now I would rather take that money from someone who's not going to need it anymore. Someone going to jail. That way it will be money that nobody is going to miss and isn't there to help anyone."

Thomas mulled that over in his mind. Even he would have to admit that it was a reasonable request to be able to keep some of the bounties of his handiwork. It had been that way in the past with privateers and bounty hunters, so why not a superhero.

"Uh oh." Walter put his hand to his ear.

"What's wrong?"

"Apartment building on fire." Walter replied, moving toward the window. "I've got to go. We'll talk again later."

With that Walter jumped out the window. There was silence for a few seconds, then a tremendous crash as Walter smashed into a dumpster five floors below. He then righted himself and took off again, and headed toward the apartment fire, hoping he would be in time.

CHAPTER 10

Walter made his way through traffic as fast as he could. He really wanted to fly, but he also wanted to arrive without smashing into a burning structure. It was one thing he hadn't really tested the suit against and had no idea how the heat would affect him. Still, he was a hero, and a hero has to try.

When he arrived on scene he took in the picture before him. The building was fully engulfed, with flames shooting out every window of its three stories. For a moment there was a thought of despair as he couldn't imagine anyone being alive anywhere in the structure. It was then that he heard the scream.

Walter didn't know when he made the decision to go. It was not as if he had some kind of internal debate with himself. It was simply the fact that he found himself in motion, heading toward the gaping maws of flame. Being that he had evidently decided to help, he poured on the speed, figuring the less time he spent in the building the better.

He didn't know from where the scream had emanated, but he was certain it was up high. As the building only had three stories he figured he would start at the top and work down.

Seconds later he found himself on the top floor looking around. The fire was fascinating and beautiful to behold. The yellow, orange and red flames twisted and danced in a destructive display of beauty within unholy terror. It was hypnotic in its own sinister way.

Walter found that his vision was enhanced by the suit and he could see much better than he should have been able to. The smoke was still somewhat of a hindrance, but not nearly as effective of a barrier as it would have been without it.

He also found that the mask filtered the air. He wasn't getting so much as the smell of smoke, let alone the lung-choking clouds of noxious fumes.

The heat did permeate the suit and was uncomfortable, but it was bearable, and he judged it must certainly be better than being in this hell without it. The firefighters that were in full gear weren't even able to get close, and here he was inside this superheated oven.

Using his super speed, he was able to make room to room searches in just a few seconds. In no time at all he found four people in an interior room that had not been reached by the fire as yet. Running them downstairs, two at a time, took only seconds and the people were then handed, coughing and blackened but safe, to the firemen.

It was then that a mother's cry pierced the night.

"My daughter!" She yelled in the kind of blood-curdling cry only a mother in anguish can manage. "My daughter is still in there."

"Which apt?" Walter yelled, his voice amplified by his suit.

"Three-oh-eight." She shrieked back at him.

Without so much as a thought Walter was running back into the building and up the badly damaged stairs, which crumbled behind him. It barely registered that he now had no way down, he was too consumed with trying to find a helpless little girl.

Walter ran through the appointed apartment to no avail. He had already searched the area once and found nothing. This time, however, he paid special attention to anywhere children traditionally hide, the closets, under the bed and cupboards. It wasn't until he made a second pass in the bathroom that he saw her. The vision his mask presented him must have been confused by how the little girl had worked to stay alive.

There, laying in a tub of water, wet towel across her face, lay the unharmed little girl who could be no more than eight-years-old.

Smart girl. Walter thought as he scooped her up and looked her over. She was still conscious and seemed in good shape.

"I don't know about you," Walter began, trying to make his voice sound as friendly as possible. "But I'm thinking we should get out of here."

The girl nodded enthusiastically and did not appear disturbed by the black shadow that had her in its arms.

Walter then wrapped her in a couple water-soaked towels and headed toward the roof. Once there he ran from side to side, trying to find a way down. Even with his enhanced vision it was difficult to see through the thickening smoke. That meant that there was no way anyone down there could possibly see him and know to get a ladder to him.

"What do you say princess?" Walter gave her the best wink his mask's overly large white eyes could manage. "You want to go for a superhero landing?"

Again she nodded and clung even tighter to him.

Walter stepped off the roof and prayed that there was no one below him. He checked the best he could, but the smoke was not being cooperative. Fortunately, he hit the ground without crushing anyone, his body acting like a shock absorber and reducing the feeling of impact for his precious cargo.

Loud cracking sounds alerted him to trouble above and he bolted forward away from the crumbling structure. Large chunks of masonry and lumber smashed into the ground right where they had been located just an instant before. Seconds later the entire building was nothing more than a pile of furiously burning debris.

Walter was easily able to find the distraught mother and with the largest smile he would ever have, handed the little girl to her.

The tears the two shared would be all the thanks Walter would ever need. The sweet reunion was something he would treasure forever. It was almost blissful, but it was not to last.

Walter was still standing there, his hands on his hips in a superhero pose when he heard the laughing shout from another youngster. A boy of maybe ten years of age.

"I can see the Shadow man's winky." The boy called out, bringing forth several gasps, and a torrid string of laughter. Catcalls soon followed and a couple of other wise-guy comments.

Walter looked down to see that his bicycle shorts had been melted away in the fire. He stood there, looking as naked as a jaybird in front of a large crowd and some news media.

"He's naked." One firefighter pointed and nearly laughed. "Isn't he?"

"It's got to be some kind of protective covering." The other replied. "No way he could have withstood that fire without something."

"He still looks naked." The first one laughed.

"The boy's got game." The second one joined in the chuckle. "I'll give him that."

Walter stood there dumbfounded for a moment, not sure of what to do. Then, more out of reflex than any conscious decision, he took off. Straight up into the sky he went, disappearing into the clouds in a matter of seconds.

The laughter and jeering ceased instantly as the fact that the people were dealing with a true superhero was demonstrated to them in such a dramatic fashion.

****

Walter arrived at home and transformed back to human looking configuration. He couldn't believe the exhilaration and embarrassment the night had dealt him in such rapid-fire fashion. It was insanely comical when he looked back at it even now, fresh in his mind. He just hoped that people would forgive this little superhero breach of etiquette.

Walter decided, correctly, that it was too late in the evening for him to make that night's news cycle as it was after most of the evening news shows had aired. He was even dubious that he would make the early edition in the paper. It was always possible that someone would 'stop the presses' and insert something about him at the last possible second, but it was doubtful.

Convinced he would not be a newsworthy event until the next day, Walter went to bed. His superhero work had been taxing and his calorie intake was low for the day. Those factors conspired together to make him sleepy enough to want to crash. His coming out, would have to wait until tomorrow.

Walter's analysis would have probably been correct twenty years ago. However, like many others, he neglected to consider the influence and wildfire speed of social media.

****

Memory Foam download: Subject was successful in evacuating a structure rendered dangerous by extreme heat and fire. Subject was also successful in evacuating five persons trapped inside the superheated structure.

After completion of the rescue, subject was dismayed by his own appearance. Although this unit is confused as to the entertainment seeming brought to spectators when the subject's outer garments no longer hindered his superhero appearance.

This unit requests clarification of terms Dong and Wang.

****

Walter awoke the next morning to a plethora of shared social media alerts and messages. Even though he wasn't all that active himself on social media, didn't meant that he didn't have accounts for himself, or follow some people. When he opened up his pages, it seemed that everyone was talking about the possibility of a real-life superhero. Even if many of the names hung on the scantily clad shadow were less than flattering. Dong-man, Super Wang, and several names unsuitable for print were hash-tagged everywhere. Most of the comments seemed to be positive. There were always going to be a few negative comments about anything, but they were in a distinct minority. The ones that upset Walter slightly were the conspiracy nut theories and the ones claiming the entire incident to be a fake, fraud or computer CGI.

Walter could understand the CGI crowd and their disbelief. There was so much fake stuff on the internet that perpetuated as real, that it was difficult to know what to trust anymore. The comments that bothered him were the conspiracy nuts and their government oppression theories. Many of the comments were indicating that this shadow man was some kind of black project the government had begun in order to conquer people and keep them submissive. They had no evidence, of course, but to many that was just all the more proof that this was a secret program.

The logic of that argument was lost on Walter, but he still couldn't help but be bothered by people thinking he was there to oppress them, when all he had ever done was sought to help. He was well aware of the axiom that you couldn't please all of the people all of the time, yet he still wanted to be known as a good guy.

Finally, he just shrugged and decided that he would do the best he could and if too many people came out against him, he could always quit. Just using his powers to stay ahead in his working life would be worth having them.

****

Jimmy Fang was working at his desk in his newly repaired office. The same one he had caused so much damage to when he was working out his frustrations about his son. New paintings hung upon the wall, pictures on his desk had been replaced, in fact the desk itself was brand new. All of the furniture was new, as Jimmy had taken to stabbing and slashing the old furniture with an ancient Katana he had hanging on the wall. He knew, culturally speaking and according to his heritage that a Butterfly sword would have been more appropriate, but there was just something he liked, something sexy about the curve of the Katana.

Jimmy was far from happy, but the message he had gotten from his son's doctor had at least been a relief. His son was out of danger and stabilized. Now they just needed to work on getting his back fixed. It was going to be a long, hard road, but Jimmy was prepared to do whatever it took where his son was concerned.

Jimmy got up from his polished mahogany desk, which was so large it had to be lifted in through the window and began to pace. Many things weighed upon his mind, and he needed to focus.

"Boss!" One of his junior lieutenants yelled out as he stormed into Jimmy's office. Something that was only allowed under the direst of circumstances. "You've got to see this."

Jimmy was contemplating chopping the man up into little pieces on the spot, but the man had been a loyal operative for many years, was well aware of the rules, and wouldn't be interrupting his contemplations without good reason. Jimmy was prepared to dismiss the summary execution idea for now. Unless the interruption turned out to be unwarranted.

The lieutenant grabbed the TV remote and fumbled with it for a moment. He was nervous in his boss' presence and was well aware of how his life now hung in the balance if he failed to appease his employer.

"This is all over the morning news." He directed his boss' attention to the large, new, flat-screen on the wall. "I think this is the guy that hit Johnny's crew.

Now Jimmy was all ears and eyes. He would be riveted to the television for the entirety of the news cycle. The interruption of his morning ruminations forgotten, his lieutenant was safe for now."

"In today's headlines." The talking head of the local news began turning her much too pretty face toward the camera and plastering a flawless smile on her face. "Superhero or super fraud? Do these videos show an honest to God superhero or a clever computer-generated hoax?

"Several videos taken by multiple witnesses show a figure, dressed all in black, running into a burning apartment building and pulling out survivors. What impressed these people more than the deed itself was the speed at which the savior seemed to operate."

"Well there is no doubt that the people on the scene believed that they saw something real." Her cohost, in his expensive suit, perfect hair, and equally debonair smile, replied. "Many are crediting the shadowy figure with saving no less than five lives. One as young as eight-years-old."

"We go now to Alex Wynn who is on scene at the apartment complex where the hero made such a dramatic entrance."

"Thank you." Alex, the poor guy who was run all over the city to get on the spot background shots, replied. "The fire started late last night and spread as quickly as the terror. Residents had no warning and little time to flee. Seeking higher ground, the people caught inside the building could only hide from the flames and try to survive long enough to be rescued."

File footage of the burning structure replaced the image of Alex on the screen. Fire seemed to be shooting from every opening

83

of the building. Anyone looking at it would never believe that anyone was alive in there.

The footage then changed to show a black figure running into the building and emerging with people over his shoulder. Three times the figure went in, the third time exiting the building via the roof and landing on solid ground. Seemingly unphased by the three-story fall he had just taken.

"I'm here with Trevor Tailor a witness to last night's incredible events." Alex then held the microphone toward the witness and nodded at him to begin.

"I was here, I saw the whole thing." Trevor excitedly began. "The guy all in black moved like lightning. I mean he ran in there, three or four times in less than a minute. And he carried people out each time. Then he just took off."

"He ran away?" Alex inquired for clarification.

"No." Trevor shook his head defiantly. "I mean he took off. Whoosh, straight up into the sky. The guy could fly. I got it on my phone, but the cops took it."

"Thank you, Trevor." Alex then took several steps away from the witness and continued his report. "Many of the other witnesses also complain that the police seized their phones and videos, but not before several of those videos were shared on social media."

File footage of a splicing together of shots of the hero then replaced Alex on screen. A blur was added to cover the more pronounced details of the shots after the shorts he was wearing had been burned away.

"Back to you in the studio." Alex then ended his segment.

"Thank you, Alex." The much too perky woman turned from the screen she had been looking at and faced the camera directly again. "Social media is awash with this hero guy. Especially with his pronounced details. Many have taken to calling him Dong-man and Super-Wang due to his lack of coverings."

"The boys got game." The male talking head threw in. "I'll give him that."

"But is this anything we want to promote?" The lady pressed. "I mean children see this guy."

"I don't really know there." He sighed. "But if this is real, the man saved five people. I'm prepared to cut him a little slack if his protective suit is a little risqué."

"Let's just hope that others see it your way." She admitted. "As for who this hero is, or was, no one has been able to make a guess. But whoever you are, thank you. And a word of advice, pants."

Jimmy clicked off the TV and turned to the lieutenant that had never left.

"Bring me Mister Koi." He commanded.

The underling nodded profusely and quickly backed out of the room. After he was gone, Jimmy turned the TV back on, backed up the picture on the DVR and froze it on the best image of the man in black he could find. He took special note of the face and the oversized white eyes on the mask.

Jimmy's mind now spun with anger and hope. It also spun with all of the painful things he would do to this superhero, if and when he caught up with him. He might even start by rendering the name Dong-man, irrelevant.

****

Thomas watched the news from his hospital bed with an angry scrutiny. He still couldn't understand why he garnered such dislike for the man who had saved his life, but until he could put a finger on it, he would watch the daring-do of this shadow like man with distrust and distaste.

"This guy again." Thomas mumbled as he watched the multiple camera footage spliced into a seemingly coherent timeline.

One thing Thomas did like about the man in black was his approach upon arrival. There was no showboating or mugging for attention. It simply seemed as though he arrived in the background, assessed the situation and got to work.

Thomas' attitude also started to change as he watched the man carry people, two at a time, out of the building and run back in for more. Then his heart just melted as the man handed the last victim, the eight-year-old girl back to her mother.

The heartwarming reunion was ruined, however, as people started to focus on the fact that the hero looked naked. There was simply no way someone could not notice it, especially after the first cry went out about the man's 'winky', from a young child.

Laughter and gasps were prevalent as the hero in black, took a seemingly embarrassed pose and took off. Straight up into the sky.

Thomas knew his attitude toward the hero in black had changed, when he discovered himself getting angry at the people that were mocking him instead of being mad at the man himself.

"I see you're watching the news about our very own superhero." The captain announced as he made his presence by the door known.

"I just can't put a finger on this guy." Thomas didn't even bother to try and deny his interest in the man that had saved him. "First, he appears to be going around looking for trouble, to try and be some kind of hero. Then when he gets the chance to possibly bathe in the spotlight, he takes off."

Thomas was going to play dumb about the late-night visit from the clad in black superhero. There seemed to be no reason he should alert his captain as to his communication with the man. It might put the captain into an awkward position, especially since the captain seemed to be a supporter of the vigilante.

Another thing then struck him. He had known the man was covered when he visited him in the hospital. There were certainly no protrusions from him. He must have been wearing something when he visited, but why would he take it off? Did it burn away? That seemed to indicate a pretty substantial flaw in the man's superpowers. That was, if all of his coverings were subject to that kind of deterioration in heat.

"I talked to your doctors, by the way." Culpepper pressed on as he fully entered the room. "They are amazed at the speed of your recovery."

"I've always healed fast." Thomas explained, not really giving it any thought. "When I played football, I would be back from sprains and pulls in days when other guys took weeks."

"Well that being the case," Culpepper continued. "I heard them say that they are going to take you off traction and put you in a regular cast. That means you'll be out of here in a couple days."

"Well that's good." Thomas was smiling now. It was the best news he had heard in days. "If I actually have to stay here for weeks, you might just find me finishing out my time in the psych ward."

"Well even if they do let you out and you come back to the station, you're going to be on limited duty for quite a while." Culpepper cautioned him. "You also have to go through the standard review for being involved in a fatal shooting. But with the witnesses involved, the camera footage, and the injuries you and Rebecca sustained, I think your statement is just going to be a formality.

"By the way, the kid leading that disaster was Johnny Fang. Jimmy Fang's son. So you might want to stay outta Chinatown for a while. Word on the street is that he doesn't blame you, but he's got a raging big one for our superhero there. Blames him for his son's injuries. Our CI's say Jimmy is sparing no expense in trying to track down the man in black."

"Wow." Thomas gasped. "He managed to piss off the Mayor of Chinatown himself. I just hope our hero is either very good at concealing his identity or is actually as super as he thinks he is."

"Time will tell." The Captain shrugged.

****

Walter watched the local morning talk shows with a bit of a cringe on his face. Although he was happy with his performance the previous night, his grand finale left a lot to be desired. He still couldn't believe that he didn't even consider the effect of the heat on his outer garment. The only saving grace was the fact that it didn't stick to him when it melted away.

Another facet to this being in the public eye that he hadn't considered, was the prolific use of cell phone cameras by witness and their willingness to share everything on social media platforms. Walter had never seen the need for investing too much time into social media. His parents had passed on, he was an only child, and he lived in the same area his whole life. There was simply no one to post anything new to. He saw his coworkers all the time and shared real-life stories with them, so why go through the trouble of having a social media account, just to see the same reports that he got from them in person? Not that he didn't have a few, employers liked employees to have accounts to keep up on office announcements and things like that. Walter even followed a few coworkers, mostly because he was invited and was too polite to say no.

Not this younger generation though. Everything they did or saw had to be posted for the world. It was seemingly a gigantic cry for attention from a generation that was used to instant gratification. This, by proxy, led to the sharing of the things that they saw, which included Walter in his superhero guise.

Walter now cringed at every mention of Dong-man or Super-wang. Regardless of the fact that he had run into a burning building to save five people, the only thing anyone really seemed to be able to fixate on, was his wardrobe malfunction.

Deep down, Walter knew that he wasn't having a fair reaction to his portrayal in the news and on social media. The news, at least, seemed to be very positive and did repeatedly mention the lives saved and the apparent risk he had taken. Social media, on the other hand, was a little more vile in his portrayal and did tend to focus on the more negative aspects of his debut.

On the bright side of the social media beratement, he did seem to get a lot of compliments on his build and apparent package size. There were even several offers to get together sometime, from several people of both genders. Not that Walter wanted to risk that just yet. After the damage he caused the massage parlor, he wasn't exactly sure he wanted to get intimate with anyone until he had learned better control over his more involuntary actions.

Walter watched the news until one of the anchors concluded the segment with the unimaginative line of 'who was that masked man?' and turned off his television. It was getting time to start work and cram a week's worth of work into a half an hour. Then he would go practice some more.

At least my flying is getting better. Walter thought as he sipped his coffee and turned on his laptop.

CHAPTER 11

To say that Jimmy Fang was upset as he perused through the news channels, would be one of the understatements of the century. However, he did have his emotions under enough control as to not destroy his office again. Those who knew him well would definitely see through the façade and see the tense muscles, the lines on his face, and the slight grinding of teeth. Those details spoke volumes about a man who was normally as emotionally detached as he could get.

Mister Koi definitely noticed the rage lurking just under his boss's surface. To avoid doing anything to provoke him further, he simply stood there, his hands on one another, ramrod straight, and took in every detail he could from the footage Jimmy was showing him.

Bulletproof, fireproof, and he can fly. Mister Koi thought as he watched the video over and over from multiple angles. *How in the hell am I going to bring him down?* These were sentiments he dared not voice aloud or even allude to. His employer was just mad enough to forget about all the loyal years of service, friendship, and duty, at this point.

"Any progress on finding out who this man is?" Jimmy demanded of his friend and colleague of many years.

"None." Mister Koi replied with dispassionate honesty. "We simply do not have enough to go on. No facial recognition, no vehicle to track, and no voice samples to try and match. What little audio that has been captured from this man, has been altered in some way. It does us no good."

"I want him Mister Koi." Jimmy growled. "No excuses."

"It is possible that this man, who fancies himself a hero, would respond to a situation where someone is in danger." Mister Koi continued, seemingly unfazed by his employer's frustration and anger. "I would suggest creating a situation where our hero has the opportunity to do something heroic. I believe that might just bring him to us."

"A sound plan." Jimmy nodded and rubbed his chin in thought.

"I have a plan in the works that might just lure him to us." Koi revealed, making his boss perk up with interest. "However, it is quite possible that it will present certain problems."

"Such as?" Jimmy pressed for details.

"It is quite similar to the axiom of the dog chasing the car." Koi began. "Once we get him to us, what do we do with him?"

"I'm not sure I follow." Jimmy leaned forward his face thoughtful and curious.

"This person has demonstrated great speed, fire resistance, bullet resistance and tremendous strength." Koi explained. "Once we get him to any desired location, we may not be able to do anything with him. It would only suffice in letting him know that we were after him.

"We either need to get him somewhere too secure for him to escape or find out how to kill him in a single blow."

"How do we know how to kill him?" Jimmy was up and pacing now. He was agitated by the delays in getting his revenge, but smart enough to know that Koi's caution was prudent. "Or what would be strong enough to hold him?

"We watch, wait, and test him when the opportunities arise." Koi returned. "We even bring in outside muscle if we have to."

"I hate using outsiders." Jimmy grumbled. "It shows weakness in our ranks."

"I understand." Koi had to tread carefully here, and he knew it. This was a point of pride for the great Jimmy Fang. "But if we use our own people we run two distinct risks. The first being that unsuccessful attempts to test this hero would result in a depletion of our available manpower. Something the other minor clans might try to take advantage of.

"Secondly, if suddenly every person his man faces can be traced back to Chinatown, our hand will be effectively tipped. Something we are trying to avoid."

"In other words, if every bad guy this hero faces is of Asian ancestry, it won't take a rocket scientist to figure out where they are all coming from." Jimmy summed up correctly. He was then quiet in thought for some time before finally turning back to face his longtime friend. "Alright. I'll authorize the bringing in of outside talent. None of the Russian gangs. They've been sniffing around the edges of our operations for a while now and I don't want to give them any access. The last thing I need is for the other gangs to accuse me of Russian collusion."

"Actually sir," Koi began. "That was exactly why I was considering using them."

Jimmy gave Koi a curious look but knew him well enough to know that Koi would have an angle in mind and so he didn't interrupt him.

"If we can convince the Russians to go after this hero man, we might just be able to turn him against them for us." Koi explained. "Even if they succeed in taking out the target for us, they will almost certainly lose people in the process. If this strategy even cuts down their ranks by only a few soldiers, it will have proven worthwhile for us."

"Two birds, one stone." Jimmy nodded. "I approve Mister Koi. I most definitely approve."

****

Officer Thomas Cantrell was not in his uniform as he entered the station. Technically he was still on medical leave, but he was bored at home and still needed to give a statement anyway. That being the case, he figured he might as well come in and get it over with.

Captain Culpepper had been correct when he said that the statement would be merely a formality. There was simply too much corroborating evidence that he had acted correctly and with due diligence. His interview was short, and the shooting was quickly ruled a righteous shoot.

Moments after the interview, Thomas was knocking on the office door of his commanding officer.

"Come in Thomas." Culpepper called out and waved at the plain clothed officer, who still had his arm in a sling. "How are you feeling?"

"I'm going to go stir crazy in the house sir." Thomas replied quickly. He didn't want to mince words, and even though he knew the response would be no, he wanted to ask something of his captain. "I want to get back to work."

"You're not fit for patrol." Culpepper replied firmly. There was an iron to his voice that let Thomas know that he was not going to be flexible in this case. "But I think there is something you can do."

"What's that, exactly." Thomas was suspicious. The captain gave in too quickly.

"I'm moving you back to detective," Culpepper dropped his bomb on him and smiled as Thomas' eyes went wide. "I'm creating a new position of 'investigative auditor'. I want you to run it."

"Sir I quit being a detective because…" Thomas was cut off by his captain.

"Because you couldn't stand watching your hard work be undone by shifty lawyers, legal technicalities and possibly corrupt judges." Culpepper finished for him. "That's exactly why I created this position. You are going to review cases that are about ready for arrests. You are going to make sure that every I gets dotted and every T gets crossed. It is going to be your responsibility to review cases before they go to the DA and make sure that there is enough evidence. You get to decide if the detective on the case has to go back and get more evidence or if what he has will fly."

"Sir, that sounds like a job for a lawyer, not a detective." Thomas protested.

"You were a lawyer, as I recall." Culpepper picked up Thomas' file, which just happened to be on his desk. He knew full well that Thomas would never settle for sitting around the house doing nothing. "Lawyer to beat cop, to detective, to sergeant and back to beat cop. You even did time as an instructor. Looks like you are more qualified for my job than I am."

"Even if that's true sir," Thomas shrugged, knowing in his heart that he was more qualified than most of his peers, possibly even the captain. "I don't want a desk job. I'm a cop. A beat cop."

"You are what this department needs you to be!" Culpepper shot back with perhaps a little more sting than he intended. "And right now, you're off beat duty. So you might as well take what I'm offering at least until you are well enough to get back out there on the street."

"Yes sir." Thomas could scarcely argue that. He felt it was better to be at the station doing something useful, than at home watching soap operas and overeating. "I'll report to my new office on Monday."

"One more bit of wonderful news on that front," Culpepper shot him a cringed look. "Your new office is B113."

"No!" Thomas had an incredulous look on his face. He couldn't believe that the captain would be so cruel.

"It's close to the evidence room and it's vacant." Culpepper shrugged.

"It's in the basement, the airflow sucks, it's damp, and it smells like mold and burnt coffee." Thomas protested.

Office B113 was the lowest of the low when it came to offices. Not even the lowliest rookie would be assigned that desk. It was out of the way, cramped and stunk. For the past several years, it had been doing time as overflow storage for the records room, but recent modernizing of the records had reduced the number of paper copies on hand, and thus freed up the office. Now it was empty, except for the crumbling ceiling dust, bugs and years of dust. It was in desperate need of a good cleaning, painting, and fumigating. All things that the captain ended up promising Thomas, would be done by Monday.

Thomas wouldn't hold his breath when it came to his Captain's promises about his new workspace. But if the work didn't get done, Thomas might just end up holding his breath *in* his new workspace. But duty was duty and work was work. Better to be in a cramped, smelly, bug-ridden office than home. Just not much better.

****

Walter's stomach was grumbling and growling as he checked his fridge for the fourth time. He needed food but wasn't thrilled by anything he was seeing. He wanted protein, good old Angus beef. A ribeye cooked medium-rare with a piping hot baked potato smothered in sour cream and bacon. That was what he wanted, but he had hit most of the food places in town recently and didn't want them pointing fingers at him as the freak that ordered tons of food every day. Not to mention it was a little early to be ordering steak and potato. People tended to get strange looks when they cooked a cow at eight in the morning.

Walter sighed and decided to go with the old standby of power bars, pancakes and sausage. The power bars were filling and packed with calories while the pancakes and sausage would provide the taste for his breakfast. Of all of the superpowers he wished he had, was the ability to make some of these high calorie, protein-packed smoothies and bars taste better.

"They can make man live in the moon, but they can't make broccoli taste like chocolate." He mused to himself.

Suddenly Walter froze. He had just realized what he had said. It was the first time he had been able to put his finger on where the aliens were, that had given him the suit. His memory in that department had been less than reliable. Up until now he had been giving credence to his dreams and vague notions because of what he had been experiencing. This was the first time he was certain of his experience.

Out of reflex he walked over to the window and looked up at the moon, vanishing in the morning sky. *I wonder if I can fly up there?* He thought silently. *I wonder how much of what is going on they can actually hear and see?* Although he hadn't quite pegged this entire affair as an experiment that was being monitored, he considered it foolhardy to believe that someone would give him all this power and not try to keep tabs on him in some way. From now on he would proceed on the assumption that the place was bugged, or possibly even the suit itself.

I need someplace to go where I am shielded. Walter racked his brain and finally came up with an idea. He retreated to his bedroom activated the mask of his suit and using his x-ray vision to guide him, cut a hole in the floor of his master closet. He was careful to not destroy the floor or the carpet covering it. If all went well, he would be able to lay down the floor and no one would be the wiser that there was anything underneath.

Much to his relief he found that the soil under his home was the same as most everywhere in his neighborhood and was the bane of every gardener's projects. A thick, brown clay. It was so horrible for growing plants in, that tons of topsoil had to be trucked in for any kind of landscaping to take. But for Walter's purposes this clay was perfect.

Using his heat vision, he superheated the clay and caused it to push to the side and harden. He then kept it going, deeper and deeper, creating a super hard ceramic tube as he went down. This ceramic shaft was going to be the entrance to his very own secret hideout. Finally, he hit bedrock at approximately a hundred feet down. Now it was time to build the real hideout.

Again, using his heat vision, he cut blocks out of the bedrock and pulled them up out of the tube. It was then, that the flaws in his plan hit him. First flaw was that he had nowhere to put the massive blocks of stone he was pulling up and out. Second flaw was that the ceramic tube had acted like a chimney, moving the heat upward. Before Walter could do anything else, he would have to put out the fire he had started in his closet.

Putting out the fire was fairly straightforward, although it did cost him most of his clothing. Using his super speed, he was able to get the hose and put out the flames in a matter of minutes. Basically, every bit of clothing that was in the closet was ruined. And he had a several ton block of granite sitting on his floor, threatening to buckle his floor joists.

After the fire was out and his situation normalized he took a quick stroll out into his backyard and looked around. The sun was bright, the wind soothing and most importantly, none of his neighbors were out. He then took advantage of that time window to move the large granite stone out into the backyard. He took a moment to cover it with a tarp, lest anyone ask what he was going to do with it and how it got there. Later he would move it out to the desert. For now, however, his work on his new lair would have to come to an end, and breakfast was calling anyway.

Later in the day, after Walter had eaten and completed a week's worth of work in a half an hour, he decided to head out to the desert to drop off the granite block and do a little practicing.

The first test on the agenda was the speed test. Walter knew he was fast enough to appear like a blur on camera, but just how fast was he? To find out he mapped out a distance and set his stopwatch. Calculating a speed would be simple after he knew those two variables. Each run he would try to go faster until he had a max speed figured out.

His first runs were at a respectable speed, topping out at just over seventy-miles-an-hour. That was an easy pace and kept from exerting himself too much. At two-hundred he was breathing heavily, but still not reaching his limit. It was at four-hundred that things got interesting. Not only was that incredible speed hard to maintain, but his vision did not quite keep up with his speed. It was as if his body didn't have a problem with that speed, but how fast his brain could process what he was seeing was difficult. Things turned into a blur and he tended to trip and run into things. A painful discovery that culminated in the stepping in an unseen gopher hole. He tumbled for over a mile and emerged from the dirt a sore and battered man.

After that he decided to work on his laser and heat vision. Using the powers the mask gave him, he easily sliced the granite block he had brought out in two. He then decided to try varying the strengths as to just punch partway through the block instead of slicing straight through. He judged that it might be useful to be able to cut someone out of a situation without slicing the rescue in half in the process.

One extra thing he decided to try, over and over, was some kind of super breath. Preferably a freezing kind of blow that would put out house fires and keep his working areas cool as he cut through more bedrock. Unfortunately, as hard as he tried, he simply wasn't able to conjure up anything more than a blow that might put out a dozen birthday cake candles.

Flying home, after practicing all day, Walter took a side trip and stopped in at a scrapyard. There he scrounged up the end of a tanker car that he could use to cover the entrance to his secret lair and protect his house from the heat that would be generated by his stone cutting. Getting it under the house was going to be a little difficult, but Walter already had an idea as to how to accomplish that.

Upon arriving home, he lifted the house a couple inches, slid the cover inside, and set the house back down. He would have to crawl under the house later and reattach some things, but nothing he wasn't capable of. He had put himself through college doing residential construction during the summers. The long hot hours were what pushed him on to get his degree, so he could work in a nice airconditioned office somewhere. The skills were still there though, albeit a little bit rusty. It was not that Walter looked down on menial labor, the opposite in fact, but sunburns, working in the rain, long hours and sore backs were not something Walter wanted to put up with for the rest of his working days. So even though the pay was good and the work steady, he decided to go the suit and tie route.

Once Walter got the cover situated and everything the way he wanted it he fixed himself a big dinner, spent a few moments relaxing, and then got to work on his secret hideout. With night having fallen, he was able to cut the massive granite blocks out and remove them unseen as he flew them out and dropped them in the desert. No doubt some geologist or archeologist would find them someday and be at a complete loss as to how these perfectly cut stones got to where they were or what purpose they served.

A humorous thought then struck Walter. Were the seemingly laser cut ancient stones, found all over the world, the work of others like himself? Was he not the first person to have this power bestowed upon him? Could Walter have just solved one of the mysteries of the ancient world?

A moment of wonder then hit him as well. One of the stones in the Wailing Wall in Jerusalem was estimated to weigh in at sixty tons. Archeologists have no idea how the block was moved or lifted into place. If it *was* someone like him that placed the stone block, was he really going to be able to lift sixty tons? That would be something indeed.

Walter had tried different things to test his strength, but the problem was that he didn't know the exact weight of the items he was picking up. He had no clue what a cut block of granite might weigh or how much a train car had in it or if he was more powerful than a locomotive. Exactly how strong he was, was a thing that he felt he should know but had no idea how to find out.

Walter pondered all this while he worked late into the night. Eventually he had a large space cleared out of the bedrock and was ready to call it a day. Turning the place into something comfortable could wait for a while.

CHAPTER 12

Mister Koi was cautious as he met with the member of the Russian mob. The place chosen for the meeting was an abandoned warehouse next to the train yards. The kind of place where a lot of unsavory individuals had met their end. The kind of place where you could fire a weapon, and no one would notice anything over the noise of the trains constantly passing nearby.

Wanting the meeting to look sincere and not wanting to risk any other members of his clan, Koi had gone alone and was currently leaning against the hood of his car, waiting for the Russians to arrive. He was the kind of man that didn't look like a threat to anyone. Average height, thin and showing his age, he wouldn't pass for the deadly assassin that he had been an experienced fighter that the still was. Sword practice, pistol practice and sparring were all parts of his weekly routine. He was good, and sneaky enough to not advertise the fact.

He stirred from his comfortable position leaning against the car as he heard another vehicle approaching. He then stood up straight, adjusted his tie, and steeled himself. This meeting was not guaranteed to go smoothly and if things went badly he was out on a limb, by himself.

The limousine that pulled up was long, black and bulletproof. To state the obvious, trust was not running high on either side. Two SUVs pulled in behind it and several bodyguards piled out of them and started looking around. Automatic weapons were plentiful as walkways were scanned, doorways covered, and Mister Koi suspiciously observed. Once the muscle was satisfied that there were no threats in the immediate vicinity one of them knocked on the driver's window of the limo.

Quickly the driver got out and moved to the rear door, opening it for his very important passenger.

Sergi Grogon was not the most intimidating man one could lay eyes on. Small compared to his bodyguards and a little wiry. His dark hair had gray at the temples and his hands were gnarled by arthritis. One would be quick to dismiss the man until they looked into his sharp, dark eyes. The kind of eyes that burned right through to a person's soul and then destroyed it. They were the eyes of a man who had seen horrors and caused many of his own. They were evil and would send a shiver down the spine of most people.

"Mister Koi." Sergi called out to the Asian man standing next to his vehicle. "Good of you to call. I missed our little chats."

To call the two friends would be a stretch, but when they were younger, they would meet every month to discuss the stresses and responsibilities of the job. They would never talk strategy or give anything away that their bosses were planning, but it was a way to speak to a likeminded person and have a micro support group. The meetings faded and then stopped as the two climbed their respective organization's ladders and took on more duties. Finally, it got to the point where it would be unseemly to be seen together so the meetings came to an end. Both of them missed the old days.

"Our positions would no longer accommodate such communication." Koi nodded to his boss's rival. "But I too missed the time we spent together."

"I assume that you are not here to reminisce." Sergi cut to the heart of the matter. "What is it that you want?"

"I believe that we are about to gain a common enemy. I assume you have been watching the news." Mister Koi then went on to fill Sergi in about the man in black. How he was a vigilante with great power and was already testing the waters in an attempt to bring down the drug trade in the city and rid it of crime. Most of what he was saying was fiction, but there was enough truth in his words that Sergi would be able to make the right connections if he knew anything about the mystery man or watched the news.

"What is it you want us to do?" Sergi was curious. He had indeed heard about the new superhero in town, but as yet he had no dealings with him.

"We would like to work together to eradicate this common enemy." Koi explained. "Much like we did when the gangs from the islands tried to take over years ago. We have already determined that this man, or the protective suit he wears, is invulnerable to bullets, heat and significant impact. What we need to do is find a weakness."

"You want me to spend my soldiers like water, just so you can find a way to kill this man?" Sergi spat.

"The burden of resources would be shared between us. We simply need some of your…heavy equipment specialists to complete our ranks." Koi pressed. "Possibly some assistance in drawing the man in."

"This is curious to me." Sergi finally admitted. "Tell me what you would like us to do."

The rest of the meeting hashed out more details between the two. Plans were laid, and each made arrangements. They also made plans for the inevitable double-cross that was sure to happen as soon as the cooperation was no longer needed or convenient.

Sergi got back into his limo as his son, who had been sitting in the back, was finishing winding up the cord for the long-range microphone he had been listening on. The cheap novelty item had become a useful tool as one could listen in to see if the other needed assistance while still maintaining the fiction of a secret meeting.

"I'm not sure I understand father." Nikoli admitted as his father poured himself a drink. "Why not let Jimmy Fang take on this guy alone? If he wins, ok. If he loses we move in and take his territory."

"Several reasons." Sergi began, counting on his missing fingers. The ones that he had lost working in the salt mines as a boy back in Russia. "First of all, this will get us in deeper with Jimmy's organization. We will be able to learn more of his operating habits and possibly the locations of several operations.

"Secondly, this cooperation, or at least the appearance of it, is a good thing for us. Occasionally we all will face outside threats, such as this hero or the Islanders. There are times that we must work together, and this is proof that we can do it.

"Thirdly, and most importantly, this suit that our hero wears must be very advanced tech. If we can procure it for ourselves, or even just a sample, its worth could be immeasurable. Imagine an army of soldiers that do our bidding that are invulnerable to weapons fire. We could take over the entire trade in the city, possibly even the country."

Nikoli nodded at that. He hadn't considered taking the suit intact or parts of it to reverse engineer.

"we could even sell the technology to the government and go legitimate." Nikoli added in.

"Bite your tongue." Sergi shot back quickly and the two started to share a laugh.

****

Thomas was tired and ready to call it a day. Tomorrow marked his first full day back to work and he was less than thrilled by that fact. It wasn't as if he wanted to stay at home and do nothing, but his new job assignment wasn't the one he was dreaming of. There was, however, that nagging feeling in the back of his head that he might just be able to do some good in that position. That spark of hope that let him cling to the possibility that he might just be able to help some of the other guys avoid the burnout that had plagued him.

There was a time that Thomas was excited every time he went to work. He genuinely looked forward to climbing the ladder as fast as he could, become a detective and save the city. The years he spent in law school had put him in good stead in that regard. That was before the bureaucracy, paperwork, lack of support from the community and lawyers dragged him down. Years of watching hard work on investigations go down the tube wore on him. So much that he threw in the towel and requested to go back to patrol. There were even times he had considered quitting altogether and becoming a lawyer again. Maybe even go to work for the other side for a while and make some real money.

Thomas pushed that thought out of his head. There was nothing wrong with making money, even the thought of occasionally relieving a bad guy of some of his stash had crossed his mind. Thomas had never crossed that line, except for a twenty here and there for lunch. Unlike some of the guys he had known who had paid for entire vacations with a bankroll they had lifted off some dealer they busted. There was a limit to how far Thomas would dip his toes into that pool. Yes, he knew it was just as wrong to take the couple of bucks sitting on the table as it was to rob the safe under the bed, but it just seemed different and therefore for him it was different.

Thomas' thoughts were interrupted as he turned the corner into his bedroom and found a black shadow-like person standing in the corner.

"Now take it easy officer." The man in black requested. "I'm not here to hurt you."

"Damn straight you're not." Thomas growled back as he quickly reached for his gun in the nightstand. Unlike his service pistol this was a .44 caliber. Significantly more powerful than the 9mm he usually carried. "Now put up your hands."

"Do you know what's going to happen if you fire that gun at me?" The man returned, causing Thomas to look down at the hand cannon he was pointing. "Nothing. Nothing is going to happen, at least not to me. You'll stink up your bedroom, waste a bullet, probably get the police called down here all for nothing. Do you really want to have to explain to your cohorts why they are responding to a discharged firearm, with no victim, in a cop's home? Go ahead and try to explain that away."

"I'll just tell them I was shooting at a vigilante lunatic who then ran away." Thomas spat back.

"Cops are cops." Walter shrugged. "Do you really think they'll believe you? More likely they'll just think you are trying to cover up an accidental discharge by blaming me. The good guy. Oh, some will believe you, but there will still be whispers and chuckles about the cop who shot up his home on accident."

"Alright you got me there." Thomas grudgingly admitted. It was true, what the man in black had said. Cops who have the police called on them for accidentally firing their weapon never live it down. The ribbing is usually in fun and very few times do the officers get in any real trouble, but they never live it down. Rubber and paper guns start showing up in their lockers, bills from fictitious drywall and flooring guys get scattered around, and the jokes never end.

Beaten by cop logic, Thomas finally tossed his revolver on the bed and held up his hands.

"Now what do you want?" The glaring officer inquired.

"What I've always wanted." Walter sighed. "I want to help. I want to help the police, the public and everyone I can, but I don't know where to start."

"I told you before, I'm not setting up targets for you to kill nor am I helping you line your pockets." Thomas barked back.

"Oh don't worry about that." Walter assured him. "I'm not looking to kill anyone, and I've recently taken care of my money problems."

"And how, exactly, was that accomplished?"

"Turns out," Walter began, a white, happy smile appearing on his mask like a giant emoji. "That there is gold in them thar hills."

Thomas didn't need or want any other explanation than that. Even he would have to admit that it was the perfect way for a superhero to make an honest buck. Just fly around using x-ray vision to find a vein of gold and use your super strength and speed to dig it up. Perfect. If the man actually had x-ray vision. Thomas wasn't sure what the superpower infused man could do, or how he did it.

"Makes sense, I guess."

"And it's all perfectly legal." Walter confirmed. "I checked."

"Alright, suppose I agree to help you find the most dangerous criminals on the street." Thomas was being both hypothetical and realistic. "What are you going to do?"

"Whatever you need me to do." Walter replied. "Gather evidence, tip off the police, or take them down with extreme prejudice."

"I thought you weren't an assassin." Thomas gave him the eye, trying to gain any insight into the man's motivation.

"I'm not." Walter replied indignant. "I will defend myself, hopefully without killing anyone, but if it does happen…" He simply shrugged, leaving his sentence unfinished.

Thomas couldn't really argue against that. He was guilty of killing a suspect or two in defense of his own life. He was also a great supporter of the armed victim and often had to hide a smile when informed of a suspect being shot by a potential victim when a robbery or assault had gone bad.

"If, and I mean if, I agree to help you," Thomas finally sighed. "How would I get in touch with you?"

"Uhh…" Walter now scratched his head, which he couldn't even feel through the suit. "I was actually hoping you would have some ideas about that. I'm kind of new to this covert operations stuff."

"There's always a burner phone." Thomas suggested. "A cheap, disposable cell phone that isn't registered to you. The time is prepaid and you use it by the minute."

"But it can still be tracked, right?" Walter replied, trying to feel out the pros and cons of his suggestion. "I mean if I keep getting calls in the same place, someone could figure out where I am? Like they do in the movies."

"In real life it's not as easy as they make it out to be on TV. But it is a possibility and that's going to be a risk no matter what we use." Thomas replied. "Computer message boards are going to have an IP address, cell phones can be tracked, and we are not setting up a special spotlight for you."

Walter was crushed by that last part. He was so looking forward to some kind of sky signal. Something that people could look up at and know that there was a hero out there. He knew it was an illogical, impractical and childish desire, but that didn't mean it didn't exist.

"Well, for now, I have an online email for you to use." Walter grabbed a pen and notepad from his other nightstand and began writing. "I check it from different areas, cyber cafes, libraries, work centers, those kinds of places. At least it's as secure as I know how to make it."

Thomas took the paper from Walter and committed it to memory. He would destroy it later, after he sent a few emails to it.

"Where did you get your powers from anyway?" Thomas finally asked the million-dollar question.

Walter thought long a hard about how to answer that question. He didn't think that his new cohort was ready for the talk about nanite robots, aliens and the moon being a space station.

"It was an accident." Walter informed him. This deception being the one that eliminated many questions and hopefully kept him from digging too deeply. "I wasn't even supposed to get powers, it wasn't even me that set up the entire experiment."

"What experiment?" Thomas pressed.

"I can't answer that." Walter dashed Thomas' hopes with that. "I don't really know how it all happened anyway."

"Probably best that way."

"I hope so."

****

Memory Foam Download: Subject spent the evening in the presence of a law enforcement officer. Subject appears to be planning to work with said officer in pursuit of defeating the criminal element on a local level.

Item of interest: This unit does not comprehend why the subject's wardrobe needed to be destroyed, but the offending garments were eliminated by fire caused by the subject's heat vision. This unit only hopes that the reason behind the purification of the clothing was not due to some kind of contamination. This unit has no desire to be purified by fire.

CHAPTER 13

Alex Wynn, field reporter, was busy this morning. He already had several people to interview and a handful of background shots to get. This was the part of the job that wore on him. He wanted to be the one investigating the story, digging deeper and getting the accolades that went with it. There was a time when reporters did the digging and broke the story. Now it seemed like it was all producers and internet searches that were responsible for the content. All the reporters did was interview a few witnesses or the information was passed on to a talking head in the newsroom. People chosen more for their charisma than their journalism skills.

It wouldn't be fair to say that he was a reporter of the old school, he was much too young for that. But his mentors had all been old school guys and even his neighbor down the street he grew up on was a grizzled veteran of the news trenches. The man most responsible for getting him hooked on the journalism bug was an eighty-year-old, Pulitzer Prize-winning neighbor enjoying his retirement. He was an old war correspondent that had seen action in Korea, Vietnam, Israel, and Lebanon. He had been wounded on assignments, brought down corrupt politicians and had even taken on the mob more than once. Alex would sit on the man's living room floor, wide-eyed as the man would take out old photos of himself with famous people, in foreign places and in dangerous situations.

It was the kind of romantic sensationalism that was intoxicating for a young lad. It was a pity that those days were mostly over.

Even the new generation of war correspondents were all far from the action. Oh there were a few that were embedded with active troops that saw action from ambushes and patrols, but by and large the talking head reporter sat on a hilltop, with a smoking ruin far in the background, hand to his ear and regaling tales of the this oppressive regime or the struggles of brave rebels. It didn't seem to matter that most of the footage they showed on air was the same recycled footage of people running and screaming, the hospital footage was all stock and the carnage all canned. It was rare for new footage to be used, and even when it was, it was usually a lone cameraman or someone with a cellphone camera that sent it to the news outlet.

To be fair, things happened so quickly that it was nearly impossible for reporters and cameramen to get anywhere before the action was over. People catching it on their phones was probably the best way to get new footage these days. Still it disgusted Alex that the talking heads seemed to take all the credit, win the awards and participated in none of the actual work.

Alex himself was somewhat guilty of that as well. Something he wanted to make right. He wanted to do the digging, wanted to get his hands dirty and wanted to break the story. Even if it was just one.

Those were his reasons for being out this night, in a sketchy part of town, his small handheld camera at the ready and recorder ready to take in what he saw. Today he was hunting for a superhero. One that seemed to frequent this area of town looking for danger. One that had already foiled robberies, braved structural fires, and saved a couple of police officers.

This was the story that Alex Wynn had chosen to try to get to the bottom of. This was going to be his magic moment. If only he could find him.

"Hey buddy," A wretchedly dressed man, who had been sitting on the curb, called out in a raspy voice. "You got a dollar?"

"I'm sorry," Alex shook his head at the man. "But I don't give money to people on the street."

"Too good for it?" The man snarled.

"Fifty-three percent of chronically homeless people have a substance abuse problem." Alex replied. "I can't risk that I would simply be feeding your addiction."

"Can you risk what we'll do to you if you don't give us your money?" Another voice asked from behind him. As the man Alex had been too distracted to see came upon him. "Now don't do anything stupid and give me your money."

Alex raised his hands and turned around slowly. He wasn't an expert when it came to weapons, but he reasoned that the size of any weapon pointed at you, probably looked like a cannon.

"Now take it easy." Alex soothed. "There is no need for this to become violent." Alex then removed his wallet and held it up for the man to take.

The man who had been sitting on the curb then got up and liberated the wallet from Alex's hand.

It was then that the weapon the man had in his hands suddenly got very hot.

"What the hell?" The man shouted as he dropped the glowing red weapon from his hand.

****

Walter was on patrol, making his usual rounds when he heard the threats from the street below. It was not the easiest thing for him to pick up or at least pull out of all the other noise his super hearing was picking up when he was using it. Practice had allowed him to listen to keywords or phrases. Much like an internet keyword search.

He had just reached the point where he could clearly see the two holdup men without any enhanced vision and decided that it would be a good time to try his laser vision on a real target. Walter concentrated on the gun in the man's hand and sure enough, a thin beam of superheated light shot from his eyes and struck the weapon. Walter didn't know a lot about weapons, he didn't even own one, but he knew enough to shoot only for the grip of the weapon lest he cook off a round in the chamber.

Walter then landed, a little harder than he wanted to, between the reporter and the two would be muggers. Everyone froze at his sudden appearance. Giving Walter a chance to glance down and make sure he didn't break the street, and that his bicycle shorts were in place.

"Gentlemen" Walter greeted the two shocked thieves. "I would appreciate it if you two would return this man's property.

"Get bent." The first man, who was the one originally on the curb, yelled out, drawing a pistol of his own. His fluid movement from drawing to discharge was an indicator that this was a man well versed in the use of his firearm. It was obvious that Alex had not been his first victim.

The gunshot sent Alex diving toward the pavement, but he quickly looked up in awe as Walter just stood there as the bullet flattened against his body and fell to the ground. Four more quick shots followed all having the same effect. Walter then reached out and crushed the weapon in the man's hand, breaking many of the bad guy's fingers in the process.

"I was prepared to let you both off with a warning. But now that you've fired your weapon the police are going to get involved." Walter then used his super speed to tie both men together, using their own coats to make the bindings. "That should hold you until the proper authorities arrive."

Alex was quickly on his feet and backing away slightly, from the white-eyed shadow before him. Fortunately, the more logical part of his brain kicked in before he had moved very far. This was the person he was looking to meet, after all.

"Uhhh, Thank you." Alex was able to stammer. "Mister…?"

For just a split second, Walter nearly answered with his real name. This was not something he had actually practiced.

"I really don't have a name." Walter finally admitted. "It seems that all of the cool superhero names are taken and I don't want to get sued."

"OH, you're getting sued." One of the robbers yelled out. "You broke my freaking fingers."

"Shut up." Alex and Walter yelled at the two in unison.

"Look, I'm a reporter. Alex, Alex Wynn." Alex introduced himself. "I've been hoping to meet you."

"Oh yes, I've seen your work." Walter replied as he remembered the segment with Alex at the apartment building fire.

"I'd like to set up an interview with you." Alex pressed, hoping to get some access with this man.

"Well, I'm not really an interview kind of guy." Walter replied. "I'm not doing this for fame or fortune."

"So why are you doing it?"

Walter cocked his head to the side and thought for a moment. Finally, he found a kind of an answer.

"Because it needs to be done." He decided. "Now if you'll excuse me."

"Wait, before you go, Here." Alex pressed his card into his hand and stepped back. "Just in case you change your mind about the interview."

"Uh I really don't have pockets." Just then Walter's suit adjusted in response to his instinctual need and seemingly absorbed the card into it. "Oh, I guess I do."

"Well take it easy I guess." Alex waved.

Walter then waved back and shot upward into the sky. In less than a second he was invisible to the naked eye, his black suit blending into the night sky.

Alex just hoped he could run into the man again. He had a good feeling that he might just find himself that interview after all.

****

Nikoli looked over the trap he had set. The car was positioned perfectly on an isolated stretch of freeway that was closed for construction. He had worked hard to make it look like a driver had gotten disorientated and driven into an unfinished area. The driver was, in fact, the sister of one of his more junior employees.

She was supposed to act scared, scream a lot, and call out for help. All in an effort to draw in this superhero. As it turned out, she didn't need to act. The car was precariously balanced, and she was in real danger of plummeting to her death. The result was a young woman that was terrified out of her mind.

The screams emanating from the vehicle were exactly what Nikoli wanted to hear, the fact that she kept cursing her brother's name in Russian, was not. He did consider it unlikely that the hero in question would understand any Russian, but there was always the chance. Unfortunately, it was too late to do anything about it now. They simply had to sit and wait.

Walter had his ear to the ground, so to speak, as he flew along a couple hundred feet up in the air. His night had been productive, with robberies foiled, another person saved from a fire, and a contact made with a reporter. All of these experiences had combined to put him in a euphoric state as he flew along on cloud nine. It was then that he heard the first scream.

It took Walter no time at all to home in on the source of the distress. The car, hanging off of the edge of an unfinished freeway was easy to spot. To him it appeared as though the driver had taken the wrong entrance and gotten themselves into trouble.

Quickly he positioned himself in front of the vehicle and hovered out where the driver could get a good look at him.

"Hello." Walter waved at the distraught woman. "I'm going to try to help you. Do you understand?"

She nodded vigorously, her nervousness clearly evident in her eyes.

Nikoli smiled as he watched the black-clad superhero come to a halt in front of the car. It was just as he had hoped. Now all he had to do was make the shot.

His rifle had been in position for hours. He had spent a great deal of time making sure that it was sighted in perfectly, right where he had hoped the hero would stop. Now he gazed through the sight once more, flicked off the safety with his thumb and took aim. Acquire, aim, breathe, aim, hold, aim and squeeze. The mantra a lot of shooters have drilled into them over the years repeated in his head. The report of his rifle surprised him, just as it should, and the fifty-caliber round sped toward the back of the superhero at supersonic speed.

Walter was just about the attempt to push the car backward when it occurred to him that he had never really attempted to move or carry anything heavy while hovering before. It was quite possible that he wasn't supposed to be able to carry anything heavy while remaining stationary in the air, perhaps he needed something to push against to move massive objects, even if it was just the air. That thought caused a small doubt that disappeared in a chuckle. He wasn't supposed to be flying or have any other superpowers anyway, so why not just assume he could carry something heavy while doing it?

That doubt pushed aside, he edged closer to the vehicle. It was then that the heavy caliber bullet, slammed into his back. The impact landed right between his shoulder blades in a perfect shot.

Walter felt like he had been hit by a truck. The kinetic energy of the bullet caused his suit to ripple and the impact drove him forward, slamming him into the front of the vehicle. Out of instinct, he grabbed onto the car to keep himself upright. He had just enough time to realize his mistake before the vehicle tipped forward and began to fall with Walter still clinging to the front end.

The woman screamed as she saw the ground rushing up to meet them. The sight of a black-clad figure hanging onto the front of her car only added to her confusion and fright. If she ever got out of this, she was going to kill her brother.

Walter pushed with all his might and attempted to fly straight ahead. He could feel the vehicle slowing as he gradually reversed the momentum of the plummeting car. The problem was distance. He simply didn't have enough time to stop the car from hitting the Earth, he just had to hope that he slowed it enough.

His impact against the ground was brutal, kicking up clouds of dust and inflicting a decent amount of pain. The vehicle then plowed into his midsection, causing him to utter a tremendous grunt.

As he laid there, a car protruding from his midsection, he gave the terrified but very much alive woman as good of a smile as he could through his mask. Which effectively made him look like a creepy emoji. The woman then screamed again, as the car tipped and came falling toward Walter's face.

"Uh oh." Was all he could utter before a fresh crash, new screams and even more dust filled the air.

Walter wasn't exactly sure what happened in the immediate aftermath of the car falling on his face. He didn't know if he had lost consciousness or not. All he was sure of was that the car was still on him and he was having difficulty moving it. Not really because of the weight, but because he had no leverage and it was difficult to move along the ground, on his back, while lifting the car off of him.

While he was attempting to extract himself from under the vehicle the woman crawled out and took a moment to meet his eyes.

"Thank you for saving me." She whispered to him as she moved her long dark hair away from her face. A beautiful face at that, one that Walter committed to memory. A large white smile crawled across his face as her thanks made it almost worthwhile. Then in the blink of an eye, she was gone.

By the time he got the car off of him, *everyone* was gone. The shooter, the woman, everyone. There didn't seem to be any witnesses to the incident anywhere. Using his enhanced vision, Walter looked around and was disturbed by what he saw. There were cameras everywhere. Multiple angles and viewpoints, mostly duct taped in place and wireless. Whoever set these up, wanted to be able to record what happened, possibly to study it later.

Walter then made a few mental calculations and flew over to where he believed the shot had come from and headed off in that direction. It did not take him long to find the shooter's nest. There sat the rifle used in the assassination attempt, left behind lest it slow the shooter's escape. There was also a bullet casing on the ground, but there was no other evidence of the shooter.

As Walter stopped to contemplate what all this meant for him, the pain began to grow. His adrenaline was wearing off and his injuries were becoming apparent. Doing his best to hide the fact that he was in any discomfort at all, lest he still be in view of a camera he hadn't detected, he picked up the casing and the rifle and took off into the sky. He wasn't sure what exactly he was going to do with them, but they were clues as to who had just tried to set him up. He also just happened to know a police officer who might able to help him track them down.

Walter seethed at the thought of revenge, but that would have to wait. He was in pain and needed to get home. His tormentors could wait, for now. What he needed at the moment was protein and rest.

****

Memory Foam download: Subject appeared to engage in battle with a vehicle and despite receiving several injuries the subject emerged victorious. The offending vehicle was dispatched, and its occupant saved.

This unit is concerned by the fact that it is evident that not all witness to the heroic act were inclined to celebrate the achievement of the subject. It would appear that one or more bystanders decided to make an attempt on the subject's life. As a result, the subject suffered a high-velocity impact from an exceedingly large projectile. The subject sustained multiple injuries as a result, and the offending vehicle was able to get in a strategically placed blow while the subject was distracted. The result was even more injuries sustained when the devious vehicle made a desperate attack that caused the subject to become trapped underneath its weight. This effectively destroyed the vehicle and allowed the would-be assassins to make an escape.

Query: Meaning of the term 'Sucker'. Unit's research does not find a definition which correlates to the subject's attitude toward himself.

CHAPTER 14

Nikoli was not happy with himself about his performance in taking out this superhero. His father, on the other hand, was much more philosophical about it.

"I cannot believe I let him get away." Nikoli spat as he paced angrily in front of his father's desk. "I should have used something bigger. Something with even more punch. Now he may be wary and on his guard."

"Nikoli." Sergi soothed. "You were dealing with a complete unknown. There are factors here that we cannot even begin to calculate. You did fine."

Sergi then called up the footage of the cameras onto his laptop and went over it again.

"He didn't even look all that affected by the shot I took." Nikoli grumped. "Such a large bullet should have torn right through him. It was even an armor penetrator. I just don't understand it."

"He was affected." Sergi corrected him. "As much as he attempted to hide that fact. We also learned that there are limits to his strength. You see here, when the car fell on top of him. He couldn't just toss it off like it was nothing. He had to work his way out from underneath."

Sergi's eyes then narrowed as he watched the woman bend down and say something to the man in black. There did not appear to be a mutual exchange and it was only a second, but it was not something he would have allowed.

"The woman you used," Sergi pointed at the screen. "Who is she?"

"Sasha." Nikoli replied easily remembering the attractive brunette. "It's Tupov's sister."

"What did she say to the man in black?" His father pressed. "I can't make it out."

"I wasn't aware that she had spoken to him." Nikoli confessed. "I rushed the footage to you, so we could go over it together. I haven't studied it in detail myself."

"It might be wise to bring her here to ask her." Sergi leaned back, folding his hands together under his chin. "The man in black seemed to react positively to her, judging by his smile. It might prove useful to have her close."

****

Thomas went over the case files that were flooding onto his desk as quickly as he could. The high number of investigations that looked as if they needed some tweaking was disturbing to him. As he worked, he took note of the investigators, the locations, and the suspects that were being looked at. The more he looked, the more he solidified that he was looking at a disturbing trend.

Most of the cases being worked seemed on the level. Random people with random crimes. The problem was when he started looking at those that weren't so random. Namely the crimes involving different mob bosses and underlings. Those cases had holes in them that one could drive a truck through. It was almost as if the detectives on those cases purposely left things undone to guarantee that no conviction would result. In his eyes that meant only one thing, that these cops were on the take.

As Thomas pressed deeper into those files two groups kept popping up. Those from Chinatown and those from Russia. All people belonging to Jimmy Fang and Sergi Grogon. To Thomas it was evident that Jimmy Fang and Sergi Grogon had bought most of the police force. Whether or not that extended to the DA's office he couldn't say, but he suspected it did. It would be very hard for the DA to not notice the holes in the cases that were coming in.

This kind of police work burned Thomas. He knew these people were guilty of the crimes they were being investigated for but looking at the evidence and what was likely to get thrown out, it was clear that they were going to walk away scot-free. Thomas would do his duty and his job and send the cases back to the detectives to gather more evidence or fix mistakes, but he was pessimistic as to the outcome.

It was then that he remembered what the man in black had said about wanting to help him, even if all he had to do was gather evidence. This might just be the tipping of the scales Thomas was looking for. If only he had a way to contact him.

****

Walter had a decision to make, and one that would not come easy. He wanted to get up with Thomas and go over his discovery that someone was actively trying to kill him and that he had clues to possibly unmask the identity of that individual. The problem was that he had no reliable way to contact the officer other than calling the station directly. He didn't even have the officer's cell phone number. But that wasn't really the problem. No, the problem was Walter wanted to fully bring the officer into his world. To work together in his secret lair and share his identity as a sign of trust.

Walter had no idea how Thomas would react to such a bombshell and had no plan as to what he should do if Thomas were to simply make his identity public knowledge or attempt to arrest him.

He wrestled with the idea for a while and came up with a compromise of sorts. He only hoped he could pull it off.

****

Thomas decided not to go home right away. His head was swimming from the revelations of the day and he needed someone to talk to. Fortunately for him, the only good news that he had received all day was that his partner, Rebecca, had come out of her coma and was responding well. Now he was on his way to go see her. Not only to check on her and let her know he was thinking about her, but also to use her as a sounding board. He had a lot on his mind and hated the thought of burdening her with even more than she was dealing with now, but she was his partner and would be pretty damn pissed at him if he didn't treat her the way a partner should.

Thomas walked into Rebecca's hospital room, flowers and stuffed animal in hand. He was going to do everything possible to embarrass her and treat her like a kid. He even had a balloon in mind for his next visit.

"Oh hi stranger." Rebecca greeted as she bid him entry. "Get in here you big lug. I'm sorry that you just missed Carl." Carl, her husband, had just left a few minutes before. He wanted to stay longer, but the baby needed to be fed and put down.

Rebecca and Thomas had a quick embrace, he was being careful not to hit her with his cast, and she was being cautious not to squeeze his broken ribs too tight.

"I'm glad to see you're getting better." He began as he handed her the flowers.

"Oh how sweet." She gushed over the carnations, her favorite. "I'm glad to see you're up and about as well. The captain told me about all the injuries you sustained. I'll take a bullet to the head over broken ribs any day."

"Well they did say you might have brain damage, but I know its got to be difficult to hit such a small target."

"Ha Ha." That is so funny. "Actually, the damage is minor. I'm fuzzy on a few details and my right arm feels numb, but it's functional. That appears to be the extent of the damage."

"Glad to hear it." Thomas instinctively looked down at her right arm and noticed the tremor. Hopefully that was something that would clear up in time.

"So what's on your mind?" Rebecca blurted out of the blue, completely blindsiding him.

"Who says…" He began to protest, but she cut him off.

"I've known you long enough to know when something is on your mind." She gave him the eye in return. "You've got trouble pressing down on you so hard you're about to make wine."

Thomas laughed at that but didn't bother to contradict her. Instead he filled her in about his new job, and what he was discovering about the possibility of dirty cops in the precinct.

"You know you need to go to the captain with this." She informed him, reaching the same conclusion he had hours ago. "He's the one that gave you this detail, so the odds are that he's not in on it."

"I know." Thomas agreed. "The problem is I either have evidence of corruption or incompetence. Neither is very good for the department, but incompetence isn't a crime. What if all I've got here is a couple of lazy cops, not bent ones?"

"What does your gut tell you?"

He didn't look at her for a moment. She had hit the nail on the head. She knew what he was thinking and why.

"My gut says that these guys are dirty." Thomas finally replied, his head lowered.

"Then get the evidence and take it to the captain." Rebecca commanded him. "Now suck it up and get out of here. I'm tired."

Thomas looked at her with a crooked grin and gave her another hug. He then turned and left without a word. He had work to do and it was not the kind he was going to enjoy.

****

Walter was waiting for Thomas when he got home. He had been sitting on the roof, killing time, waiting. He had expected him a long time ago.

As soon as Thomas got out of his car, Walter drifted down and landed on the man's front lawn.

"Good evening Officer Cantrell." Walter greeted before he even touched the ground.

"How did I know you were going to show up today." The unsurprised Thomas observed as he turned to face the man in black. "And it's detective now."

"Congratulations. That might make my request a little easier. I have a favor to ask you." Walter began, dispensing with the small talk and expected banter.

"Everybody needs a favor." Thomas huffed. "Everybody has their hand out."

Walter willed himself not to play the 'well I did save your life' card. It was not something he wanted to hold over the man.

"All I want is for you to come with me and take a look at some things." Walter attempted to explain. "I'll let you make the call from there as to what to do."

Thomas sighed, he didn't want to go, he didn't want any of this. But the fact that the man had saved his life was prevalent on his mind, as well as the fact that he wanted a favor in return from the man in black.

"Ok, ok." Thomas held up his hands in surrender. "I'll go with you."

"Oh and by the way," Walter stammered a bit. "I'll need you to be blindfolded."

Walter carried Thomas, who was complaining the entire time, toward his house. In fact, Thomas was so vehement in his protests that Walter threatened to drop him more than once. It was only after Walter did let him go, then caught him again, did Thomas calm down. After that, he was surprisingly cooperative.

Walter did make a slight miscalculation while trying to get Thomas into the house. After knocking his head against the door frame, he was able to readjust and get him in unseen. From there it was a quick trip to the closet and then he lowered him down into his secret lair.

Finally, he felt safe letting the police officer remove the hood he was wearing and take a look around.

"Nice digs." Thomas voiced in awe as he looked around. "Computers, television, a wet bar, is that gold over there?"

Thomas walked over to a stack of probably twenty large bars of gold. They were crudely formed, as if made in a makeshift mold, but they were still bars of gold.

"That's how I've been financing myself now." Walter confessed. "I found a vein in North Carolina, one in Alaska, and another in California. They were all on public land so I'm not stealing anyone's personal property. I found a nice vein in Colorado as well, but that one is on private land and I would have to buy it first."

"Nice." Thomas had to admit.

"Go ahead and take one if you want it." Walter offered. "It's honest money."

"Sort of."

"I've filed all the claims I need." Walter defended. "Everything has been done on the up and up. I even pay taxes on it."

"Is that a rifle?" Thomas pointed over to a weapon peeking out from the corner of the room. "It is isn't it. Are you planning something?"

"That rifle," Walter walked over and grabbed it from the corner and placed in on a table in the middle of the room. "Is what I wanted to talk to you about. Someone set me up and tried to kill me. That weapon was used to take a shot at me." He then put the casing down next to it. "It hurt like a son of a bitch too."

"They actually hit you and it didn't kill you?" Thomas was impressed. He knew enough about that particular weapon to know that it would have torn through a normal person like paper. Several normal persons for that matter. "Did you find the bullet?"

"No. I didn't even think to look for it." Walter confessed. "I figured that with the rifle you could duplicate any ballistics."

"We can. The bullet sometimes has a story to tell all its own though."

"Well between getting shot and having a car dropped on me, I was in a little discomfort." Walter explained. "I needed to come back here and heal up."

"How are you now?"

"I'm as good a new." Walter shrugged. "I guess it's good to know my limitations."

"Alright." Thomas nodded as he took another look at the weapon. "I'll look into it. But I'm going to need something in return."

"And what's that?"

"I might have a problem with some dirty cops." Thomas then spent the better part of an hour laying out the reasons for his suspicions and what he might want the man in black to do about it. "You offered to get me some evidence. That is what I'm asking for."

"How?" Walter was no expert when it came to police work. He was also pretty certain that most of the crime shows exaggerated the capabilities of the police and FBI.

"If these guys are on the take, they'll have to meet somewhere to get paid." Thomas explained. "This isn't exactly the kind of thing one gets direct deposit for. I've got an informant in Chinatown that says payments like this would happen around the first of the month so I'm thinking you discreetly follow a couple of the guys I think are dirty and bust up the meet."

Thomas then looked Walter up and down and cocked his head to the side.

"Do you think you can do discreet?"

"OH, check this out." Walter then made Thomas go wide-eyed as he stripped off his bicycle shorts and stood in front of him.

"Well, I guess that's impressive." Thomas mumbled awkwardly. "But I don't really see how that's the least bit subtle."

Walter then faded from view, making Cantrell gasp out loud.

"Ok. Now I'm definitely impressed. That is really cool." Thomas walked around where he believed Walter to still be standing. "Some kind of adaptive camouflage I'm guessing?"

"As I understand it, yes." Walter confirmed, not really knowing how everything worked. "I can change what I look like." Walter then changed his looks again and went through a myriad of different designs and emblems before changing back to all black and slipping his shorts back on.

"You can change at will, with all those cool options, and you go with simple all black?" Thomas as shaking his head now.

"I couldn't decide what I should look like." Walter protested with a bit of a whine. "All the good graphics, and names for that matter, are taken by comic books. You really don't appreciate how prolific comic book writers are until you try researching a cool name, only to find out that it has been taken."

"I was kind of partial to Super Wang, myself." Thomas laughed.

"Very funny."

As Walter flew Thomas home he listened to the detective list one superhero name after another only to reply that each one was taken.

By the time the two had parted ways for the evening each was left with questions about the other. Still a partnership seemed to be brewing and both were left hopeful for the future.

****

Memory Foam Download: Subject was able to establish a cooperative agreement with local law enforcement agents. Although specifics were vague it would appear that a great deal of undercover work will be required.

On the way back to his domicile, the subject stopped to break up two robberies, helped push one disabled vehicle off the road, and rescued a little girl's feline from a tree.

Note for future reference. When rescuing a feline from a tree, do not attempt to pull down the branch and pluck the cat from said tree. Subject attempted just this type of tactic and the branch he was holding suffered a catastrophic failure. Cat was launched approximately one-hundred-feet before it was recaptured by subject using super speed. It is unlikely that the feline will attempt tree climbing anytime in the near future.

Blikzak and Raknid were riveted to the reports coming in from the memory foam pillow. Not only were the reports getting more interesting, but the pillow was finally showing real signs of the AI built into it.

"Well it just may seem like we will get the results we wanted from this experiment after all." Blikzak observed as he reclined in his chair.

"Let's not get ahead of ourselves here." Raknid cautioned. "It is true that all indications are that the subject is going to remain a good guy, and he even has the assistance of local law enforcement, but he could still fall into hero burnout when he sees just how much he has to do.

"It is such an odd thing that for all the art, music, poetry and kindness that this species is capable of, it still goes out of its way to commit so much horror on itself. Once our hero gets a real face-full of the despicable crime of which man is capable, he might just change his spots."

"I'm willing to bet that he stays on the side of good." Blikzak stated flatly. "I would wager that he destroys only one villain. As in kills only one. After he gets a taste of how bad that is, he never does it again. And even when he does do it, he is left with little choice."

"I'm less optimistic." Raknid shook his head. "After a little while of watching the revolving door of the criminal justice system, I believe he will begin sentencing the evildoers he catches himself. I think he will stay a good guy, but he will take a darker path."

"How much you want to bet?" Blikzak perked up, smelling easy money.

"Two cases of beer?"

"It's a bet." Blikzak quickly agreed.

CHAPTER 15

Jimmy Fang was not at all happy as he scrolled through the report Mister Koi had put together on his computer. He was even less pleased when he watched the video files the Russians had provided as well.

"What kind of armor is that man wearing that he can withstand a hit like that?" Jimmy demanded to know but was well aware of the fact that there were no answers coming.

"We don't know." Mister Koi admitted from the corner of the room where he often stood. "We have yet to divine how he sustains flight, his armor and its weaknesses, and the source of his super strength. I have shown this footage to our chief chemist, as he is the closest thing we have to a scientist, and he cannot see any evidence of a mechanical exoskeleton, thrusters or anything that would explain any of these things.

"His only suggestion was that this might not be a person at all."

"What do you mean?"

"His theory is that we are looking at a machine." Mister Koi explained. "A machine that is controlled wirelessly by a human operator and is designed to look almost human. If that is the case, then the hydraulics, actuators and metal framing that would have to be on the outside if it were a human, can now be run inside and out of sight if it is a machine.

"It still doesn't explain the powers of flight, but it goes a long way toward explaining everything else. The speed, the strength, and the durability of this masked man."

"Which may not be a mask at all." Jimmy threw in, grasping the gist of what was being explained to him. "If this truly is a robot, it would explain why some of the facial expressions we have witnessed, seemed clunky and artificial. Almost as if it were a computer displaying emojis."

Mister Koi was impressed by how quickly his friend reached the same conclusion he had. All he needed was a nudge in the right direction.

"All of this is terribly fascinating," Jimmy then switched gears. "But it does nothing to alleviate our problem, nor does it grant me the revenge I seek for my son."

"It may not, but if the robot theory proves to be correct, that would mean that someone, somewhere is controlling it." Mister Koi continued on, undaunted by his friend's tendency to change moods quickly. "And if they are controlling it, then there must be a signal."

"And if we can discover that signal's frequency," Jimmy finished for him. "We can trace it to its source."

"Just so." Koi nodded in the affirmative.

"Very good Mister Koi." Jimmy smiled, satisfied. "Very good work indeed."

"My honor is to serve." Koi bowed.

****

Walter did his usual efficient job while working from home and had all of his messages returned, and normal work done in less than thirty minutes. He had considered quitting when he discovered how easy it was to get the gold he needed to provide for himself, but he felt that this was part of his operational cover and it wasn't as if his job was all that hard to begin with. Focus on your work, return all calls, dot the 'I' cross the 'T' and done. The biggest complaint he heard about anyone at his place of employment was that they didn't return calls. People could handle mistakes, delays, or anything else as long as they were kept informed. It was when they felt ignored that they would lose their cool. That being the case, Walter was a very attentive employee.

It was shortly before ten in the morning, when Walter's workday and start of his practice sessions were interrupted by a knock at the door.

Walter was mildly surprised by this event as he was not expecting any visitors, none of his neighbors knew he was working from home now, and he had no outstanding orders for delivery. Still it was a curiosity that called to be investigated and good manners demanded that he not simply ignore the potential visitor.

Shock, surprise and confusion reigned upon his face as he opened the door to find Detective Cantrell standing there.

"Hello Walter Scrum, you really should invest in a better-quality blindfold." Cantrell informed him as he stood there reading the shock on Walter's face. "I could see right through the one you gave me."

Walter's face fell, and he simply motioned for the detective to come inside.

"I was really hoping to keep the deep, dark secret going for a little while. We don't exactly have the deepest reservoir of trust at the moment." Walter grumped as he let the detective in. "But since you aren't here with a SWAT team trying to take me in, I guess I'll let it slide."

"There were times I had considered it." Thomas shook his head. "Especially if there was a chance to catch you without your suit on."

"Good luck there." Walter chuckled. "I can't take the damn thing off."

"What?" Thomas didn't understand, instead he waved his hand at the khaki and polo shirt wearing man standing in front of him. "It doesn't look like you're wearing it now. Is the mask retractable or something?"

Walter activated the suit, complete with the mask, and Thomas gasped as the man in black appeared before him, still wearing the casual clothing over the top.

"What the hell is that thing?" Thomas was finally able to gasp out.

"It's a bonded suit made of tiny robots, called nanites." Walter shrugged. "It's bonded to my skin, I can't take it off."

"And you said it was an accident?" Thomas remembered the conversation they had earlier. "How and where were you when this happened?"

"Actually, it was aliens who gave me this power." Walter watched as Thomas' mouth dropped open. "As far as I can remember they live in a base on, or more accurately, inside of the moon."

"Wait you expect me to believe aliens are real and gave you this power, come on." Thomas nearly rolled his eyes but was being too serious for that.

"Let me get this straight," Walter began, a distinct sarcastic tone emanating from him as he shut down the suit features and returned to normal. "I have super strength, super speed, I can fly, shoot lasers from my eyes and am bulletproof, and *aliens* is the part you have trouble with?"

"Good point." Thomas was forced to concede.

Thomas then reached into a bag he was carrying and pulled out a file folder, which he immediately handed to Walter.

"What's this?" Walter inquired as he took the contents and began to leaf through them.

"That weapon you gave me has a colorful history." Thomas then watched in amazement as Walter breezed through the entire report in a matter of seconds.

"Evidently it was purchased eight years ago and then promptly stolen from its original owner, then ballistics matches it to three murders and one attempt on a judge in Boston." Walter tossed the folder on his table and continued. "Then was seized locally in a bust and supposedly destroyed two years ago. Now it has found its way here and is shooting at me."

"It is that seized locally and destroyed part that gets to me." Thomas spat. "Again, this points to dirty cops in the department."

"You're thinking that cops intercepted this weapon on its way to the furnace and redirected it toward the criminal element?" Walter deduced correctly.

"I'm willing to bet that this one isn't the only one either." Thomas grumped. "I doubt it's a lot of small arms, as those would get picked up often and people would notice that they were due for destruction and somehow back out there. But if one rather exotic weapon made its way back into the bad guy's hands, you can bet that there are others."

"What kind of exotic weapons?" Walter cocked an eyebrow at his new friend.

"I pulled the destruction list over the past three years to get an idea of what the bad guys with money might want and I found something interesting." Thomas sighed. "All of the weapons I think would really appeal to the professional criminal element aren't destroyed locally. Things like grenades, RPGs, and other kinds of explosives are sent to a private contractor to be disposed of. That .50 caliber was one of the items sent to them for destruction."

"And if that one weapon made it back out onto the streets then the chances are that other stuff did as well." Walter finished for him. "Sounds like we need to pay a visit to this contractor."

"We?" Thomas scoffed. "There is no we here. This is a law enforcement thing, not a vigilante thing."

"Ok, if you want to raid a company that has access to high explosives and high caliber weapons I'm not going to stop you." Walter then shrugged. "It probably wouldn't be useful to have someone with you that is proven to be bulletproof, super strong, can see through walls and move at super speeds."

Unfortunately for Thomas the arguments he was making were completely logical and couldn't be disputed. After a moment or two of thought, he finally admitted as much.

"I'm going to regret this." Thomas sighed.

****

Sergi and Nikoli were sipping tea in the enclosed solarium of Sergi's mansion in the upper-class suburb that they both lived in a few blocks apart. Both filled the time with small talk about how the kids were doing, school, work for them, and how the wives were getting along. It was just filler until the real business of business could be discussed.

It was finally the elder that brought the conversation around to the problem at hand and how to best deal with it.

"How goes the hunt for the man in black?" Sergi inquired as he put down the paper he had been leafing through.

"Fang has been good enough to share some of his ideas on the man with us." Nikoli replied as he refilled his cup of tea. "His people seem to think that this man is actually some kind of artificial entity. A robot or android for a lack of a better word. They believe that it is being intelligently controlled from another location. The thought is that if we can disrupt the signal we can take control of the robot. Also, if we can trace the signal, we can follow it back to the person doing the controlling."

"Sounds logical, but I can tell in the hesitation in your speech that you don't agree." Sergi correctly surmised.

"You've seen the same footage I have Papa." Nikoli began. "The man in black is too fluid, too graceful. I have seen the research our contacts at DARPA have shown us over the years. Everything artificial is clunky and clumsy. It moves in a very robotic and predictable way. This man doesn't do that."

"What do you propose to do then?" His father pressed.

"We are going to make another attempt to destroy him." Nikoli informed him bluntly. "I've already put the plan into motion. The bait is ready and all we need is the correct timing."

"What are you using for bait this time?"

"The same woman as before." Nikoli winced a little at that. "She was most uncooperative after the last attempt and threatened to go to the police. It would seem that she was rather upset at being put in a situation where she could have been killed. This, if successful, will eliminate two problems with one solution. Even if it is unsuccessful in killing the man in black, it will probably result in the death of Sasha Tuplov."

"And her brother?" Sergi raised an eyebrow at his son. "What does he think about the possible loss of his sister?"

"He did not seem to have much of a problem with it." Nikoli assured him. "He informed me that the two weren't all that close."

"And…?" Sergi pressed.

"I had his employment terminated on the spot." Nikoli shrugged. "Any man that won't stand up for his own family would probably fail to stand up for us."

"Good boy." Sergi nodded. "I see I've taught you well."

The two then returned to their tea and resumed the small talk about their family.

****

Memory Foam Download: Subject spent most of day researching possible criminal connections of a major corporation. Is now working with the police on regular basis and has revealed secret identity to at least one other person.

This unit is unclear if the revelation of his secret identity was on purpose, but both parties seemed satisfied with the results.

Item of interest: Nightly patrols continue as the subject requires less sleep. The interfering with petty crimes such as assaults and robberies have continued.

Item of interest: Metabolism seems to have stabilized and the subject seems to have found a balance in his required nutritional intake.

****

Blikzak and Raknid both read through the reports from the microcircuitry pillow with a sense of relief. They were quite happy that Walter had gotten the hang of his powers, they were even aware that Walter seemed to have managed to gain a nemesis in the form of organized crime. This was getting good and seemed it would only promise to get better.

"When would you like to call our bet fulfilled?" Blikzak inquired of his superior officer and friend.

"When I get back from vacation." Raknid replied.

"Oh, I had forgotten about that." Blikzak was almost excited about being left alone for a few months. "When do you leave?"

"In ten cycles or so." Raknid sighed. "With the next automated supply ship."

Raknid was not looking forward to a long space journey with no one on board to interact with. He had hoped that he would get a manned ship, so he could practice his social skills a little bit and get filled in on any homeworld news that wouldn't make the downloads. This would be his first vacation in over a thousand years, so he was a little out of practice when it came to dealing with others of his kind. Blikzak had been his only companion for so long that their interactions had taken on a life of their own. It was very probable that others of his kind would be using entirely different speech patterns, phrases and references. That didn't even begin to address any changes in customs or manners.

He couldn't help but remember the last time he was on his homeworld and tried to interact with others in a social establishment. The phrases they used were so different than the ones he was used to. It was like being a time traveler without the benefit of having skipped years of boredom.

Truth be told, he wasn't going just for a vacation. He felt that some of the data they had collected on the new generation of nanites needed to be looked at and studied. He was going to make sure someone took the data seriously. If he simply sent the report it would probably just get buried somewhere. After all, this generation of nanites that he had access to was probably several generations behind the ones the people of his home world were using. The ones he had bonded to him were tenth generation and the ones he had bonded to Walter Scrum were twentieth generation. Some of the reading he had gone through indicated that most people were up the thirtieth generation with a gen-three-five due to be released any day.

Raknid toyed with the idea of upgrading to the latest and greatest, but really couldn't see the point. The ones he had worked just fine and unlike Walter's suit, turning on the industrial/superhero modes was illegal and regulated. It could be done in an emergency, or when carefully licensed, but that was all. The planet patriarchs didn't want millions of super-strong and super-fast citizens running around. The damage could be enormous.

"Well don't forget to turn your clothing options back on when you get home." Blikzak chuckled. "We've been running around not worrying about configuring clothing for so long, you might not even think about it."

"I'll try to remember." His reply sounded sarcastic, but in truth it was a genuine concern. With just the two of them alone for so long they didn't even bother with clothing anymore.

"Are you going to get a new body while you're there?" Blikzak poked a little at his own expanding midsection in consideration of his question.

The duo's race had long ago gone to cloning as a means of reproduction. That was not to say that they didn't engage in intercourse, but for most that was purely a basic pleasure function and not a means of making babies. Instead original material was harvested from the first body, then it was preserved and duplicated. Original material could be used for eons, and thus helped avoid the problems of replication degradation.

There were still a few traditionalists that had children the old-fashioned way, but they were in the minority. Not rare by any stretch, but uncommon enough to stand out.

Blikzak and Raknid had all of the necessary equipment to create new cloned bodies with them on the moon, but all the genetic material they used came from the copy of their body that they arrived with. This led to a micro amount of replication degradation but wasn't enough to worry about. Still, when they got the chance, they liked to procure a new body from the original source.

"I probably will." Raknid confessed. "This old model is beginning to show its age. The joints are beginning to wear out and the digestive tract has never worked quite right."

"I am aware." Blikzak indicated as he put his hand over his nose.

CHAPTER 16

Walter flew high above the road below that Thomas was currently driving on. He was still able to keep his vehicle in sight. Thomas could not say the same thing about Walter, as he couldn't take his eyes off the road long enough to look for him. Even if he did, Walter was currently using the adaptive camo option on his suit and was nearly invisible.

Walter didn't like Thomas's plan, such that it was. Thomas had simply vied for the knock on the door approach. He had set up a meeting with the head of Dark Forest, the company that had been contracted to destroy all of the confiscated military quality equipment. That man, one Victor Jackson, was all too happy to meet with any representatives of the city's finest boys in blue.

His enthusiasm for the meet immediately put Thomas on edge. Most guilty people were either stubbornly uncooperative, or extremely helpful. The people that were innocent, were usually cooperative, but complained about wasted time, grumped about inconveniences or were simply a little nervous about being any kind of a suspect and tended to run on with information that wasn't really relevant to what the police were looking for.

The long drive to the Dark Forest compound did nothing to put his mind at ease either. He understood the reason the compound was so far away from any population centers. It was a company that trained specialized security, tactical police units and even helped out the government by training active military and those that did off the books work. They had access to heavy weapons, explosives and armored vehicles. Not the kinds of things you wanted rolling through the suburbs and shattering the white picket fence illusions. Having shooting and grenade ranges nearby public schools and parks would probably never be classified as a good thing.

As Thomas made the turn into the compound's front gate, his apprehension was ratcheted up even higher as the guard, complete with automatic weapons, checked his ID, compared it to his schedule and eventually waved him inside.

"I sure hope you're up there." Thomas mumbled softly as he drove toward the main building.

"I am." Walter replied, even though Thomas couldn't hear him. Walter, on the other hand, could not only hear Thomas' every whisper but he could even make out the accelerated heart rate the police officer had going on.

They had toyed with trying to get communications going both ways, but Thomas didn't want to take the chance that he would be spotted with them or searched. There were already signs everywhere warning about unauthorized recordings of both the video and audio nature.

"Going in." Thomas unnecessarily informed his invisible partner as he exited his vehicle.

The walk through the lobby was full of all the things one would expect to find in a paramilitary establishment. Plaques and displays embellishing the glories of warfare were in abundance. There were jeeps, weapons, and even old military aircraft hanging for display purposes. It was exactly the kind of place Thomas would have loved to have taken a while to view if he were not on the job.

"Detective Caldwell?" The woman behind the desk inquired as he made his approach.

"Cantrell." He corrected.

"Oh Cantrell." She gushed. "I apologize."

"That's ok." He assured her. "It's a lot better than what I get called most days."

She dutifully laughed and gestured for him to follow her. She then led him down a short hallway to a large set of double doors and didn't even pause before throwing them open.

"Mister Jackson will be with you in a moment." She assured him. "Is there anything I can get you in the meantime? Coffee, soda, water?"

"No, No." Thomas declined, even though he would have loved another cup of coffee. "I'm fine."

She nodded and left him alone, closing the doors behind her as she departed.

Thomas used his alone time to appreciate the office and the myriad of military memorabilia that had made the transition from the foyer to this office. He was especially interested in some of the displays containing larger caliber weapons. Some, that he was willing to bet that had made their way from the scrap pile to the display case. He was intensely interested in one weapon in particular, an old .50 caliber machine gun.

"Almost a hundred years old and still the design is basically unchanged." A well-dressed man announced as he walked toward Thomas at the display case. "It is hard to improve on perfection.

"I'm Victor, Victor Jackson." The man stuck out his hand and firmly grasped Thomas'

"It is an impressive piece." Thomas admitted. "It also reminds me of why I'm here."

"That so?" Victor shrugged slightly. "Why is that?"

Thomas fumbled with his briefcase for a moment, his left arm, still in its cast, not being very cooperative. After much effort he was able to remove a picture and handed it to Victor.

"This turned up at the scene of a crime." Thomas then handed him another photo, one with the serial number clearly visible. "Its serial number matches one that was scheduled for destruction. Scheduled for destruction by your company, as a matter of fact."

"Now Detective," Victor put up his hands in a defensive gesture. "Certainly you're not accusing us of any wrongdoing?"

"Put yourself in my shoes, Mister Jackson." Thomas continued, levelly meeting the man's gaze. "If you found a weapon that was supposed to be destroyed and wasn't, where would your first stop be?"

"Probably right here." Victor admitted. The man then walked back and sat behind his enormous glass desk. "Can you give me that serial number again?"

Thomas read off the serial number and watched as Victor typed it into the computer that was tied to his glass desk.

"Ah, here it is." Victor announced as a readout appeared on his desk. "Batch 1201. It was stolen. In fact, the entire contents of the container were stolen."

"I suppose there is a police report to verify that?" Thomas was suspicious but couldn't dispute what the man was saying. At least not yet.

"We are a long way from the city out here, Detective." Victor explained. "The report was made to the county sheriff. I doubt word of it would have made it back to you. But the short answer is, yes, there is a report on file."

"So where was this container when it was stolen?" Thomas pressed.

"It was here." Victor sighed. "Waiting in its cue for destruction."

"Let me get this right." Thomas returned, his suspicious gaze meeting Victor's. "Someone drove a truck, a large truck, onto this heavily guarded and armed compound, broke into a storage container full of heavy weapons and explosives, and drove away unchecked?"

"As you can image detective," Victor's tone was controlled, but there was the edge of anger in it. He was not a man that was used to being questioned. "The container is not parked in populated areas or close to anything important. It did have some high explosives in it so I'm not about to keep it close to my office.

"That being said, it was set in an area that is designated a safe zone in the event that something were to happen. You could imagine that it is an area where people don't spend a lot of time."

"I can certainly understand that." Thomas then sighed and attempted to defuse the man's temper that he had intentionally irked. "I have to ask, you understand. When weapons that were slated for destruction end up taking pot shots at my fellow officers, it tends to raise my dander."

"Understandable." Victor was beginning to calm a little.

"I would like to request a list of everything that was stolen." Thomas was well aware that this wasn't really his jurisdiction, but he was hoping that Victor was fuzzier on the law than he was. "If these weapons have made their way back into the city then we need to know what to keep on the lookout for."

"Of course." Victor nodded. "I'll have my people email you a list. I'm sure it was in the report we gave the sheriff, so it should be in a file here as well."

"Did they catch whoever stole the weapons?" Thomas inquired, cocking his head in curiosity.

"Not to my knowledge." Victor sighed. "We gave them camera footage of what we think was the vehicle used for the robbery arriving and departing, but to no avail."

"I see." Thomas then got up to leave. "That's about all I have in regards to questions, but would you mind terribly if I took a look around your facility. I've never been here and have no idea if I'll ever be out this way again. It seems very interesting."

"Be my guest." Victor invited graciously. "Go where ever you wish. I'm sure a man of your experience can tell which range is hot and were to stay out of."

"Thank you. I'll try to not get myself hurt." Thomas laughed and turned to leave.

Victor watched the policeman go and then picked up his phone as soon as Thomas closed the door behind him.

"Yes, we have a detective walking around the facility." Victor informed the man on the other end of the line. "Please make sure some harm comes to him, and make sure it looks like an accident. There are a lot of trucks moving around here, it would be a shame if the good detective were to step out in front of one."

"Understood." Came the one-word reply.

Thomas was moving from building to building, looking for any evidence of wrongdoing that he could use to justify a more in-depth examination of the place. The problem was, that he wasn't finding anything useful. Most of the buildings were garages or storage areas. There were a few areas set up for tactical scenarios that would be acted out with paintball guns, but the hard ammo and live fire ranges were all a good way away from the main office areas. It wasn't until Thomas exited one of the garages and stepped into an open courtyard that things began to get interesting.

The truck that came backing toward the detective was moving at a high rate of speed. Thomas barely had a chance to acknowledge that he was in danger before it became evident that there was going to be nothing that he could do to avoid impact. He wouldn't even have time to brace himself before contact would be made.

He had just resigned himself to the fact that he was going to be hit when the entire back end of the truck caved inward onto itself. It was as if the truck had just run into an invisible concrete post. The driver was pushed deep into his seat and given a good case of whiplash. He was expecting to hit a soft human target, not an immovable object.

Thomas could barely make out the outline of Walter in his adaptive camouflage as he strained to arrest the momentum of the high-speed vehicle. The detective had no idea where Walter had come from, or how fast he was moving when he hit the truck. He was simply grateful that his new friend was there.

"Are you ok?" Thomas whispered to the vague shape that kneeled behind the truck.

"I've been better." Walter replied as he staggered to his feet. "I had to come in awful fast to get here before you went splat."

"Well I appreciate it." Thomas then moved to the cab of the truck and saw the man there rubbing his neck, with a confused look on his face. "Are you alright?"

The driver simply groaned in reply, still shaking the cobwebs from his brain. He would never really know what had just happened, but he knew he had hit something a lot more substantial than the detective standing a few feet from him.

"Where the hell did you come from?" The driver finally managed.

That sentence ruined any chance that Thomas may have had of proving that this was an intentional act. There was going to be no way to even infer that this was anything more than the random act of an impatient and inattentive driver. Even Thomas would have that irritating nag of doubt, even though he knew full well that this had been an attempt on his life.

Thomas didn't stick around to explain what had happened or make any accusations. The last thing he needed at the moment, was to try and explain what had happened to the back end of the truck. He couldn't very well say an invisible superhero was responsible for damaging the vehicle. And he certainly couldn't claim to have done it himself. An admission like that would never be believed and the implications that he was friendly with the superhero working about the city could have disastrous implications as well.

Relief was in abundance as Thomas exited the compound without anyone attempting to stop him. He had even made it several miles away from the place before the groan from his backseat startled him so badly it nearly made him run off the road.

"What the hell?" Thomas yelled out as he got his car back under control.

As he looked back he watched Walter change from invisible mode to all black with no facemask this time.

"You scared the hell out of me!" Thomas protested, his heart still racing from the experience.

"You're welcome." Walter replied, his black suit fading to reveal the deep purpled bruises on his midsection. They were beginning to shrink and fade even as he looked at them, but they were still clearly visible.

"Wow, that truck really did a number on you, didn't it?"

"I've had more pleasant experiences." Walter grumped back. "That guy was aiming directly at you, the truck was armored for military use and weighed in at several tons, and the velocity he had attained was impressive to say the least."

"Well I do appreciate you taking the hit for me." Thomas admitted sincerely. "That's two I owe you."

"I'm not looking to keep score." Walter replied with a weak smile. "But I am going to ask you to pull over, so I can get my clothes out of the trunk. I need to sleep, heal, and recharge a bit."

"You can't sleep in your suit?" Thomas then immediately corrected himself. "I mean, in this configuration?"

"I have no idea what my body looks like when I'm sleeping." Walter confessed. "It might look like this, it could look like my pajamas, or it could just look like me in my birthday suit."

"Why don't you know?" Thomas inquired.

"Because I'm unconscious at the time." Walter shot back with a bit of a chuckle. "Plus, I live alone. I've not had a real lady friend since this happened to me."

"Real lady friend?" Thomas arched an eyebrow at his friend.

"I went to a massage parlor once." Walter confessed. "It didn't end well."

"No happy ending?"

"Oh, I got a happy ending, but the massage parlor didn't." Walter then went on to fill Thomas in on his experience of shooting a hole in the roof of the massage establishment. A story which filled Thomas with much delight and provided him with much amusement. Walter could tell that this was not a story he was going to hear the end of any time in the near future.

"Did you learn anything of use back there?" Walter inquired, trying to change the subject.

"Just a list of items that are probably on the street." Thomas sighed. "They are too good at covering their tracks for me to get them on anything right now. If it is true that they filed a police report about items being stolen from here, there is going to be zero I can do to them."

"Wasted trip then?" Walter groaned. "Because my flying around using my x-ray vision didn't turn up anything obvious either."

"I wouldn't exactly say it was wasted." Thomas countered. "If this list is accurate, and I suspect it is, we at least have an idea what can be used against you. I have to tell you, it's not a pretty list."

"Didn't think they'd be throwing flowers." Walter replied.

****

Nikoli looked over his plan to eliminate the man in black for the hundredth time. He had prepared for this event as best he could, but his main source of research was the imaginations of dozens of comic book writers and movie producers. Even so, it led him to take certain precautions where the hero was involved.

One of the takeaways he managed from his reading was the fact that his nemesis might have X-ray vision. He therefore reasoned that the same precautions that medical technicians used to protect themselves from X-Rays might just be used to block the hero's vision.

There were other things as well. Some comic book heroes were susceptible to sonic waves, some were vulnerable to certain colors, and others had weaknesses where certain radiations were concerned. Nikoli had no idea how to handle or reproduce any kind of radiation, but he could put some of the other information to use.

His plan consisted of placing the bait, Sasha, in the middle of an abandoned cement factory. Once the hero had been lured in, men that were hidden in lead-lined boxes would emerge and attempt to take out the man in black. Large sonic weapons, the kind used on cruise ships and for riot control, would open fire from three different locations. Then a barrage of rockets, launched from shoulder-fired launchers, would be thrown into the mix. The crescendo of the battle would be the multitude of claymore mines that were spread about the factory floor.

If this didn't combine to bring the hero to a spectacular end, Nikoli would have no idea what to do. Short of dropping a building on this man, he couldn't see being able to bring the kind of firepower needed to destroy this man if this didn't work. Anything more he attempted would be sure to bring the entire police force down on him, possibly even with help from the national guard to try and hunt him down.

Nikoli briefly wondered if he could get the Army to do his dirty work for him and destroy this man. The problem was, that even if he could get the Army involved, it would destroy his objective, which was obtaining the secret of the man in black's power. That was a something he would only sacrifice if the man in black became a direct threat to his and his father's organization. And right now, he doubted that the hero even knew who was attempting to take him out. Heroes made enemies. That much was true of the comic books, and of real life.

Nikoli then looked back at the diagram he had laid out and decided that it was possibly the best he was going to be able to do. It was now time to call in his lieutenants and figure out how to best execute his vision.

****

"Our sources within the Russian's organization have provided my news as to their progress in hunting down the masked vigilante." Mister Koi announced as he entered his boss's office.

"What did they reveal?" Jimmy inquired as he looked up from his work.

"After the first attempt on the man in black, they decided to use more firepower to accomplish their task." Koi began, pacing as he spoke. "They are now going to attempt to blow him up using a combination of landmines and rockets. As I understand it, they are even going to throw in some kind of sonic weapon that I am unfamiliar with."

"Do you think it will work?" Jimmy gave his friend the eye.

"Even if it does not, it will seriously deplete the weapons stores of our adversary. Possibly even his manpower reserves as well." Koi was trying to put a good face on possible failure, but that was why they were using the Russians to begin with. "I understand that this has already cost them one mid-level man. Although I have yet to ascertain whether he was killed by the hero or by his own people."

Jimmy nodded absently. He had no idea what to think about all of this now. Personally, he was more than happy to let the Russians run point on this, even if his organization had to take a temporary blow to its prestige. Jimmy played the long game and if reducing the Russian's capabilities was all he was going to get out of this grand game, then that was what he would accept. Knowing what the Russians were capable of might just be useful when the time came to wrest control of their territory from them.

"Keep me informed." Jimmy finally said in dismissal.

Mister Koi, recognizing that his boss wanted to be alone, simply bowed and backed out of his office.

Jimmy called up the items he had been working on, on his computer. Blueprints and structural schematics filled the screen. He had been studying them intently trying to find the weak points of several major buildings in the city. It was his failsafe. If he couldn't kill the superhero he would make him afraid to act against him. This provision included planting explosives in several buildings around the city. If the hero became a persistent problem and wouldn't back off, Jimmy would destroy one of the structures and threaten to do the same to the others.

It was a bold plan and somewhat insane, but innocent lives meant nothing to Jimmy, especially American lives. Jimmy still viewed himself as a patriot to his homeland. Americans only existed to fill his pockets and provide him with material possessions. If he had to kill them all and return home, he would do so. He even thought about doing exactly that someday. Perhaps when he was ready to retire, or flee the country, he would lace his already poisonous product with something more lethal. Then sit back and watch as thousands of drug users overwhelmed the country's infrastructure and medical networks. But until then, he would work to squeeze every dime he could get out of the users and abusers of this country.

Money wasn't the only motivator where the man in black was concerned, although it was high on the list. Jimmy still wanted revenge for his son's injuries. The man had dared to attack his house and he would pay for it. That revenge, however, was now viewed as a bonus to his agenda. Jimmy recognized the danger an invulnerable man posed to his organization and realized that it was only a matter of time before the hero turned his sights on him. Getting ahead of the game and either killing him or finding out how to do so was to his benefit. And if he couldn't be killed, he could be neutralized, hence the failsafe.

Jimmy sighed and pinched the bridge of his nose in frustration. He was learning all he could about structural integrity and architecture, but it was slow going. What he really wanted was to consult an actual expert in construction. That, alas, was one of the industries that he ran legitimately and couldn't risk consulting people there on how to commit mass murder. Nor did he know of any engineers that would be willing to help him on that front.

Just getting his people on board, when the time came, was going to be hard enough. Most of them were hardened fighters that would dispose of their enemies and his with great enthusiasm. Getting them to arrange the murder of thousands of innocents might not be as easy to do. Most of his men had a twisted moral compass, but even those had limits. It was the reason that Jimmy had never put any stock into the 9/11 theories that populated the internet. Trying to get as many people together that were willing to commit mass murder of innocent civilians without at least one of them talking, seemed problematic at best. The government couldn't even manage a DMV, let alone a conspiracy on that grand a scale.

Jimmy imagined that if it came down to rigging this failsafe, he was certain that he would have to be directly involved and even get his hands dirty. It had been a while since he had to do that kind of manual labor, but he was no stranger to it. He might be one of the wealthiest men in the city now, but that was not always the case. There had been a time when Jimmy had worked his hands raw in the fields of his homeland. That seemed like a lifetime ago, but the memory refused to fade and served as a reminder of how far he had come.

An idea then occurred to him. A way to get the setup he desired and get the help he needed. It would cost, but not more than he was willing to spend, and it would deflect blame should things go wrong. A smile that would shrivel the hearts of most men then crawled across Jimmy's face as he contemplated the pros and cons of his new idea.

CHAPTER 17

Thomas was not the most confident person when it came to high places. He had been able to stand flying with Walter mostly because of a combination of keeping his eyes shut and the fact that Walter had him in an iron grip. Not that Thomas would admit to feeling safe in Walter's arms, sometimes guys just act like guys. That was not the case at the moment, however, as Thomas and Walter stood on top of a tall building and waited for a meeting that was supposed to be taking place on top of the parking garage across the street.

"I hate this." Thomas whined as he scratched his arm under his cast. "I hate the heights, I hate the cold wind, and I hate the waiting."

"You also hate the fact that your cast is itching like crazy." Walter replied, not bothering to look over at his new friend.

"Thanks for reminding me." Thomas griped.

"It's hardly reminding you, when you're already scratching."

"Do you see anything yet?" Thomas attempted to steer the subject away from his complaints.

"A tan sedan just pulled up." Walter replied, his magnified vision cutting through the darkness. "Looks like it's a police vehicle. Looks like your informant was on the mark."

Thomas adjusted the video camera and the parabolic microphone. He just hoped that the wind didn't drown out the voices he was trying to catch. No sooner had Thomas gotten everything on point when a second sedan pulled up.

"Looks like a couple of Jimmy Fang's boys." Thomas muttered as he looked through the viewfinder. "They've got a bag with them. Can you see what's inside of it?"

"Looks like money to me." Walter replied, squinting a bit. He then shifted his gaze back to the police officers. "The bag your boys in blue have looks to have some paperwork in it."

"I didn't even catch that." Thomas focused in on the bag his coworkers had in their possession and waited. "Looks like a classic exchange."

"Do you want me to bust it up?" Walter asked a little too eagerly.

"Not just yet." Thomas dashed his enthusiasm. "If my contact is correct, these guys will now drive across town and meet with some members of the Russian families to do this all over again. I want evidence of both meets so I can go to the captain."

"What about the guys Fang sent?" Walter inquired. "Can I disrupt their daily routine?"

Thomas thought for couple of moments, all the while filming the exchange of bags.

"I actually do want to find out what is in the bag my guys gave them." Thomas finally sighed out loud. "If you are confident that you can retrieve the bag and still get me across town to the Russian meet, then yes you can bust them up. A little."

"Got it." With that Walter was up like a shot and searching for the vehicle he had seen on the roof. It did not take him long to locate it as there was not a lot of traffic and even fewer cars on the road with that many people in it.

Walter then dived down and positioned himself in the middle of the street. The driver of the car saw him and accelerated toward the man in black who never moved a muscle. The impact of the irresistible force meeting the immovable object was epic. The vehicle folded around Walter, who was now experienced enough with such an impact to adjust himself to limit any injury. That was not to say that the impact felt good, but at least it wouldn't leave bruises or hurt like the armored truck did.

The men in the car were not wearing seatbelts and were launched forward, impacting the front seats, the steering wheel and the windshield with great force. None of them punched through it, as their speed never got up that high in the short distance they had to accelerate, but none of them would be walking away from the crash or were free from injury.

Walter casually walked around to the passenger side of the vehicle and tore the door off. He then scanned all of the occupants of the car to make sure that none of them was in any real danger of expiring. After he was satisfied that there were no internal injuries beyond broken bones and bruises, he grabbed the gym bag that the police had given them and launched himself back into the sky.

Seconds later he was back on the roof with Thomas and started gathering up the equipment. Thomas had been packing it up since Walter had left, but he hadn't gotten very far. Between his arm still being in a cast and his lack of familiarity with the equipment he wasn't packing it up very quickly.

To his credit, Walter said nothing, he simply handed the bag to his friend and used his super speed to not only read the packing instructions, but to get it all secured for flight. Moments later, Walter was carrying Thomas on his back while carrying the surveillance equipment in a large net below himself. To the casual observer he looked almost like a helicopter with a large sling-load dangling underneath it. It was not something that one would see every day, but it wasn't anything that would stand out either.

"You need a saddle or something." Thomas complained as he struggled to maintain his balance and grip upon his friend's back.

"You were the one that didn't want to pre-stage anything." Walter shot back.

"Not only could we not take the chance that the stuff would be discovered and tip our hand, or get stolen, the brass wouldn't let me check out duplicate sets of gear." Thomas grumped back. "I'm supposed to be on desk duty, they were doing me a big favor letting me check out anything in the first place."

The police officers they were trying to intercept had a big head start, but if they had to follow the road and obey traffic laws, whereas Walter could literally travel as the crow flies. He could also move at speeds that the people on the ground could never imagine, not that he could tap into all that potential at the moment. With Thomas struggling to hold on his speed was reduced considerably. Still, they made it to their destination in plenty of time.

"We need to hurry to get all this set up." Thomas announced as he set foot on the relative security of a firm apartment building roof. "We don't have an unlimited amount of time."

"Leave it to me." Walter assured him. "I read the instructions. I'm sure I can get this up and running in time."

Fortunately, the instructions for set up and for storage were plainly laid out in each item's hard-sided case. It was almost as if the police acknowledged that it was full of people that would never admit they needed help and stop to ask for directions. That being the case, the directions were kept in plain sight and made as simple as possible.

Walter used his super speed and got all the equipment connected and tested in record time. While he worked on that, Thomas started going through the files that Jimmy Fang's boys had purchased from the police.

"This is rotten." Thomas sighed. "Patrol routes and times, shift rotations, and even a couple of confidential informant names.

"These guys are selling all kinds of information to Jimmy and I'll bet they are doing the same to the Russians. These guys are definitely dirty."

"Well here is your chance to get more proof." Walter pointed at a sedan that was arriving. "I'm willing to bet your boys in blue aren't far behind."

Thomas picked up his binoculars and got a bead on the guys that had just showed up.

"That's Nikoli Grogon." He gasped. "He's the son of the head of the Russian mob around here. This must be important if he is showing up in the flesh."

Thomas quickly switched to the video recorder and made sure the microphone was properly positioned. He then started recording just as the crooked cops showed up.

Unlike the previous meeting with the Fang's men, this meeting was much chattier. The men acted more like old friends then compatriots who were simply beneficial to each other. Whereas before it was all cold, professional and in a hurry.

"Can you hear what they are saying?" Thomas whispered to Walter, who was focused on the meeting taking place.

"Yes." Walter nodded. "Are you getting all of it?"

"Except when the wind picks up." Thomas griped.

To Walter it didn't sound like too much information was being shared. It was a lot of small talk about work, the kids and such. It wasn't until the groups were about to separate that anything remotely interesting was talked about.

"They are talking about the same kinds of things that they sold to Fang." Thomas cocked his head, listening intently. "Times of patrol routes, and things like that."

"The Russian guy just asked about me." Walter suddenly perked up and became much more attentive. "Do they know who I am, or where I can be found?"

"Doesn't seem like it." Thomas replied, to which Walter sighed in relief. "They are admitting that they don't have much to go on where you are concerned."

"Looks like they are saying goodbyes." Walter observed. "Did you get everything you needed?"

"Got it." Thomas nodded. "This is definitely a meeting where you might want to go and introduce yourself when it's finished."

"Sounds good." Walter agreed.

"We might have one more problem." They both heard someone say.

Thomas and Walter suddenly turned their attention back to the meeting when he heard one of the police officers make that little announcement.

"And what is that?" Nikoli asked as his eyes narrowed.

"We have a new procedure to run our investigations through." The detective explained. "Someone that weighs our investigation and decides if it goes to the DA or not. "He has already made some inquiries as to some of our cases and commented on how thin they were. He could be a problem if he wants us to go back and add things our cases."

"Is he for purchase?" Nikoli asked, indicating he was open to bribing Thomas if need be.

"Doubtful." The officer replied. "This guy's an idealist."

"Keep me informed." Nikoli nodded at the man's assessment. "Let me know if and when, liquidation becomes necessary."

"Will do." The detective nodded and took that as a dismissal. He then moved back to his car and got in with his cohorts.

Likewise, Nikoli and his crew mounted up and prepared to disembark.

"That might be your…" Thomas began, but Walter was nowhere to be seen. He had already launched himself into the sky and was streaking toward the rooftop parking lot.

Walter set himself down directly in front of the exit route from the rooftop. The cars had to come toward him in order to leave so there was no way he could miss them. The first car to approach belonged to Nikoli.

"Run him down!" Nikoli shouted to his driver as recognition of who had just appeared in front of him dawned. "I want him dead!"

This time, Walter did not wait to be hit by the fast-moving vehicle. Instead he timed a punch and brought his closed fist down on the hood of the car as hard as he was able. The momentum of the car was too much to simply be arrested by the impact and instead it launched the back end of the car upward. It nearly reached ninety-degrees before falling backward and smashing hard onto the pavement.

Nikoli and his henchmen were thrown forward in their seats. The windshield, steering wheel and backs of the front seats all became barriers for them to impact. Nikoli's driver was the most fortunate as he was the only one actually wearing his seatbelt. He would be bruised and sore the next morning, but able to function.

The man in the passenger seat was not as lucky. Since Walter had punched downward onto the front of the car, the bumper did not register an impact. No airbags deployed to slow the man's contact with the dashboard and windshield. He wound up halfway through it, face down on the hood of the car, groaning.

Nikoli was the one in the best shape as he had been riding in the back. He tumbled out of the door, gym bag in hand and raised his gun at the man in black.

"I don't think you want to do that." Walter shook his head at the mobster.

Nikoli looked at his gun in confusion. He knew it was going to be useless, but why not take the chance? Fortunately for him, he never had to make the decision.

Bullets from the police started raining down on Walter as they witnessed his interference, slid their vehicle sideways and were all firing at him.

Walter started strolling casually toward the four firing policemen. His suit barely even registering the impact of their weapons. His plan was simple, use his superspeed and disarm them, then leave them there in their own handcuffs for the proper authorities to sort out. He wasn't going to hurt anyone, and it would be a simple thing, with Thomas' video, to prove that they were all dirty cops.

The fly in the ointment for that particular plan, was Nikoli. Nikoli had posed no threat, so Walter made no move against him. He figured he could always come back to him after he dealt with the police. There was no way that Nikoli could get far enough that he wouldn't be easy to catch.

Nikoli, on the other hand, was well aware of this fact and also knew that his handgun was useless. But he had other weaponry with him in the trunk. Moving quickly, he popped the trunk and pulled out two hand-grenades. He then waited patiently for Walter to be fully engaged with those in the police car, pulled the pins and threw them both.

The first grenade landed directly behind Walter and went off a fraction of a second before the second one. The second one had bounced farther and rolled under the police car before detonating.

The first explosion drove the air from Walter's lungs and propelled him forward, he smashed into the car with a tremendous impact, just as the second grenade went off. The car vanished in the fiery explosion that combined the propellant of the grenade and the gasoline of the vehicle.

The sounds of screaming, burning men was etched into Walter's brain as it became evident that not all of the police in the car had been killed in the initial explosion. He attempted to get up and was racked with pain. He could tell that there were areas where shrapnel had gotten through his suit and penetrated his body. He felt like there were even areas that were now unprotected, and he could feel the heat from the fires burning him in different spots. His focus quickly changed from arresting an evil doer to surviving the night himself.

It took almost all of his energy to get to his feet. His head rung, and his body protested his movements, but he was able to push past all that and move away from the burning car. It took several more moments of sitting there, collecting himself, before he was able to launch himself up and take flight.

Walter basically smashed into the roof that Thomas was on. There was no real grace or control in his landing. Thomas rushed over to him as the hero laid down on the ground and proceeded to check him over.

"That was a hell of a shot you took." Thomas informed him unnecessarily.

"Yeah, I was there." Walter groaned back, pain beginning to take the place of the surge of adrenaline.

"Do you think you can make it back to your place?" Thomas inquired. "It's not exactly around the corner."

"What about all this stuff?" Walter groaned, looking at all the gear.

"I'll make some calls and get it taken care of." Thomas assured him. "I'll take personal possession of the recordings. No one will see them until we are both ready."

"Then yeah." Walter nodded as he rose unsteadily to his feet. "I can make it home."

"Alright, you head out and I'll get up with you tomorrow." Thomas then looked him over one more time. "I know you are going to say no, but are you sure you don't want to go to the hospital?"

"Naw." Walter brushed it off and put on his full bravado. "I'll be fine."

****

Memory Foam Download: Subject was instrumental in police investigation into corruption. After attacking and being attacked by several vehicles, the subject was successful in gathering evidence requested by law enforcement officers.

Injuries were sustained as a small explosive device was used against the subject. Impact was severe enough to separate several bonded nanites and penetrate the subject's body. Injuries are being treated by the emergency medical protocols and should be healed within three hours if enough genetic material can be located to effect repairs. The subject's massive ingestion of protein products should assist in that regard.

Item of interest: The subject has begun several stretching exercises, known locally as yoga, in order to gain more flexibility in his physical operations. The bonded nanites are assisting in that regard by conditioning muscles while the subject sleeps.

Item of interest: The subject has begun an obsessive study of martial sciences. Evidence has indicated that the programmed nanites are using the information the subject has gleaned about combat and evolving its own martial arts program. This unit believes that this will result in increased fighting efficiency by the subject as the nanites are literally learning martial arts from the internet and passing that information to the subject while he sleeps.

****

Blikzak couldn't believe what he had just read in the memory foam report. This was unprecedented. The nanites should not have the abilities that the microcircuitry pillow was describing. They were there to augment, assist and basically take orders. The fact that they were learning on their own and passing that information and abilities onto the wearer was unprecedented. The problem was, he didn't know if it was all due to the nanites. It was possible that this had something to do with the differences in physiology between the parent species of the nanites and the humans of Earth.

Questions still danced in the back of his mind as to the viability of continuing the experiment. Those questions were mostly moot, as his superior officer had already departed on his scheduled vacation.

Blikzak's mind wandered back to the surprising arrival of the automated supply ship and the leaving of his commander and friend. It seemed like it was going to be a supply drop off like any other. The kind they had experienced a thousand times, or more. This time though, the ship was empty. There were no supplies aboard. Not even a new vid for them to watch.

Raknid had not been concerned by the development. He argued that this particular ship was probably on its way back from another outpost and had already dropped off its cargo. It had happened a couple times before, but never since the outpost's sizes had been so drastically reduced. With the outposts now being only manned by less than a dozen observers, one ship could make a complete circuit and drop off the needed supplies to each station in one trip.

Blikzak supposed it was always possible that a new station had opened up, or that one of the other stations had required a large replacement part that took up too much space for them to all get resupplied. Besides, it wasn't as if they actually needed anything at the moment. They still had enough food, power cells, and fuel on board the station to last several centuries. More than long enough for the Earthers to have started colonizing the moon and force the decision to abandon the place and seek diplomatic relations.

At least if the humans didn't either kill themselves or blow themselves back into the stone age, again.

CHAPTER 18

Jimmy Fang sat across his desk from a man he detested but was willing to use as a means to an end. It was not very difficult finding a religious zealot that was willing to murder thousands of innocents in pursuit of their goals but arranging the meet without alerting the plethora of three-letter organizations that monitored for the kind of threat he was proposing was more problematic. His men did finally manage to come through, however, and after a series of dead drops and car changes, the meeting had been made.

"Thank you for coming." Jimmy began, offering no reverence for the man's position as a religious leader.

"Thank you for having me." The man, Ezekiel Bashir, responded in kind. "It is good to meet such a prominent businessman and supporter of our cause."

"I care not for your cause." Jimmy corrected quickly. "If you and the rest of your zealots were to fall off the face of the Earth I wouldn't bat an eye."

"Then why did you seek us out?"

"Because although I don't care a rat's behind about your cause, we do have a common goal." Jimmy explained. "You wish to spread fear and terror to advance your cause. To call attention to your goals of your religious utopia. To that end you and your fanatics, have planted bombs in buildings, demolished bridges, and derailed trains. You have demanded areas of land be ceded to you to establish your kingdom. And despite all of your prolific work all over the world, no progress has been made toward your goal."

"Very true."

"It is almost as if you, and your followers, are more about killing and creating chaos then you are about truly establishing your utopian vision."

Bashir simply shrugged and cocked his head. He neither confirmed nor denied the allegations. If pressed, he would have admitted that the euphoric adrenaline rush of being in control of who lives and who dies, was intoxicating. That was reason enough in itself to continue his killing spree. If his utopian vision never came to pass, then so be it.

"If you are so against my…philosophies, then why did you request this meeting?" Bashir finally inquired, his dark eyes intense in their curiosity.

"Because I want to help you spread chaos." Jimmy Fang replied, his smile as dark as the heart of a dying star. "And in doing so, I will use you to my own ends."

****

Nikoli awoke from his bed soaked in sweat. The events of the previous night had replayed over and over in his dreams, often with exaggerated results. He had barely made it home before news of what had become of his men had broken. The other three men that had been in the car with him had all been taken to the hospital and were then scheduled to be taken into custody. None of them had given up the fact that Nikoli had been there, but that might not last. It looked as though they were going to be questioned hard about the deaths of several police detectives when their vehicle mysteriously exploded.

Nikoli was confident that his men would hold out for a while though. He was aware that the police would not be gentle when questioning them about the deaths of a few of their own, but while his men were in the hospital, there was only so much the police could get away with. The question then became whether or not to try and silence his people permanently. Normally this was not a question he would even dare to contemplate. Loyalty was key and a boss that had a reputation for killing any men that were placed in inconvenient situations was a boss that was not likely to last for long. This circumstance, however, was a little unique. He had just killed several police detectives and the fact that he was attempting to kill a superhero and accidentally killed the police was not likely to get him off as an excuse.

In the mean-time Nikoli consoled himself with the fact that the grenade did seem to have an effect on the man in black. He now had solid evidence that a concentrated attack would destroy the so-called superhero. Soon it would be time to execute his plan to execute the man in black.

****

Thomas let himself into Walter's house as quietly as he could. He was no expert in picking locks, but he could do it in a pinch. Just don't ask him to do it on any door you wanted to get through quietly or quickly.

He then made his way toward the back bedroom he knew was his friends and slowly pushed the door open.

It took him a moment for his eyes to adjust, but soon he could see his friend face down on his bed, his torn-up bicycle shorts still on and barely covering him. He could also see several blood spots on the sheets and a half-dozen chunks of metal that had been pushed out of Walter's body by the nanites in his super suit. Thomas wasn't sure if the metal pieces had come from the grenade that Nikoli had thrown at him or from the car explosion, or both. He only knew that his friend had suffered a great amount of pain because of him and he regretted it.

A dull moan from Walter made Thomas straighten up and back toward the door. He then put on his game face and waited for his friend to come around.

"What the hell was I drinking last night?" Walter groaned as he rolled over to see Thomas standing in his open doorway. "I suppose I should get you a key. I would say we should start meeting in my secret lair, but I neglected to put in an elevator."

"Being able to fly has its advantages, I guess." Thomas shrugged. "I imagine the money saved on airfare alone would be worth it."

"I need some breakfast." Walter sighed as he sat up.

"And a shower." Thomas added. "You smell like a combination of smoke, nitrate and gasoline. Your bed sheets are a mess as well."

"Did we get married when I wasn't looking?" Walter shot back, but not denying a single thing Thomas had said.

"You get yourself cleaned up and presentable." Thomas chuckled. "I'll start breakfast. What do you want?"

"Everything, and a lot of it." Walter stood up and stretched. "I feel good, but I think my body is still being repaired. Even if it isn't, I'll probably need it for the next time."

Thomas was about to protest and let him know that there might not be a next time. Evidence of the car's hood getting punched in was a pretty good indicator that Walter had been there. Add dead cops to the equation and you had a lot of people asking questions about the man in black that really didn't have any good answers.

Thomas had shown the video to the captain via an email late last night, but the captain had chosen to sit on it for now. Let people wonder about what had happened and keep the department's black eye shielded for the moment. If nothing came out of Walter's involvement, then no one ever need know about the crooked cops. If some started calling for the superhero's head, then Culpepper said he would release the tape to protect him.

Instead of telling his friend all about the firestorm brewing with his involvement, he simply closed the door to let Walter finish his morning routines in privacy. He then retreated to the kitchen and started withdrawing a mountain of food from the refrigerator. It was going to take some time to cook everything, but he could see that Walter wasn't going to be in a rush this morning.

****

Blikzak was confused as he looked at the proximity warning light on his console. He had scanned the region of space that it was emanating from just the previous night with no results. For anything to have come close enough to set off the warnings in that short of time, it would have to be traveling faster than light. And if it was traveling faster than light, it wasn't anything natural.

Blikzak called up his schedule and checked it, but there were no scheduled arrivals for at least two more weeks. Raknid's return should correspond with the next supply run and that was the next thing on the schedule.

It would take another ten minutes for the anomaly to get close enough for a detailed scan and so Blikzak used that time to set up the defenses. It was interesting to see the ion and graser cannons move into position. They hadn't been moved in years and had never actually been used to fire a shot in anger. The most they had ever done with them is to vaporize a couple of large asteroids that could have made a mess of Earth had they been allowed to hit. One of those rocks had nearly gotten through. Blikzak had managed to hit it well within Earth's atmosphere. But that had been years ago, over Siberia.

Blikzak was wearing his sighting helmet, just in case, as the data from the approaching ship started coming in. It turned out to be one of his own supply ships, but there was something wrong with it. It was venting atmosphere, and trailing ion radiation. Burn marks covered the exterior and several panels were missing. It was, to use and Earther phrase, shot to shit.

"Earth-Moon Base, this is…(Static)" Blikzak started working controls on his communication's panel trying to boost any signal and clean up the static.

"Approaching vessel." Blikzak began, trying to sound as authoritative as he could. "Your transmission is breaking up. Please say again."

"Earth-Moon Base, this is….(Static). We have suffered major damage and are coming in to dock." The transmission still wasn't perfect, but it was better. "In other words, Blikzak, this is Raknid, open the doors."

Blikzak jumped up as he recognized his commander's voice. He then turned and started toward the docking area. It would be a while before the ship would dock, so there was no tremendous hurry. Still, Blikzak put an extra pep to his step and started getting things ready for the incoming ship.

When the ship was finally approaching docking area, Blikzak got his first good look at it with his true eyes. He couldn't see how the drifting wreck that was approaching had even managed an FTL journey. It smoked, it lurched, and it was still trailing debris.

"I'm docking on manual." Raknid announced over the coms. "Many of the autopilot functions are disabled."

"Understood." Blikzak replied, as he activated a plethora of safety bots and fire suppression carts. "I have things as ready as possible."

"This isn't going to be subtle." Raknid came back over the coms, mostly speaking to himself in an effort to calm his nerves.

Blikzak barely breathed the entire time the ship was docking. Every screech of metal, every clunk of debris and every spark from the power circuits, made him jump and took eons off his lifespan.

Finally, all motion stopped, and the docking board showed mostly green, with a couple of cautionary yellows thrown in. Fortunately, there were no red icons that would have meant delays in disembarking and possibly fires or other such hazards.

Raknid wiped his brow after he had made sure that all was secure. If a good landing was one you could walk away from, then a great landing should be classified as one that the vessel is usable again. This was not a great landing, but already the repair bots appeared quickly and got to work. They should be able to make the long-range resupply ship as good as new, given enough time.

Outposts like the one Blikzak and Raknid manned were equipped with a plethora of short ranged vessels. Short trips to the planet being monitored for supplies, analysis, and good old-fashioned recreation were condoned and accommodated. Long range transports, however, were strictly forbidden and tightly controlled. It was always a concern that one of the observers would leave their post or go nuts and try to mutiny to return home. The high council decided that it was preferable that any such lunacy be kept off the homeworld. It was much easier to ignore a problem when it was millions of lightyears away.

Raknid, bringing in a supply ship off schedule and on manual was a serious breach in both protocols and regulations. But Blikzak was certain that he wouldn't have done it without very good reason. He looked forward, with a great deal of trepidation, to finding out what that reason was.

Blikzak was eager as he waited at the gangplank for his friend to open up the ship. It seemed to take forever for the ramp to lower and the heat dispersing jets to rid the external body of any radiant heat. His jaw then dropped as he saw his friend standing there. Not that that was a surprise, but what was a complete shock, was what was behind him.

CHAPTER 19

Jimmy Fang had told Bashir that he would pay him, but he neglected to specify whether the payment would come in silver or lead. As it was, Jimmy had no remorse in killing the man who was now face down on his carpet, bleeding out all over the floor. Nor did he have any compunctions about eliminating a good number of the man's zealot followers.

Had the circumstances been different, Jimmy would have been viewed as a hero for eliminating such a vile terrorist threat. Now any such praise would have been muted by the fact that he had financed the zealot for over a month as he planted bombs in certain structures all over the city.

Jimmy was careful to make sure that Bashir educated him on how to activate and detonate the bombs before he caused his expiration. It would have been rather embarrassing to eliminate the man who knew how to bring about the destruction Jimmy sought before he knew how to cause it.

Now his failsafe was fully operational. If the authorities got too close he would threaten to set off a dozen bombs across the city, killing thousands. He was reasonably certain that if that meddlesome hero got in his way, he could be convinced to back off rather than be responsible for the deaths of innocents. Even if Jimmy could only buy time, he could probably manage to slip away and retire back to his homeland. It wouldn't be the triumphant return of the man who destroyed America, but he had enough money stashed all over the world that it would be a comfortable life with many of the amenities that the rich enjoy.

Capitalism might be the evilest form of economy, but it did have its benefits.

****

Nikoli had been keeping his head down for the better part of a month now. His plan to destroy the man in black had come to fruition and now only waited to be executed. The hardest part of his delay was the fact that he had to keep that infernal woman on ice for so long. One would think that after her brother so willingly set her up to be bait and possibly killed that she would have welcomed his elimination, but family is a funny thing and she took the news of her brother's death hard. In fact, her reaction was downright violent. She had actually managed to clobber one of Nikoli's men and get his gun before others could subdue her again.

Now all of Nikoli's preparations were for what he planned to be his final confrontation with the man in black were-complete. The abandoned cement factory was rigged with traps, explosives and places for his men to hide. He had his unwilling bait ready to be laid in place. He also had a timetable where he knew the police would not be about to stop him.

Not that many of them were feeling too charitable toward the so-called-hero at the moment. Nikoli had not been able to deflect all of the blame of the dead police toward the hero, but he had muddied the waters enough that he was still a free man, and a mountain of suspicion had landed on the man in black. After all, men in masks cannot be trusted.

Not that he had escaped the incident scot-free. He had more police sniffing around him and his operations then he had ever had before. If he hadn't been able to bring in experts to claim that the video that surfaced had been altered, he might have very well found himself in jail. There was also the fact that no warrant had been issued for the video surveillance in the first place. Although the video might go a long way toward convicting him in the court of public opinion, legally it did him very little damage. The other bright spot in the court of public opinion was that the video had not been released to the general public yet. The only reason he had seen it was because he had been brought in for questioning.

It had been a bold plan by Captain Culpepper to bring in Nikoli and accuse him of the killing of several police officers. It was possible that he had hoped to bluster and rattle Nikoli enough that he would confess or that maybe he would be so ignorant as to not know that the video would probably be ruled inadmissible. Fortunately, neither Nikoli or his lawyer were stupid enough to step into the trap. There was no real evidence of what had happened except for the video that judges were going over. Nikoli blamed the man in black for everything that happened, and if the evidence of the film was thrown out, he might just be able to make a better case of it. Nikoli smiled a shark's smile as he already knew how the judges would rule. The men of the court had been expensive to buy, but they had proved to be worth every penny.

That little dilemma considered and shelved, his mind wandered back full circle to his plan to eliminate the man in black. Another day, or two and he would pull the trigger on the operation. All was proceeding according to his design and he was going to enjoy every minute of it.

****

Walter was working solo most of the time now. Thomas couldn't afford to be seen with him and was swamped with work at the moment anyway. Evidently his captain was not pleased with Thomas going maverick on him and working a case without authorization. In punishment, he had shortened the time Thomas had to review some cases and was making him go back through the cases of the officers who were questionable in their dedication to law and order.

There was also the fact that he *may* have been working with a masked vigilante, but that was easy to muddy as Thomas never actually said they were working together, only that he had caught him on camera.

The two were still able to get together on Thomas' off time. At least what precious little of that he could spare.

The last time the two got together, Walter remarked on the lack of a cast that Thomas was no longer sporting. Thomas had gone to get it replaced earlier in the week, but the doctors were so amazed at the speed of his recovery they refused to put another one on. They did, however, tell him not to exert himself too much and to still take it easy. They also refused to clear him for full duty, so he was still stuck in the office, longing to get back on patrol.

Walter snapped out of his ruminations when his super sensitive ears picked up an alarm bell. As he was out doing his day job and driving to see a client, he was not dressed for the occasion as such. However, he did have his bicycle shorts on under his business suit. It seemed that this was the time to attempt to be a hero in broad daylight, instead of hiding in the shadows as he had been.

The alarm turned out to be emanating from the first national bank. One police car had already arrived and was waving everyone back. The poor officer had no idea what to make of the man, dressed all in black with large white eyes, that simply strolled past him into the bank.

The scene inside was chaos. Clearly the robbery had not gone according to plan as the robbers were huddled together arguing when Walter walked in. There were four in total, with one holding a gun to a woman's head.

"Gentlemen." Walter called out as he walked in. "I would advise you to release your hostage and put down your guns. It will go a lot easier on you in the long run if you do."

"And if we don't?" The man holding the woman growled.

"One way or another you are leaving this bank without any money." Walter crossed his arms in front of his chest in a display of emphasis. "Whether that is conscious, dead, or in great amounts of pain is up to you."

"Gun that freak." The man in charge shouted to the other three who promptly emptied their weapons into Walter.

Walter had learned to control the suit a lot better in the past month. He could now modify its density so that the bullets would absorb slightly, then fall to the ground. Which was a lot better than them bouncing off of him to possibly hit someone else. That meant that instead of rushing to try and get the men disarmed, he could wait until their ammunition was expended.

Walter feigned a yawn as the three shooter's weapons ran dry. While they were looking at each other, wondering what to do next, Walter sprang into action. The three men were sent sailing backward to smash into the counter at the far end of the bank, before they could even come to terms with what was happening. Walter simply looked like a blur of motion as he slammed into the three henchmen and removed them from the board.

"Looks like it's just you and me." Walter announced as he moved to stand in front of the man and his hostage.

"Look." The man indicated the gun in his hand. "The trigger is already pulled. I'm holding back the hammer with my thumb. If you come at me, jostle me, or even make me sneeze, I'll blow this woman's head off whether I want to or not."

"Let me get this straight," Walter began calmly. "You're holding the trigger in the pulled position with your finger and your thumb is holding the hammer back? Do I have that correct?"

"Yes." The man nodded.

"But if I back off, you can release the trigger and the hammer won't fall." Walter pressed. "And she'll be ok?"

"Yeah." The thug replied as if Walter were stupid. "That's how guns work. So back off because if anything happens to her or me, the blood is on your hands."

"Why do people always say that?" Walter began, as he looked closely at the man's trigger finger. "Why do they always want to put the blame on the person trying to help? I didn't try to rob a bank, I didn't mess up the robbery, I didn't take an innocent woman hostage, so why would I feel the guilt if she dies?"

At that, the woman whimpered, and Walter so wished he could wink at her in reassurance, but there was no way to communicate his intentions without tipping his hand.

"It would seem to me that the crux of this problem rests with you." Walter finally continued.

Walter's sentence was followed by a flash of light, which caused many in the bank to shield their eyes. The flash was quickly followed by the wafting aroma of a disgusting smell, reminding many of burnt hair.

Several people in the crowd had recovered enough from the surprise of the flash to theorize what had just happened. They believed that the man in black had just used his laser vision to disarm the man, possibly even cut his weapon in two. It took several seconds for the crowd to realize that the facts were a bit different.

The robber couldn't quite calculate what had just happened either. It wasn't until the pain began that he started to register what had just happened. The problem was, even though he was coming to intellectual understanding of what had just happened, he was in complete emotional denial about it. To that end he released the hammer, which simply remained in the cocked position. He then attempted to pull the trigger several times, despite the fact that his trigger finger was now laying on the floor, severed from his body by Walter's heat/laser vision.

It was not until the pain of his burns began to hit him full force that the man dropped his weapon and fell to his knees, clutching the stump of his burned finger with his other hand. There was no blood at the wound, as it had been cauterized by Walter's heat vision, but the smell was tell-tale and left many in the audience feeling queasy.

The woman simply stood there, unable to move. Her panic beginning to subside as she took in the sight of the gun sitting on the floor.

"He is the victim now." Walter informed her. "You may deal with him as you wish."

It still took several moments for her to grasp what he was telling her, but when she finally looked down at the pathetic human being that just moments ago had held her life in his hands, she knew what she wanted to do. Her knee contacting the man's jaw would be a sight that Walter would never forget. She not only managed to break the bone in two places, but she rendered the man unconscious for the rest of the day. As the man toppled to the floor, the woman seemed quite satisfied.

By the time it was over, four bank robbers had been taken into custody, no innocents had been hurt, and Walter simply slipped away out a skylight and took off toward his car.

It was not until he was at his car, that he realized that he had locked the keys in it.

****

Blikzak walked toward his commander's office with a little more trepidation this day than most. It had been this way since his friend's return from vacation in a shot up resupply ship. Blikzak couldn't help but replay the events of that day over and over again in his head.

As the gangway lowered from the ship and the cooling jets fired their last, Blikzak could finally see his friend standing there among several others of his species. The problem was, that he shouldn't have had anyone with him at all. And were those children? He had children with him. What was going on?

"Commander," Raknid began, using his title in the presence of so many onlookers. "I wasn't expecting guests. What the hell happened to you?"

"It's gone." Raknid informed his friend. His bluntness indicating that he had found no easy way to relay the truth during his voyage. "It's all gone. Everyone, everything, it's all gone."

"The planet?" Blikzak was still confused and rightly so. His friend didn't seem to be making any sense. "Our homeworld, the planetary colonies, it's all gone?"

"No, the planet is still there." Raknid assured him. "But everyone on it, and the colonies, are dead. Everything is destroyed. The spaceport was the last thing still standing."

"What the Blark happened?" Blikzak cursed for the first time in centuries.

"It was the new generation of nanites." Raknid explained. "They became sentient. They not only became self-aware, but they became a kind of collective intelligence. It evolved and learned, using each independent nanite as if it were a brain cell in a gigantic mind. It networked itself together and then decided it didn't need us bossing it around anymore."

Blikzak's jaw dropped. It was a lot to process and he wasn't exactly sure he was up to the job.

"And the people you arrived with?" Blikzak decided to push past what he couldn't wrap his mind around and keep on driving. Maybe it would all make sense later.

"The few survivors that were holed up in the spaceport." Raknid revealed. "It turns out that the security scanners that were designed to penetrate the nanite clothing to look for contraband, could be ramped up and used to repel the nanite hoard. But even though they could keep the nanites at bay, they couldn't destroy them. They had no choice but to stay put and hope for rescue."

"Which you provided." Blikzak was ahead of the game on that one.

"The resupply ship was on automatic and docked itself routinely, but when my supply ship opened up, they poured on and let me know what was going on." Raknid sighed heavily. "We made a run for it, but the nanites were waiting for us. They had no problems with letting a ship in, but getting out with life forms on board was a definite no-no. We were severely damaged in the escape, and we had to stop to make repairs several times, but we made it."

"I take it our observations about the nanites evolving turned out to be correct." Blikzak nearly cursed again, but once a century was probably enough for him.

"Yes." Raknid confirmed. "We don't have to worry about that yet. It took many more generations for the ones that destroyed our home to reach that point and the ones we have and the ones we put on Earth have certain safeties that the new generation did not. But you'll notice that the survivors I brought back are all wearing physical garments. They used the security scanners to separate themselves from the nanites. Not all of them had been upgraded either, so the process was simplified."

"But where does all this leave us?" Blikzak suddenly realizing the consequences of his question. "No home, no resupplies, no support. What do we do?"

"As to what we do, it is simple, survive." Raknid put his hand on his friend's shoulder. "As to where does this leave us? I would say that this leaves us alone."

That conversation had been a month ago. Since that time, the duo and many of their new additions had been working to establish contact with any other observation outposts like theirs. Or if there were any other survivors who had fled the planet before it's destruction.

In all there were forty-eight survivors in addition to themselves. There had even been six natural children in the mix. Natural children had not been the norm for reproduction for eons, but it still was chosen by some. It was happenstance that six of them would be in the spaceport when everything went wrong, but since natural children were an exception to the rule, they got paraded around a lot. Which put them in a location used for travel in a higher concentration than anywhere else. Another bit of luck had been that none of them were completely orphaned. Several had lost one parent, but none of them had lost both.

The new home of these alien refuges was also fortunate in the mix of specialists that had survived. Although when a race is basically immortal and simply switches bodies when one gets worn out, they become experts in many fields over several lifetimes. For the most part, however, the ones that had arrived were quite familiar with the station and its technology, as outdated as it was, and were able to smoothly take up jobs, fire up unused areas of the station, and even get the hydroponics up and running. A supply trip to Earth was going to be required to obtain some soil and seedlings for food, but that shouldn't present a problem.

"Commander?" Blikzak called out as he stood in his friend's office doorway. It was not an office that had seen much use in decades. They both pretty much lived in the command center so the offices they both possessed went unneeded.

"Come in." Raknid sighed, preparing himself for more bad news.

"I have some news on the other outposts." Blikzak handed his boss the electronic reader. "No word from outpost nine, eleven, or twelve. We already knew that outposts one, two, four and seven had been abandoned. Outpost three, six, eight, and ten all report that they are up and running, but their personnel counts are much like ours. The largest staff is four persons and the others are all at two."

"What about outpost five?" Raknid inquired.

"WE are outpost five." Blikzak replied with a nervous chuckle.

"Oh wow. That's right." Raknid laughed. "It had been so long since we talked about ourselves in that sense that it had jumped out of my tiny little brain."

"Other bits of good news." Blikzak continued, ignoring his commander's brain malfunction. "The supply ship you procured for your return flight has been completely repaired, and there is another on the way. Evidently there was one more ship on an automated circuit launched before things went to hell back home. It should be here in three days."

"We will override the automatic docking and hold it at the outer limit." Raknid replied with a bit of uncharacteristic hardness to his words. "We will then inspect it and make sure that it is not a…what do the humans call that…?"

"Trojan horse." Blikzak finished for him, latching onto his thought process and agreeing with it wholeheartedly.

"That's the one." Raknid agreed. "I want you to work with Sapcara and Togatta and learn everything you can about the planets that we still have outposts observing. One of them might just have to become our new home."

"I understand." Blikzak was still in the mindset of going home and taking back their planet, the problem was that he had no idea how to do it. No one did. They had, as a species, created a monster beyond their control. Instead of arguing the point he simply nodded and got back to work.

****

Memory Foam Download: Subject is progressing in regard to the use of his superpowers. Today's actions included the foiling of a bank robbery and the rescuing of a hostage in a rather unique way. This unit has committed to researching the subject of hostages and negotiations and has found the subject's approach to be innovative to say the least. It could be argued that his actions were, as one witness put it, over the top. But as a deterrent it might just have some beneficial effects.

Item of note: Upon return to his mundane conveyance the subject demonstrated a level of frustration that this unit finds hard to comprehend. The use of many colorful words, that do not appear in the dictionary, seemed to project the feeling of anger and frustration. Frustration that seemed to culminate in the smashing of one of his vehicle's windows.

CHAPTER 20

Jimmy Fang was not a man who liked to waste a lot of time, so he had sent a courier to the mayor of the city directly. The courier was to wait for a reply but was taken into police custody. This was not completely unexpected as Jimmy was aware that a demonstration of his seriousness was going to be required. He had hoped that the mayor would take him seriously straight away, but he supposed that having a letter delivered with claims that bombs were placed all over the city was going to be hard to swallow. The mayor had no reason to take the threat seriously, so he didn't.

Jimmy acknowledged that a little bit of that was his fault. He couldn't exactly lay out a roadmap to the bombs and give the police time to find and disarm them before they were needed. He did, however, give them the location of one bomb. It was probably the most complicated of the bunch, as it was the one that Jimmy was willing to sacrifice. If they could disarm it fine, if they couldn't, the resulting explosion should prove that Jimmy's threats were real.

In truth Jimmy had no intentions of letting them disarm the bomb. An example of what would happen to people that crossed the great Jimmy Fang was needed and the people of this city and those who ran it, would get it. He was, however, going to wait until the maximum number of first responders were gathered before he gave such an example. Part of that calculation being, that if the best members of the bomb squad were sent in to disarm the package, then it would be the best and brightest that got wiped out first. Everyone else that was dealing with the problem from then on, would be a second stringer.

Jimmy figured it would take a few hours for the police to get their act together and get a response team over to the selected building, get it evacuated and then locate the device. He was certain that they would move slowly as threats like this were probably a dime a dozen and the device was not in a location that would be easy to find. Jimmy then set a countdown in his mind and waited until it was the proper time to make the 55th Street Library disappear.

****

Reporter Alex Wynn was in place outside of the 55th Street Library waiting for something to happen. His source within the police department had tipped him off as to the action there and told him that the bomb squad had been called but couldn't be any more specific than that.

That meant that Alex was doing the same thing a hundred other onlookers were doing, sitting behind police tape and waiting for something interesting to happen. It wouldn't take long.

In moments the quiet morning was shattered in the tremendous roar of explosives, people screaming and debris flying. It was clear that the building had just been blown up and was now tumbling to the street. People scattered, dust flew, and police shouted commands that went ignored.

People watching had no idea how many first responders had just been murdered, but they were smart enough and experienced enough to know that it was a high number.

"Superhero," Alex whispered to himself. "Where are you when we need you?"

****

Nikoli, like most of the rest of the city, watched in horror as the largest library in the city was reduced to rubble. It was not that he was a great American patriot, his first loyalty was always going to be to his mother Russia, but he had a great fondness for his adoptive country. He had even become a citizen as soon as he was able to. America was still a land of opportunity, with a reasonably stable government, good roads, wide open spaces and no restrictions on travel. Not to mention the fact that the weather was much better. That being the case, Nikoli had decided a long time ago that he would live out his life in America, or at least until the authorities made him flee back to his homeland. Something he had hoped to avoid, but he was a realist and was always prepared for it.

Thinking of preparations moved his thoughts beyond the mindless violence and destruction on the television and onto his more focused and disciplined violence and destruction. Namely the man in black who had put on such a heroic scene at the bank only a few days ago.

This was the night all of his preparations would come to fruition. At least that was the hope. Everything was ready for the command performance of the so-called hero. The men had been briefed and well-practiced, the explosives were set and armed, and the bait was sufficiently terrified. All they had to do was wait until nightfall, take their positions, and hope that they could get the attention of the shadow of a hero.

****

Thomas had been reassigned as a homicide detective, mostly because the department was now hopelessly shorthanded and looked to get even shorter. The detectives killed by Nikoli had left a hole in the department that had to be filled immediately, and now the collapse of the 55th Street Library had taken out a good number of more front-line officers. At this rate, Thomas was going to end up working as detective, beat cop, bomb squad and dog catcher very soon.

"Thomas," Captain Culpepper called out from his office. "I need you in here!"

Obediently but reluctantly Thomas got up from his desk and trudged toward the Captain's office. He knew that tone and he wasn't going to enjoy his time in front of the Captain's desk. Quickly and silently Thomas entered and closed the door behind him. He then took his place, standing with his hands behind his back, in front of the captain's desk.

Thomas looked around at the office he had been in a hundred times before. The awards on the walls, the pictures on the desk and the piles of paperwork that would never end. He often wondered how the man juggled it all. Work, family, and friends. He was one of the few that made it look easy and always seemed to keep it together. Indecision and worry did not suit this man, and it made Thomas nervous that those were the very emotions the captain seemed to be radiating.

"Thomas," Culpepper sighed. "I'm going to ask you this one time, and I had better get a straight answer."

Culpepper turned to face his junior officer and friend, his eyes pleading for the truth. It was not something that Thomas could deny the man. Instead, he simply nodded.

"I need to know, right here and now, just how well you know this so-called superhero." Culpepper finally dropped on him.

Thomas hesitated only a fraction of a second before responding. It was a question he had been anticipating for a while now. He'd always known that the conflict between law enforcement and vigilante was going to come to a head sometime soon.

"I know him well enough to get him a message any time I want to." Thomas then quickly clarified. "That is, if he answers the phone. He has been known to be out of cell phone range now and then."

"That's not really a surprise." Culpepper murmured. "He's been spotted all over the country now. California, Colorado, North

Carolina, Idaho and even Roswell, New Mexico. I'm not sure what to make of that one.

"Look, Thomas, I'm not disappointed that you didn't tell me, so put that worry to rest. I know you were walking a pretty tight line here. But the game...has changed." Culpepper handed Thomas a copy of the letter that arrived at the Mayor's office.

Thomas took his time reading the manifesto before him. He was reading between the lines as much as he was reading the document. There was just enough crazy in it to detract from the cold calculation within it. To the laymen reading it, the letter would look like a terrorist making crazy demands, but to the investigators familiar with the city and its criminal underworld, the letter made a very clear and sensible statement. Back off!

"It's Jimmy Fang." Thomas sighed, tossing the letter back on the Captain's desk. "It has to be."

"Maybe." Culpepper nodded. "Probably." He quickly conceded. "But that doesn't change what we have to do about it."

"Which is?" Thomas gave his commander the eye.

"We do nothing." Culpepper sighed. "We stay out of Chinatown and we get your friend to play ball."

"The letter says he wants the man in black killed. Killed by the government." Thomas gasped. "Hunted down like a dog."

"That, we are not going to do." Culpepper reassured his agitated friend. "But we are going to tell him to stay out of Jimmy's way. At least temporarily. He claims to have a dozen more bombs planted all over the city. We need time to find them.

"The FBI is coming in to help, especially since our bomb squad was basically executed today." Culpepper was furious, but keeping that particular emotion well checked. He was simply working the problem, just as he had been trained to do. "I know they are going to hit the ground running, but even at that they are going to need time. This is a big game of catch up and the bad guys have a hell of a head start."

"I'll do what I can to get a message out." Thomas replied. "I'm sure…my friend can be convinced to lay low for a little while. At least stay out of Jimmy's territory." Silently he cursed himself for almost saying 'Walter'.

****

Walter was having the time of his life, flying around. Now that he had gotten a good handle on it, it was one of the most exhilarating things he had ever experienced. If he had his way, he would never take normal conveyance again. No more car payments, no need for bus tickets and no need to take your vehicle to the shop after you break a window because you've locked your keys in it. A moment of humiliation that Walter still couldn't forgive himself for. It was, however, certainly a reminder of just how far one can fall after riding the euphoric high after performing acts of daring do.

Doing good things still made him feel great and he was still planted firmly on the side of law and order. There was a little bit of blowback from his performance at the bank. Dismembering a bad guy was frowned upon in certain circles, but most commentators seemed to support his actions and news articles were decidedly pro-hero. Public opinion seemed to agree with him, although no one, including himself, had really settled on a name for this superhero yet. Fortunately, the names Super-Wang and Dong-Man had faded with time. The name which seemed to be the front-runner now, came from the way he showed expressions through the nanite mask. Since his smiles, eyes and overexpressions seemed to appear like video on a screen, the name Emoji-Man seemed to be gaining in popularity. It was not a name that would strike fear into the hearts of men, but one didn't always get what they wanted.

Walter noticed how late it was getting and circled back toward the city. He now flew certain patterns, staggered and with the timing changed every night, in order to keep the bad guys from knowing when and where he was going to be at any given moment.

The previous night he foiled several robberies, a couple of car-jackings, and at least one plan of one young lady who was attempting to sneak out of her house to see her boyfriend. That one was accidental, but when one sees someone half in the window of a house, one investigates.

Walter truly believed he was getting good at this superhero gig and was happier than he had been in years. That was when things usually went horribly wrong.

Walter first heard the screams as he flew over the industrial side of town. He knew it was going to take some time to locate the source of the distress. The area below was awash with old textile plants, steel mills and other abandoned relics of industry.

It took several passes, but Walter finally narrowed the building down to the old abandoned cement factory. The problem was, that there was so much material in the way, he couldn't locate the source, even with his x-ray vision. That being the case, he settled on making a less dramatic entrance and landed near the main door.

As he slowly pushed the door open the long creaking of the hinges immediately announced his presence and amplified the creepiness of the dirty abandoned factory. The fact that the door was unlocked at all, set him on edge and made him all the more nervous despite his proven durability.

The office and reception areas were a maze of cubicles and hallways. Every area was empty of anything of value and dirt and debris was thick as thieves. Walking through this place was akin to walking through an elephant graveyard where every scrap of edible material had been stripped clean, leaving only the bones to mark the passing.

Walter was finally able to leave the creepy confines of the working offices only to walk out into the creepier confines of the heavy equipment area. The building seemed to have been built around a large central courtyard, but Walter could tell that it was actually an area for larger equipment that had long since been removed. It now was left with a large open area surrounded by a two-story catwalk. But what really caught his attention was the sobbing woman who was tied to a large I-Beam frame in the center of the courtyard.

She had a hood over her face, but her muffled yells and sobs were clearly audible. Her clothing was business attire but looked like it was in tatters and unclean. She was also missing a shoe and her hose had multiple runs in it. Walter tried to focus on her face through the hood that covered her, but his vision couldn't penetrate it. He reasoned that it must be made of some dense material, like lead. That set off alarm bells in his mind but didn't really change what he felt he needed to do.

Nikoli watched with baited breath as the hero seemed to tip-toe toward the bait. He had debated with himself long and hard about the hood she wore. He felt that if he didn't place a hood on her, the hero might recognize her and realize it was a trap, on the other hand, if he used the lead-lined sack the hero wouldn't be able to see through it and might realize that it was a trap. There didn't seem to be a good answer to the problem, so he simply flipped a coin and went with the protective hood.

He had been fortunate in the fact that the hero either didn't acknowledge the hood as an indication of the scenario being a trap or didn't let the fact that it was a trap stop him. He simply continued his slow advance toward the woman.

Nikoli's blood was pounding in his ears as he watched the man in black move closer to the target position. Just a few more steps and it would be time to spring the trap.

Walter finally reached the victim and slowly pulled off her hood. Instantly he recognized the woman who had been bait in the car on the overpass and realized that this was indeed a trap. He also recognized the look of sheer terror etched upon her face and knew that she was as much an unwilling participant in this as he was.

Walter caught the movement on the catwalk an instant before the sonic weapons opened up on him. Three of the high-frequency emitters had been place up high and had been pre-targeted on his current position. As the eardrum-shattering volume slammed into him his head felt like it was about to cave in. Fortunately, the pain passed quickly as the suit adapted and closed off his auditory canals. A millisecond later all three emitters were smoldering hunks of slag, fried by Walter's heat vision. The woman was nearly rendered unconscious by the barrage of sound. She flopped limply as he attempted to free her from her bonds. Walter wondered if her lack on consciousness would be an asset or a hindrance, but he had no time to dwell on the possibilities at the moment.

That was when phase two of the trap began. Walter had been smart enough to calculate that if there were men on the second level with sonic emitters, that there might be men up there with something else. He foiled that part of the plan by again using his heat vision to collapse the catwalk in every location where there were people, or where he couldn't see with his x-ray vision. The rocket launchers Nikoli had positioned up there became useless and either exploded, were damaged beyond use, or were buried under the falling walkway. That went a long way toward thwarting the plans laid against him, but the trap was not one or two faceted. The problem was that his vision did nothing to pick up the mines just beneath the floor.

The first claymore went off just behind Walter as he was cutting the woman's bonds. The force of the blast slammed him against the I-Beam framing and he felt multiple penetrations of his nanite suit. Unlike the bullets flying at him in the bank, Walter was unconcerned with the damage bullets would do flying away from him in this abandoned space. To that end, he set his suit to be as hard as diamonds. A lot of the shrapnel that impacted his body, wound up bouncing off and flying toward some of Nikoli's own men.

More explosions followed, and Walter spun the newly freed woman away from them and shielded her the best he could. A metronome of death and destruction followed as explosives, incendiaries and mines detonated all around him. Finally, he dropped on top of the semi-conscious and screaming woman. Protecting her from the cacophony of violence. Impact after impact slammed into Walter, nanites were driven apart from their bonds. Holes opened up and white-hot phosphorus and metal were let in.

Walter could feel his consciousness waning. Massive parts of his suit were missing or non-functional. Even his mask seemed half gone. He knew to stand-fast and fight was suicide. Running became his only real option. Mustering whatever strength he had left, he launched himself skyward. The weight of the woman, which would normally be barely noticeable, suddenly became a millstone around his neck. Through sheer force of will he took flight and disappeared into the night sky.

Nikoli looked up as he emerged from his 'command bunker' where he had directed the carnage. He couldn't see the man in black anymore, but he knew he was hurting. They had inflicted heavy damage to the superhero and more importantly gotten some very useful intelligence. They might even be able to produce a composite image from the recordings they had made. That would have to wait, however, as they had wounded and dead men strung out everywhere, fires still burned, and some of the mines hadn't gone off. Either their wires had been cut by the falling walkway or they simply failed.

Nikoli wasn't worried about the wounded as he had his own private doctor on staff for just such occasions. This was going to work the poor man hard, but Nikoli had little sympathy for that. He had made the man wealthy for him providing services only a couple times a year. He treated more runny noses from his kids than performed the duties he was agreeably retained for. Now he would earn his keep. The amount of men with injuries was bound to keep him busy for days.

"Hurry." Nikoli yelled out to his men. "The authorities are probably on the way. Something like this is bound to be noticed."

Men limped and crawled toward the trucks they had come in as quickly as they could. Bodies were carried, and the fires were left to burn.

****

Memory Foam Download: The subject failed to return to this unit for completion of his nightly rituals. No information on whereabouts is available. No download was completed as the subject never made it back to his bed. This unit has no external sensors to determine if the subject failed to make return to his domicile or simply failed to return to this unit's designated sleep compartment. This leaves countless possibilities open as to the condition of the subject. Every possibility from death to simply sleeping on the couch must be considered.

This unit seeks advice as to countering condition humans have come to refer to as loneliness. This unit does not compute as efficiently in isolation.

CHAPTER 21

Mister Koi waited patiently outside of his employer's and longtime friend's office. He believed that his friend would be pleased with the information he was in possession of. Lately, however, he was less sure of himself in these matters. As much as he hated to admit it, he was certain he was watching the unraveling of the Jimmy Fang empire, and with absolutely no help from the police and limited interference from the meddling superhero. Jimmy was simply becoming so obsessed with holding onto power that his paranoia was pushing him to make decisions that would ultimately lead to his downfall.

Koi had argued strongly against Jimmy's plan to try and shield his empire by planting bombs around the city. He felt that it was the kind of thing that was doomed to backfire and bring the focused attention of several law enforcement agencies down upon them. He did agree that it would make them back off in the immediate short term, but sooner or later their focus would shift his direction and they would come with guns blazing.

Koi had prepared for such eventualities and had money, weapons and contacts spread out around the world. When the time came, loyalty or no, mister Koi would be nowhere to be found. He would simply slip away and retire to nice beach somewhere.

That was not going to happen today. Today was a day for good news.

"Come in." Jimmy commanded from the far side of the closed door.

Dutifully Koi entered and made a slight bow to his boss.

"I have news about the Russian's confrontation with the man in black." Koi announced, cutting through any chit-chat or small talk. "It would seem that they threw everything but the kitchen sink at the hero and still were unable to destroy him. It was, however, evident that they inflicted significant damage, and had some more heavy weapons been brought into use, it is probable that they would have destroyed him."

Koi placed his tablet on the desk in front of Jimmy and let his friend watch the footage. He enjoyed watching his employer perk up as impact after impact seemed to reveal more and more of the hero's features. Even parts of his face were clear, but not enough was exposed to get a valid identification. It was the blood that was flowing that Jimmy seemed to be paying the closest attention to. It meant he was human after all and if he was human, he could be killed.

"The Russians suffered a high loss rate against this hero." Koi's voice betrayed no emotion, but deep down he was excited for what this could mean for their business empire. "It may be time to withdraw our support and move against them."

"The Russians never got that much support from us." Jimmy rubbed his chin in thought. "I have never trusted their willingness to help us so enthusiastically. They had an angle of their own to play. That thought aside, they have used up many of their heavy weapons, and their manpower is depleted. You may be correct in your assumption that it is time to make our claim on their territory."

"My contacts within the Russian households do indicate that they had their own designs on the hero. They had even made overtures to DARPA and other defense contractors." Koi shrugged. "Had they been successful in killing or capturing the man in black they had planned on selling the technology and possibly even trading it for immunity deals and retirements."

"You don't really believe that Grogon would go straight do you?"

"Not a chance." Koi shook his head. "He loves the grand game too much. His son, on the other hand, might just take the opportunity to enjoy his money without having to look over his shoulder for the feds."

"Well the point is moot." Jimmy chuckled. "They failed in their gambit against this hero and we will now attempt to make sure that they will be too busy to make another attempt."

The two men then shared an evil laugh, accompanied by an even eviler smile.

****

Nikoli walked through his doctor's work area, which was nothing more than a converted barn just outside of the city. He had always thought that if he needed an area to recover or have men worked on that the large vacant acreage and large metal structure would be perfect. To that end, he had made sure that the place was full of any amenities that his doctor might need and was kept clean and in good condition. Now it looked like all the expense and preparations were about to pay dividends.

Nikoli had served in the Russian army, his father had said the discipline would do him good and insisted, but he had never been in any combat. He now imagined, walking past bleeding and groaning men, that this was probably what the aftermath of war looked like. He had gone into that cement factory with twenty good men. He now had four dead, four dying and six that were incapacitated with wounds. All that remained functional had bumps, scrapes, cuts and bruises, but were not badly injured.

Nikoli certainly had other men to call upon, he didn't believe in putting all his eggs in one basket, but these were some of his best. It also depleted his manpower when it came to his criminal empire. That was, his father's criminal empire that he mostly managed.

This might just be enough of a debacle for his father to suspend those management responsibilities. At least temporarily.

He cursed himself for the hundredth time since his humiliating retreat in the factory, although to be fair, it was more the hero who had retreated or run away. Still the damage already inflicted on his men would have made a continued campaign untenable.

They had not even been able to find any samples of the material the hero's suit had been made out of. The only thing they found were a couple of small piles of black dust that one of his men was able to put in a bag. Nothing usable and they had no time to search further. Despite his payoffs and knowledge of the police routes, there was no way the authorities could remain away for long. Large and loud explosions, coming so soon after the bombing of the library, were bound to attract attention.

"We've lost another one." The doctor behind him announced in a sorrowful and nervous tone. "There are still good indications that we will lose at least two more, probably three."

Nikoli nodded but didn't even turn around. He was now more determined than ever to find and eliminate this man in black. This superhero would be super no more.

****

Thomas pounded on Walter's door for the hundredth time. It was now time for more unilateral action. Fortunately, Walter had delivered on his promise and had gotten him a key. Of course, Walter's sense of humor had to be displayed as well, and the key was bright pink with the image of a popular fluffy cat on it. Not something a street-hardened detective wanted to be seen with. Thomas had considered getting a duplicate made and saying goodbye kitty, but he didn't want to offend his new friend, and even he had to admit he laughed every time he took it out and looked at it.

As he made his way inside, everything looked normal. There appeared to be no damage, there was no food on the stove top and the smell was normal. It was not until Thomas made his way back toward Walter's bedroom that things indicated that all was not kosher.

The ceiling in Walter's bedroom and been punched through from the outside. Debris and dust were strewn all over his bed. Even the ceiling fan had been destroyed. He then noticed the blood trail. It led to the closet where Thomas knew the entrance to the secret lair was located.

"Hello!" The detective called down the shaft that descended down to the bedrock hewn basement. He then waited several seconds for the reply he was startled to get.

"Hello!" Came a woman's voice in reply. "Can you help me? I'm trapped."

"Hang on." Thomas was completely confused now. Why would Walter have a woman down there? "I'm coming down."

Walter had still made no provisions for people who couldn't fly to make their way to his hideout. That was why the woman was trapped down a hundred-feet below his modest home. Thomas was aware of this and had taken some precautions.

Thomas ran out to his car and grabbed the rope ladder he had picked up at a survival gear store. He had actually needed to purchase three of them to have enough length to make it down to Walter's cellar.

The descent was hard enough to make Thomas think twice about wanting to ascend the less than stable ladder, and he was covered in sweat and breathing hard by the time he reached the bottom.

Once there he took in the sight before him. Walter was on the floor, laid out flat, with blood and metal pieces all over the place. It looked as if his suit was halfway turned on as large sections of his body were flesh colored, while others were pure black. His chest still rose and fell, indicating that he was still breathing but he was completely unresponsive.

The woman was no one that Thomas recognized, but she looked to be a little worse for wear herself. She had blood smudges on her clothes, which were torn up, a couple of makeshift bandages on an arm and leg, and her hair was extremely tussled.

"And you are?" Thomas began, taking in the female standing before him.

"I am mad as hell, a prisoner, and I want to go home!" She yelled back, stamping her foot for emphasis.

"Somehow I doubt that you are a prisoner. At least not a prisoner here." Thomas quickly corrected. "But I'm guessing, by your accent, that you were a guest of Sergi Grogon recently."

"Do you assume every Russian you meet is a member of the mafia?" She shot back, not denying his assessment.

"No, it is just that given the track record between our hero here and the Russian mob, it was a logical deduction." Thomas then cocked his head at her. "I also didn't hear a denial of my charge. You work for Grogon?"

"I don't work for that Cossack." She spat. "My idiot brother did. They killed him and then told me they would do the same to me if I didn't cooperate. They used me as bait to lure in this fool. Twice!"

"It sounds to me as if this fool." Thomas pointed to his friend on the ground. "Saved your life. Twice!"

"This fool has a name." Came a weak groan from the body on the floor. "I just don't know what it is."

"Are you ok?" Thomas knelt by his friend. "And what the hell are you doing on the floor? You have a couch down here."

"I'm not sure." Walter confessed, rolling over and exposing his protruding manhood through his shot-up shorts. "It's kind of a blur, I don't really remember coming home. But I would assume, even in my semi-conscious state, that I gave the lady the couch."

Thomas quickly grabbed a blanket off the couch and tossed it over Walter's waist and lower extremities.

"It looks like you crashed through your roof and made a quick shot down here." Thomas filled him in. "Then you probably collapsed."

"We were both pretty out of it." He indicated the woman he hadn't even met yet. "The trap they had set did quite a number on the both of us. I had to shield her body from several explosive devices and I had to use my own body to keep her from getting blown apart."

"You should have just left." She grumped. "Saved yourself and come back for Nikoli."

"That's not what heroes do." Walter shook his head at her.

"You could have been killed." A thought then hit Thomas. "Wait those explosions at the cement factory? That was you?"

"Yep."

"They were still pulling bodies out of there this morning." Thomas shook his head. "I hadn't heard any identification on them though. If we can finger them as Nikoli's associates, then we can go after him. At least get our feet in the door."

"I can identify most of them." The woman volunteered. "Or at least get you pointed in the right direction."

"What is your name anyway?" Thomas finally inquired.

"Sasha." She replied a little embarrassed that she didn't volunteer that information before. "Sasha Tupov."

"What about Sasha here getting us the charges we need to go after Gorgon?" Walter jerked a thumb at Sasha. "He kidnapped her and tried to kill her along with me."

"Nobody saw her in captivity but you, and you can't exactly testify. You can also bet that Nikoli is going to have a dozen men that will say it never happened. He's pretty good at hiding the physical evidence when he needs to as well." Thomas was shaking his head. He hated what he was saying, but it was true. "Had the cops rescued her on-site then maybe there might be a chance to make something stick. But now…" He simply shrugged.

Nobody was happy about what Thomas was laying out for them, but they all agreed that it made sense. People like Nikoli didn't become a successful criminal without first learning how to game the system to their benefit.

Walter then tried to get up, staggered and sat down hard on the couch.

"I need food." Walter sighed. "Massive amounts of food. The nanites need to replicate and they need material to heal me."

"Do you think you can fly us upstairs?" Thomas inquired, not really wanting to go up the unstable ladder he had procured.

"Yeah." Walter sighed. "I think I can do it."

A half hour later, Walter was eating a tremendous breakfast, Sasha was taking her first decent shower she had had in a month, and Thomas was on the phone to the captain. Somewhere in all of this the group began to develop the beginnings of a plan.

****

Raknid was disappointed by what he was seeing in the messages that were coming in from the other outposts. Most of them were in worse shape than they were. No supplies, no ships, and the worlds they were stationed at had nothing to offer in terms of food or raw materials. The planets were simply too young to have developed into a stable habitat that would support any kind of population.

At least Earth's moon base had access to small shuttles for supply runs to Earth, and now had access to two long-range supply ships. It was the access to Earth that was actually the greatest benefit now. Earth was a planet of abundant resources. Even though the humans loved to think of their home as overpopulated and resource thin, there was actually enough food to feed everyone many times over. The fact that some countries were starving was more of a transportation problem then it was a production problem.

There was also the possibility of Mars. It was quite possible that they could keep the moon base functional until Mars could be colonized. It was not, he admitted to himself, an idea that had much merit. Humans would progress to the point that they would want Mars long before enough 'terraforming' could be completed to make it habitable for his own species.

That left his species with three basic options. First one was to not do much of anything, simply collect everyone he could from every outpost and let them all live on the moon. Once the hydroponics were up and running they could produce their own food and never have to leave. The problem was, that this would simply be surviving and not living. He could also see the writing on the walls that sooner or later someone would want to use their advanced technology to simply take Earth and kick the humans off the planet or kill them. Raknid would never be able to go along with that as he had simply become too fond of the junior species.

The second option was to move to Earth and try to live in harmony with the humans. There were several areas that were empty enough that Raknid and his compatriots could live out with as much or little contact with the humans as they wished. They might even be able to help Earth out with its energy problems, pollution problems and hunger problems. This would be entirely against the Federation's no contact policy, but as far as Raknid was concerned there was no more Federation.

The third option was to try and colonize one of the planets that had been under observation by his contemporaries. There weren't many options to choose from, but the most promising prospect were ones that they had lost contact with the observers. It was entirely possible that those outposts had been contaminated with the very nanites that they were all trying to avoid.

There was a fourth option, but it wasn't one that Raknid really wanted to entertain. That was loading up the supply ships and taking off in search of a new homeworld. The problem with that option was that the ships they had available were not designed for exploring deep and possibly hostile space. What they had were a couple of short-range shuttles and two mostly automated supply ships. Ships designed to navigate a routine circuit through friendly mapped space.

"What about the fleet?" Blikzak suddenly announced from the doorway of Raknid's office. Startling the commander.

"What was that?" Raknid was embarrassed by both the fact that he had not heard his friend approach and the fact that he had made him jump out of his seat.

"I've known you long enough to know what is on your mind." Blikzak strode in and flopped down on one of Raknid's office chairs. "You're going over our options, and I'm asking if you've considered the fleet. They must have had a large contingent of ships out on maneuvers, they always do, certainly they couldn't have all been affected."

"You are correct in assuming that I had not considered them, so let's weigh the pros and cons of that right now."

"Ok, you start."

"Con, they might try to take Earth by force and relocate us there." Raknid shook his head, as it was not an option he was willing to entertain. "I could do nothing to stop them as they would certainly have officers with them that are higher ranking than myself."

"Pro, they might be able to take back our home world." Blikzak countered. "A force of sufficient strength armed with the knowledge you possess could be just what the doctor ordered."

That thought had shot through Raknid's mind as soon as Blikzak had mentioned the fleet. He was worried that if the combined minds and military of the entire star system had not been enough to wrestle victory, then a small portion of the fleet no matter how sufficient in strength, would most certainly fail and be a waste of resources.

"Con and pro, I would not be in command anymore." Raknid sighed. "And as much as I feel we are doing the right things, I would really like this weight off my shoulders."

"Pro, they could do the exploring that we cannot and possibly find us a new home."

"And that reason right there is why we are going to do it." Raknid nodded. "All the pros and cons weighed in, we have to contact the fleet, warn them about what is going on back home and turn this problem over to people with more experience in these kinds of matters.

"In the meantime, we will continue on with what we have been doing. Trying to find a new home, sneaking supplies from Earth and trying to recover the officers still at the outposts we can reach in time."

"On it boss." Blikzak then placed a file chip on his commander's desk. "That's everything we've been able to glean about the planets under observation. It would seem the Torbid 5, is our best bet, at least as a temporary home.

"It has food, water, a stable atmosphere, a self-sustaining ecology and it has not yet entered the giant lizard phase of its development. The reason it took us so long to decide on it, is that was classified uninhabitable due to the fact that it is incredibly active seismically."

"So we can live there if we want to shake, rattle, and roll." Raknid sighed. "Ok. I'll go over it and make a decision. Regardless of what we decide, we are going to have to make a major supply run to Earth soon. Set some of our guests on getting a list together but I'll want you to coordinate the actual run. You've been down there more often than anyone else. I want your expertise leading the expedition."

"Cool." Blikzak acknowledged. "My first command."

"Just make it a good one." Raknid advised.

****

Memory Foam Download: Subject still has not returned to this unit for rest. No new instructions have been forthcoming. Nothing new to report.

CHAPTER 22

Nikoli was working late in the makeshift laboratory he had quickly thrown together in his home. Something about the black powdery substance his men had recovered from the ill-fated attempt at destroying the hero, made him curious. For one thing, he had known that one of his men had put the powder in a bag, and that bag was placed in a watertight case that had other equipment in it. When the case had been opened later, there was more of the black powder, the bags were gone and some of the equipment looked as if it had been partially eaten away.

Nikoli had not told anyone of the discovery, mostly because he had no idea what was happening. Instead he dug out some old equipment he had not used since college and began a visual analysis of the powder. He was marveling at it as he looked through his microscope the shapes and details of the microscopic robots were clearly visible. The problem was, that they seemed inert. As if they had started to get to work and used the raw materials in the case to start to replicate, but when they failed to receive any stimulating input, they ceased to function. He wondered, if perhaps the energy of the human body was required to keep them running.

He was sitting there, chewing on the end of a pen pondering such things when things suddenly got more interesting.

The crash coming from the other room made him jerk away from his work table. Everyone in the house was asleep but him, so there was no immediate explanation. At least no explanation that didn't involve foul play. Immediately he grabbed his gun, which was always close by and turned to face the door.

The first two people through the door never got a chance to say what was going on. Nikoli simply shot them as they entered. He had rules and codewords for his men if anything untoward was happening just for this very purpose. If they weren't his men, shooting them was the right thing to do. If they *were* his men and couldn't follow his rules, then shooting them was the right thing to do.

The first man through the door and to get perforated was indeed his man, but the knife in his back indicated that he was not operating under his own free will. The man behind him, the one holding the knife in his back, looked to be one of Jimmy Fang's men. Some would say that his assumption that because the man was Asian, assuming he worked for Jimmy Fang might be considered racist. To Nikoli it was simple math, Jimmy controlled the only organization powerful enough to challenge him, so the odds were good that any man coming after him would be from Jimmy's organization. The fact that the man was Asian was just another weight on the scale of evidence.

There was a slight moment of panic as Nikoli worried about his wife and kids, but that passed quickly as he remembered that they were away at her mother's house. The kids were on break and they wanted to spend as much time with grandma as they could. It was obvious that she was not going to be too long of this world, so it was a way of making some memories and saying goodbye.

Nikoli chuckled as he realized the thoughts that were racing through his mind at the moment. Such mundane things keeping him calm when he should be panicking. Still he kept his head level, killed the lights in his lab and peeked around the door the men had just barged through.

Every light was off and there was no sign of movement. Nikoli admired the way his men had been taken out with a single shot being fired to warn him of danger. It was not until his own pulling of the trigger that any lead had been thrown. Now, he was willing to bet that stealth was no longer a concern for his attackers and they would be quick to shoot.

Nikoli briefly considered the window, but it was made of bullet resistant glass and would take precious moments to slide open. Pluses and minuses to everything he supposed.

A thought then struck him and sent a chill down his spine. *Was father being hit at this same moment?* It made sense to him that if Jimmy was making a move against him here, then he would also be making a move against his father. Cutting the head off one snake would not be enough for Jimmy. That would only create a hydra but cut off both heads at the same time and his organization probably wouldn't survive.

He figured that his landline would be out. He would certainly have his men cut the phones if he were attacking someone. Instead he thought about his cell phone, which was currently in his bedroom across the house. It was then that an idea occurred to him.

He reached down and did a quick search of his man and sure enough he had his cell phone on him. He then put his deceased man's finger to the phone home button, but to no avail. The man must have had a code, but no fingerprint activation set up. Nikoli then repeated the same procedure with Jimmy Fang's man and was pleasantly surprised when the phone unlocked.

"Alright." He whispered as he punched in his father's number. Luckily, he was still of the school of thought that a person should have a few important numbers memorized. He saw relying on the phone for all that information as a weakness.

When he received no answer from his father's phone he decided to call the only number that might be able to provide him with the assistance he needed to survive the night. He grimaced, took a breath and dialed nine-one-one.

He had just given the operator his address and uttered the phrase multiple intruders when a volley of shots came flying his direction. He was able to jump behind his heavy desk before getting hit, but he snapped the cellphone in half as he dodged the lethal barrage. Which effectively ended his call.

Nikoli was weighing his options, which were scarce. There was only one way into his office, he had access to three guns but no more magazines, he was facing multiple opponents and had no idea if help was actually on the way or not. There was also the worry that his father was facing the same kind of threat at the moment and there was absolutely nothing he could do about it.

"Nikoli Grogon." A voice called out from the other room.

It took a moment for Nikoli to place the voice, he had only heard it a couple of times, but he was certain that it was the notorious Mister Koi speaking to him.

"Nikoli Grogon, I am well aware that you are in there." Koi informed him from his unseen position in the living room. "Come out and we can finish this quickly and painlessly."

"I think not." Nikoli called back. "I would prefer taking as many of you with me as I can. I hope you don't think less of me for my selfishness."

"Not at all." Koi smiled at the young man's polite brashness. "I look forward to personally sending you to meet your father. Just as my employer has sent your father to await your arrival."

Nikoli's blood boiled at that. It was foolish of him to hope that this was an isolated hit on him, but he harbored just that optimism. It did, however, explain why Jimmy wasn't here to gloat. He was busy doing just that over at his father's house.

Nikoli peeked around the doorframe again and took note of where several of Koi's men were positioned. He then took a quick shot around the corner and ducked back again. The loud grunt he heard as he hit his target was quite satisfying. Not as much as it would have been had it been Koi, but one takes what they can get.

Koi watched his man go down with apparent disinterest. In truth he was carefully controlling his emotions as the man he was sent to kill stubbornly refused to cooperate and die quickly. He knew his time was not unlimited, a fact confirmed by one his men running in to let him know that the police were on the way.

"It would appear, Mister Grogon that our time together must come to an end." He then pulled out a phosphorus grenade and pulled the pin. "Do give your father my regards." He then tossed the grenade into the office and made his way, quickly, toward the front door.

Nikoli's eyes went wide as he recognized the ordinance that Koi had just tossed into his office. He now had two choices, run out and get shot, or stay in and get burned to death. His hesitation made the decision for him and the grenade exploded throwing white-hot gas and burning phosphorous everywhere. Everywhere that the burning material landed immediately burst into flame, including Nikoli.

Nikoli rolled around in a vain attempt to rid his body of the burning material. His screams could be heard clearly over the sounds of the approaching police sirens. He threw himself onto any surface that might provide even a modicum of relief. He rolled across his desk, wallowed on the floor and even clawed at the bulletproof window, all to no avail. The only thing he succeeded in doing was getting the black powder he was analyzing all over him.

Finally, his energy was spent, his consciousness was fleeting, and his destiny seemed certain. It was an odd sensation to know he was about to die. A calm seemed to descend over him, a knowledge that his run was over and there would be nothing more anyone could do to him. It was then that his body went light, his eyes closed, and he fell forward onto his desk.

As his body smashed down onto his workspace it crushed the reading lamp which had somehow avoided all of the destruction. The current that shot through Nikoli from the burning live wires would have added insult to injury had he still been able to feel it. As it was, there was not even the slightest spasm as the current passed through him. His death seemed certain as even the curtain of dreams seemed to flee. He simply laid still and burned.

****

Thomas was on the phone with the captain as Walter was finishing up his second breakfast of the day. Thomas had scarcely left his side for the past two days, and even their new friend Sasha hung around as she seemed to feel safe there.

"Well I don't think Sasha has anything more to fear from Nikoli." Thomas announced as he hung up the phone. "You either for that matter." He finished as he pointed at Walter.

"What happened?" They both asked the detective in unison.

"Although we are loathed to prove it," Thomas sighed in frustration. "It would seem that Jimmy Fang took care of him last night. They dug what was left of a couple of Jimmy's goons out of the charred remains of Nikoli's house. His father's residence was found in similar condition. It now appears that Jimmy Fang is taking over all of the Russian's territory which is a substantial part of the drug trade in the city. Which actually brings me to the original problem I came to see you about before I knew you were recovering from bomb poisoning."

"Which was?"

"The captain is ordering you to stay away from Jimmy Fang. Stay out of Chinatown, stay away from any of his operations, don't even fly over his territory." Thomas pointed at Walter in emphasis. This was not something he could afford any misunderstandings about.

"What's going on?" Walter gave Thomas the eye but didn't protest. He knew he wouldn't be getting these requests if it weren't serious.

Thomas informed every one of the library bombing and explained how Jimmy had planted multiple devices around the city. They were busy searching for them and had located a couple, but until they were all found and disarmed, Walter was going to have to stand down from his crime-fighting activities. At least in those areas controlled by Fang and his crew.

"Ok Thomas," Walter began, shaking his head. "I'm not real keen on being ordered by the captain to do anything, but if it will make things better for you, I'll stay away from those places."

"Thank you." Thomas was relieved. If Walter had said no, there wasn't a lot he could do about it. He certainly didn't have any place that could contain him even if he managed to bring him in. Which was certainly an impossible task.

"What about me?" Sasha inquired speaking up for the first time in a while. "What am I supposed to do?"

"Well, if Nikoli is truly among the dead then I would say you've got nothing to worry about." Thomas shrugged. "Go home, go to work, live a normal happy life."

"We would simply appreciate your discretion on things such as my true identity." Walter threw in.

"And if I refuse?" She eyed the two suspiciously.

The two men simply shrugged in unison.

"Nothing." Thomas replied.

"We can't force you." Walter chuckled. "And wouldn't even if we could. I'm just asking."

"Well not that anyone would believe me anyway." She gave him a crooked smile. "Besides, I believe saving my life has earned you a few favors in my book."

Thomas and Walter were extremely relieved to hear that. Walter's secret getting out could make his life complicated to say the least.

"I only hope I still have a job waiting for me." Sasha sighed. "It was not as if I could call in and say 'I've been kidnapped, can someone cover my shift today?'."

"What is it that you do?" Walter asked.

"I'm a Nurse at Mercy Hospital."

"Well we will try to come up with something." Thomas thought for a moment. "Material witness under protection might be something that they might let you slide for. I'll even tell them that you can't talk about it to avoid any awkward questions."

"I would appreciate the attempt." She smiled at him.

"Ok, now that this is all settled, I've got some work to do." Walter announced. "For my real job, not my crimefighting gig."

"Alright. I'll drop off Sasha at work and talk to her bosses." Thomas got up, quickly followed by Sasha. "I'll see you later."

"Gotcha."

****

Andrew Cumberland had been a morgue employee for almost four years now and he hated it. But the money was good, the odd hours let him attend classes full time and the company was quiet. He also got to see all kinds of interesting, if sometimes disgusting things. He had even got to meet, or at least see, some very famous people as they came in on a slab.

Today had been a busy day and he had been forced to work overtime. Which was fine, as he was on break from school and could always use a couple extra bucks. The problem was the bodies that had been coming in. They stunk. All he had been told was that they had died in a fire, and those were the worst to bring in. They stuck to the bags, they had to be treated as evidence and they smelled terrible.

At the moment he was to prep body number six for autopsy, which was pretty straightforward. Remove him from the bag, then get the other worker to help move him to the gurney and then the table. That was all, no cleaning, no cutting, no hassle. At least that was the theory. But when the body opened its eyes upon

Andrew unzipping the bag, things got a little more interesting. At least they would have, had Andrew not fainted when the body sat up and asked where he was.

Nikoli Grogon never got an answer to his question as the poor boy fainted dead away. But upon looking around he was able to figure it out.

Nikoli watched with curious interest as Andrew fell to the floor. He then started to ponder his own continued existence. He didn't know how or why he was alive, but he was certainly glad he was. Another thing that struck him as odd, was that even though he could clearly see the burns all over his body, he felt no pain. In fact, he felt nothing at all. No heat, no cold, not even the breeze from the fan in the corner. Those were all interesting and presented a mystery he would have to look into sooner or later, but for now he shoved those questions to the back of his mind. He had things to do now that he was certain he was not dead, and questions would only slow him down.

Poor Andrew would have nightmares for months as he woke up, naked, closed in the drawer that had once held the man who had not only put him there, but had stolen his clothes.

****

Raknid came down into the cargo area aghast at what he was seeing. There were cows, chickens, pigs and a couple other creatures that he couldn't readily identify. There were also conveyors with tons of soil, bags of seed and cartons of vegetables.

"Blikzak!" He called out looking for his cohort. "What is going on?"

"Supply run is finished." Blikzak called back from somewhere unseen on the ship. "All we need to do is herd these babies down to the holding area."

"Why did you pick up livestock already?" Raknid was just shaking his head. They were months away from being able to sustain living animals. They had to get the plants growing first.

"I picked up a few tons of feed for them." Blikzak assured his commander.

"But there must be a hundred of them." Raknid was still in awe of the multitude of roaming bovines.

"Two hundred." Blikzak corrected proudly. "Took them right off a plains ranch in a region called…..South…..Dakota, I think."

Raknid sighed, shaking his head.

"We already get blamed for cattle mutilation that their own government is doing." Raknid vented. "Now we're going to add cattle rustling to the charges if we ever get captured."

"Well until then we've got a variety to breed and clone." Blikzak pointed out. "Even if we set up different colonies we'll be able to have a decent gene pool to start with. Better than we have as a species now ourselves."

That was true. Raknid thought. There were only about fifty of them with a possible dozen more on the scattered outposts. No contact had been made with the fleet, so he still had hope for more of his race to have survived, he just didn't know for sure.

"Alright," Raknid conceded. "If you're going to make me say it, I will. Good work."

"Thanks boss." Blikzak beamed.

****

Memory Foam Download: Subject has exhibited a high amount of frustration at restrictions placed upon him by local law enforcement. Although his identity seems intact, his liaison with the constables seems strained. The subject is anxious that his contact within law enforcement will be forced to reveal his secrets rather soon. This will put the subject in a somewhat delicate position.

Although crime fighting does continue, it has become, routine. The main targets of the subject's wrath remain, for the moment, untouchable.

CHAPTER 23

Jimmy paced his office, furious at his friend Mister Koi. It was not like Koi to make such a blunder. Everything else had gone according to plan, then to find out that Nikoli was not at the morgue. There were records of him coming in, but none of him going out. To Jimmy, this meant he must have survived, but was badly injured. If he was alive it could mean a long, drawn-out battle for control, or it could mean that the police had him and were milking him for information. Nikoli certainly knew enough about his own organization to do substantial damage to it. Or he could simply roll over on his own people and have them snatched up before any transfer of power took place.

Contrary to popular belief the mob was not a death before dishonor organization, at least not in the lower tier people. They would switch loyalties in a heartbeat as long as they could continue to reap the benefits of their current position. It was a simple matter of convincing them that Jimmy was now in charge of Grogon's territory. If Nikoli was indeed still alive, that could present a problem.

"How could you have let him get away?" Jimmy demanded of his friend.

"I don't believe I did." Koi replied with a calm that Jimmy found infuriating. There was no denying it, there was not a more unflappable man on the planet then Mister Koi. There was not a single ripple in the man's pond.

"Then how do you explain the lack of a body?"

"I believe that someone wants us to believe that he is alive." Koi was still organizing his thoughts, but knew he had to speak quickly. His boss was not known as a patient man at times. "I threw the grenade that exploded myself and I am certain that there was no way anyone could have survived the explosion and ensuing fire. What I believe happened is that the police identified him and removed records of him from the morgue in order to make us think he is still alive. To keep us looking over our shoulder and away from the direction we should really be fearful of."

"And that is?" Jimmy knew what he was going to say. He knew that Koi wasn't happy with all of his tactics.

"The bombs and the explosions." Koi sighed, knowing this was going to lead to another tirade. "I believe your threats and the destruction of the library was a mistake and will bring the feds down on us."

"You do not believe that it will buy us the operating room we seek?" Jimmy sat back down hard.

"Quite the opposite." Koi confessed. "I believe it will focus agencies on us in the long run. I think they will pretend to back off, and possibly get this hero to back off, but they will return with a vengeance and soon."

"Perhaps we should make some preparations to leave." Jimmy sighed. "I'll see to my son first. He has been released because of his treatments. They do not believe him to be a flight risk as long as he requires such intense therapy. But the facilities back home are just as good, if not better. I'll make sure he is out of the country by the end of the week."

"A prudent precaution." Koi nodded.

"And what will you do, old friend?"

"I hear Rio is nice."

****

It wasn't as if the crimefighting was getting boring, but Walter was feeling a bit sidelined by the restrictions placed on him at the request of the local police. He had taken down petty drug runners, dealers, muggers, robbers and an armored car heist. These were no insubstantial crimes that he had prevented, but what he really wanted to be doing, was going after the people who had destroyed a library in his beloved city.

He was also very annoyed at the thought that by not going after Jimmy Fang, that the city was effectively negotiating with terrorists. He understood the reasoning behind it. The city wanted to find all the bombs and defuse them before making their move. Two more had been found in the past couple days which left eight out there somewhere. Still, a pattern had been identified, so it shouldn't be too much longer now.

Not that Walter was wasting his time. He had been doing things for people and not just fighting crime. He had cleaned up a toxic spill on the Mississippi River, he had dug some irrigation ditches for some of the farmers that he had liberated food from, and he had helped out a rancher in South Dakota that had his herd rustled. That involved a lot of flying around the country, talking to ranchers and getting them all to donate one or two cows apiece. Walter then flew them to South Dakota and gave them to the robbed rancher.

Walter's reward had been some exceedingly delicious BBQ and the need for several showers as cows don't really like to fly. In fact, when forced to fly they indicated their displeasure by exuding fluids from both ends.

All and all, Walter was happy. He would just be happier when he brought Jimmy Fang to justice. Until then, however, he was going to do all that he could to make sure the people of his city were protected.

****

Thomas let Sasha out of his car as he had driven her to work every day since the incident. It was not as if she didn't have a car of her own, but it was parked out at Nikoli's house and she didn't want to go and get it yet. Not that she could, at the moment. The entire area was locked down and was being treated like the crime scene it was.

Thomas didn't mind driving her, as she was nice, it was on the way, and he was beginning to feel that there might be a bit of chemistry brewing between the two. They were both a little exotic to the other, he being African American was not something one saw in Russia very often even today. She, being Russian, bilingual and thickly accented had a flair that was intoxicating to him.

Neither of them had made a move on any thoughts of a relationship yet, but they both knew it was coming. Each one was just waiting for the right time, which Thomas had already decided was right now.

"So what are you doing after work?" He blurted out as she moved to get out of his car.

"I hadn't given it much thought." She admitted. "Since the incident I've been trying to pull overtime to make up some of the wages I lost. But that's not guaranteed so I could be free."

"Dinner?" His eyebrows shot up in hope. "Maybe drinks after?"

"I think I would like that." She smiled and gave him a bit of a hair flick in reply. "Text me this afternoon when I know more, and I'll let you know."

"You got it." He then watched her walk away, admiring the extra little pop she put in her hips as she knew he was watching.

"This is a bad idea." He sighed as he put his car back in drive. "But aren't all the best ones?"

****

Nikoli watched for hours as his wounds seemed to heal right before his eyes. He was beginning to understand what had happened but didn't know exactly how it had happened. Back in his study, he had realized what he was looking at. It was an item prominent in science fiction shows and bad novels, nanotechnology. The microscopic 'dust' that he was looking at in his microscope were actually thousands if not millions of tiny machines. These somehow worked together to give the hero his powers. Evidently, they also would help heal the man as well, as evidenced by the healing he was receiving at the moment.

He had already noticed a greater clarity of vision, he was stronger, and the raspy voice caused by the smoke had cleared up. His pulse no longer raced, his breathing was becoming more regular and his hair was coming back in. He sincerely hoped that all this added up to him being completely healed, and even dared to hope that he would get superpowers himself. Wouldn't it be nice, and convenient to be able to fly? He then smiled a shark's smile as he thought of all of the things he would do to Jimmy Fang if this worked out the way he hoped it would.

****

"Have you made a decision commander?" Blikzak inquired as he stood in his friend's doorway. "I mean Senior commander."

It had been agreed by all the members of the outposts that had been recovered that Raknid would be appointed Senior commander then Captain upon embarking on the resettlement mission. This would avoid any conflicts in seniority of rank since most of the other outposts had been run by commanders as well. This jump over Supreme commander to Captain was unusual to say the least, but so was their situation. Fortunately, all the military regulations actually made provisions for just this kind of promotion situation. The military believed in covering all the bases and this was definitely one that everyone was glad that they had.

They had spent a long time sending the other resupply ship out to gather up the other outposts, but now their ranks had swelled to just over sixty survivors not including the children.

"I have made a decision." Raknid sighed. "We will evacuate the moon base and relocate to planet Torbid 5 where we will begin again. We have an adequate amount of provisions, a decent technology base, and a suitable gene pool."

"And our search for the fleet?" Blikzak was not exactly thrilled with the idea of being an involuntary pioneer, but he really didn't see an alternative either. "I know there has been no answer to any hail, but certainly there must be someone out there."

"If and when we get a significant colony established we can go in search of them." Raknid knew his friend's doubts and shared them. But a decision had to be made, and he would do it. "We'll still have the ships and if we can find enough raw material and processing power, we might just have more. As far as population goes, we have the cloning technology and the traditionalists way of procreation. Between the two, we should be fine."

"Cloning for anything other than a replacement body isn't exactly legal." Blikzak pointed out.

"On which planet?" Raknid shot back with a smile.

"Good point."

CHAPTER 24

Nikoli marveled at how he had healed and how hungry he was all the time. He was smart enough to deduce that his increased appetite was directly related to the healing that was taking place, but that didn't make the procurement of food any easier. He only had the couple of bucks that were in the morgue worker's wallet and was hesitant to use the single debit card the kid had, lest he leave a trail to himself. That left only one real option and it was not one that bothered him to do, but he was concerned that it would alert others to his survival.

A makeshift mask was not difficult to create, a simple piece of cloth found in a donation bin and a little tape. The targets were easy to choose, a gas station, a convenience store and a grocery store were all in close proximity and hitting multiple targets would probably confuse the local law enforcement. Especially if he left no witnesses behind. The problem was the threat. He had no weapon with him with which to make the threat. People didn't just hand you money because you asked, you had to have a device of capital punishment with you to make them comply. Even a good club or knife would work as a device of corporal punishment in a street mugging or fight, and Nikoli had considered mugging as a way to get some quick cash but dismissed it. One could never be sure of their target in a mugging. You could get a lot, or nothing. It was a gamble. The stores represented a bit of certainty.

As it would turn out, fate's fickle charms have an odd way of working out and Nikoli was no exception to that rule.

Nikoli canvased the local convenience store, his first target, carefully. He had already made note of how many people were in the shop and where they were all standing and the best way to approach the cashier. He had made the decision that he would bluff the fact that he had a weapon with him. Most people are so flustered at the thought of facing a gun that they simply take it for granted that you have one. Not to mention, that most businesses have a policy of cooperation. If a man says he has a gun, you treat him as if he has a gun. To aid in his bluff, he had picked up a black piece of metal that had a kind of pistol-like shape to it. The outline in his clothing should aid in his illusion.

Nikoli was about to make his entrance when suddenly a car came screaming into the parking lot and screeched to a halt. Two men quickly exited the vehicle and made a dash into the store. It was obvious that they were there to rob the same store and were going to beat Nikoli to the punch. Infuriated he clenched his fists and cursed his rotten luck. An action that brought to light in interesting ability. Slowly he pulled the metal piece from his pocket and looked it over. He had crushed it. In his anger he had clenched his fists and crushed a solid piece of steel. He hadn't even realized he was doing it when it happened. This gave him an idea.

Nikoli pulled a solid concrete parking post out of the ground and stood by the robber's car patiently waiting for them to egress the establishment. It took only moments for the two thugs to empty the cash register and make a hasty exit. It was obvious that they had pulled this kind of job before and were old hands at it. They did, however, stop short at the sight of the masked man with the concrete post in his hand, standing between them and their vehicle.

"Gentlemen." Nikoli began. "Please turn over your ill-gotten gains and depart. Or don't. I would actually love an excuse for this to become violent."

The two men looked at each other briefly then brought their weapons to bear. They both fired a single shot at the masked man before them only to become completely befuddled when he didn't even flinch.

Nikoli had registered the impact of the bullets but knew that they had not penetrated. He had been shot before and was familiar with how it felt. This was a completely different and entirely welcome sensation.

They were both looking down at their weapons and preparing for another volley when Nikoli acted. With a swing of his concrete club that was a cross between a golf swing and a batter's swing, he sent the two hooligans flying. They impacted the brick wall of the store so hard that they actually became embedded in it. Expanded and flattened they hung there like so many wall mounted bear rugs all over the world, except for these rugs dripped the red blood of their bad choices.

Nikoli then walked over to them and grabbed the money and their pistols. It was then that the convenience store clerk came running out.

"Whoa dude." The young man began, admiring the handiwork. "Great job."

"It was rather satisfying." Nikoli confessed as he tossed the concrete post away.

"Thanks for stopping them and getting the money back." The man continued.

"Oh no. You misunderstand." Nikoli turned to face the kid. "This is my money now. Payment for services rendered."

"Dude, you can't do that." The young man protested. "You're the hero. The hero doesn't get paid."

"Oh my dear boy." Nikoli smiled beneath his mask. "If you're looking for the hero of this story, you need to be looking elsewhere."

With that, Nikoli then shoved the man was launched backward, right through the front window of the store and crashing through several displays. Nikoli then calmly got into the still running vehicle the thugs had arrived in and calmly drove away.

He had no idea whether or not the store clerk was alive or dead and didn't care in the slightest.

****

Blikzak looked at the data coming in from Earth, then he checked it, and then he checked it again. When it came in the exact same way the third time he called over his commander.

"Senior Commander?" Blikzak called out to his longtime friend. "I'm getting some interesting readings from Earth."

"What's going on?" Raknid inquired as he made is way over to his friend's workstation. The duo's relationship had gotten a lot more professional since the arrival of the refugees. They were seldom alone on the command deck anymore.

"I'm getting a second cooperative data stream reading emanating from the planet." Blikzak called up the signal wave indicating what he was talking about and put it on the screen. "It matches the nanites we bonded to that other fella."

"Are you saying that the nanites have replicated down there?" Raknid's mouth fell open at the possible implications. His world had just been destroyed by these things; he wouldn't be able to stand it if his own experiment led to the destruction of Earth.

"Sort of." Blikzak was still trying to make sense of the readings himself. "The ones we bonded to Walter, require a biological host in order to replicate. A transfer is possible I suppose, but it would require that the transfer takes place at the same time the recipient is exposed to a massive amount of power. Good old electrical power to be precise."

"Yes, I remember." Raknid nodded. "The human body, as well as ours I suppose, produces the electrical energy the nanites require to function. It's part of why we, and they, eat so damn much."

"We were able to replicate that energy well enough for our deep space bio-mechanical explorers to function. Actually, replicating the energy was simple, replicating the way it interacted was a pain." Blikzak nearly shuddered at the memory. "It was how we got all these star systems mapped in the first place."

"Wasn't one of those old bio-mechanical ships what crashed in Roswell all those years ago?" Raknid was searching his memory but wasn't finding the necessary confirmation.

"Sure was." Blikzak confirmed. "I still don't know where it came from though. This system shouldn't have had any in it. It had already been mapped. Guess it was a stray that got lost."

"It happens." Raknid then gave a shake and put his mind back on the task at hand. "Anyway, we need to find out who or what has the new nanite signal. See if you can get a lock on it, cross reference with any cameras or satellites in the area and see if you can get a visual."

"I'm on it."

****

Thomas once again let himself into Walter's house. To say he was angry wouldn't be completely correct. It would be more accurate to say that he was preparing to become angry. News of the incident at the convenience store had reached the authorities and they had come to the conclusion that there was only one person that could have performed the feats of strength described by the barely alive clerk and demonstrated on the security cameras.

"Walter?" Thomas called out as he entered. "Are you here?"

"I'm in the bathroom." Came the reply from the back bedroom. "I'll be out in a second."

Thomas simply stood and waited, tapping his foot and trying to prepare himself for the tongue lashing he might have to give and the possibility of taking Walter into custody. Something he was positive he wouldn't be able to do if Walter didn't want to come quietly.

Finally Walter emerged from the back, still wringing his hands from being freshly washed.

"Finished blowing a hole in the toilet?" Thomas asked, attempting to put a little levity before his accusations.

"It is a fortunate thing that whoever designed these things took into account functions that work on instinct. In other words, I have never damaged the porcelain while peeing." He then got a familiar embarrassed look on his face. "Sex took a little bit longer to conquer. My first time, as you know, was damaging, but with a little concentration and practice I am confident I can have relations without killing anyone."

"Funny you should mention killing someone." Thomas sighed and gave Walter a glare. "I'm going to ask you this one time and I need the straight and absolute truth. No games, no lies, and no excuses."

Walter got the serious tone and looked his friend in the eye.

"Ok, you got it."

"Did you kill two men at a convenience store robbery over in Clark last night?" Thomas's voice was firm but touched with regret. "And can you account for your whereabouts at approximately ten O'clock last night?"

"I didn't even go on patrol last night." Walter replied, and watched as relief filled his friend's face. "It was my mother's birthday, so I went to visit her. I didn't get back until after midnight. Several relatives were also in attendance."

"I thought your mother was dead." Thomas eyed him suspiciously.

"She is." Walter confirmed. "We still meet at her grave on her birthday when we can. We then go out for a night of remembrance. My aunt, uncle, and a couple of cousins were there. We took up a corner at a local restaurant and told stories about our time together until the place closed."

"Do you know if they have cameras that can verify that?" Thomas was relieved but was still playing the hard detective. It was his job to get the truth and he would do it the best he could.

"Don't really know." Walter shrugged. "It's not a fancy place, but it's not exactly a dive joint either. I would assume that they have some kind of security. I'll get you the information."

"You do that." Thomas nodded. "And until we get this sorted out, no more patrols. If it wasn't you that killed those men, then there is someone out there with powers like yours. We need to pin it down that it wasn't you and then we can get the focus where it belongs."

"Would my coming into the station help?" Walter wasn't sure that his suggestion was something that he wanted to do, but he was willing.

"I think it might." Thomas agreed. "Show up tonight about eight in your disguise. Sit with the Captain and myself for a while and we'll get this all straightened out."

"Will do."

CHAPTER 25

Nikoli waited outside of the dockside warehouse. One of the ones he knew was controlled by one Jimmy Fang and his boys. One that contained all sorts of contraband items shipped in from Asia. Everything from drugs to fireworks could be found inside which was what made it perfect for a first strike.

Nikoli wasn't sure how to use all of the powers he had seen the man in black demonstrate. He couldn't figure out how to fly or use his supervision, but what he *was* sure of was how to use his super strength and his invulnerability to bullets and even a bit of his super speed. He had seen firsthand how the man in black could not withstand some high explosives and was fairly certain that hand-held rocket launchers would mess him up, but in this particular case, he was unconcerned as he was sure that his opponents would not have such heavy weapons.

When he was certain that the guards inside would be busy gambling away their meager wages and drinking to get over the loss, he started walking toward the warehouse.

There was only a single guard outside, but he was armed and alert. He noticed Nikoli casually walking toward him but didn't recognize him. It was doubtful that someone so far down on the totem pole as this man would know his own boss if he were to walk up, let alone a boss from a rival family.

"You, go away." The guard called out to the approaching man. "We are not giving handouts today."

It was not uncommon for there to be some homeless wandering around the docks. Most were looking for handouts, some were looking for work, and some were looking for drugs. Still, the guard couldn't have the man get too close, it was his job to keep people away and he took it seriously.

"I said stop." The guard repeated louder. "Go away."

Just as the guard was reaching for his gun, Nikoli jetted forward at tremendous speed. His fist punched straight through the man's chest and continued out his back. Nikoli himself was surprised at the power of his impact as he hadn't even been trying to hit the man that hard. To say the man was surprised, looking at the arm penetrating his body, would be a serious understatement.

"Disgusting but effective." Nikoli mused as he stepped over the dead body and continued inside. The locked door providing no barrier at all.

The rest of the night consisted of screams, automatic weapons fire, death, destruction and ended in a crescendo of fire that consumed the warehouse and most of the evidence. Were it not for the body outside of the warehouse that escaped the fire, there would at least be the question of the event being an accident. As it was, with the evidence of a man with his chest punched through his body on the ground, it was easy to deduce that this was no accident and someone of incredible strength was on the prowl.

****

Captain Culpepper didn't know what to make of the all black figure sitting in a chair across from his desk. Walter had simply walked in with Thomas, gone straight to the Captain's office and took a chair.

His stroll through the police station had caused quite a stir, it seemed as though silence descended on the place for the first time in ages. There were a few distrustful looks, a great deal of jealous glances and a few of admiration for the man they all knew had saved two of their own. Rebecca was back at the station, still working a desk, and jumped up to nearly tackle Walter when she wrapped him up in a huge bear hug. She credited him with not only saving her, but her partner as well. Which was something that she valued even more than herself.

Even now, with Walter in the confines of the Captain's sanctuary, the occasional set of eyes could be seen peeking through the blinds, attempting to get a look at the first legitimate superhero they had ever seen.

"Just for the record," Culpepper began, looking at the relaxed figure in the office chair. "How did you get your powers?"

"I am not exactly sure how it all works." Walter began, wondering if he should leave the alien part out of the story and then deciding that he should not. "I was abducted, experimented on, and given this suit. Actually, I was bonded to this suit, as I can't take it off."

"Abducted, as in aliens." Culpepper looked at him dubiously.

Walter then reached out, grabbed the desk and lifted the steel piece of furniture without any effort at all. He then shot a laser from his eyes and warmed the coffee in the captain's mug.

"I can do all this and fly, and everyone seems to have a problem with the alien part." Walter sighed.

"Touché." Culpepper conceded. "So where did these aliens come from, why choose you?"

"They said that they were in a base inside the moon. As for why they chose me, I really have no idea. They gave me some story about an interplanetary defense force choosing me. I really didn't get too much out of them." Walter then thought for a moment about his abduction and what he could remember about his little adventure. "They really didn't seem like they were very experienced at this kind of thing."

"Amateur aliens?" Thomas muttered, from his seat next to Walter which caused him to smile a digital looking grin.

"I'm assuming you don't want to give me your name, but what should I call you?" Culpepper ignored Thomas's comment and pressed on. "The press seems to be leaning toward Emoji-man because of the way the expressions appear on your face like a pixilated emoji."

"Not sure I really care for any of the names the press has hung on me." Walter shrugged. "Especially the somewhat racy ones. But every name I've researched has already been used by a comic book or movie. I don't really know what to call myself. I guess I'm going to have to let you call me Walter."

"Is that your real name?" Culpepper raised an eyebrow.

"It's my middle name." Walter lied. He figured a small detail like that could throw them off for a long while. There were an awful lot of people with the middle name of Walter. He would also lie about where he lived if asked. He would simply say that he had chosen to protect the city, but he didn't live there. If pressed, he would argue that he had to start somewhere.

The captain managed some small talk for quite a while and was actually enjoying it. It wasn't every day that someone got the chance to interview a real-life superhero. As Thomas had called the captain with Walter's alibi, there wasn't much point in discussing what had happened at the convenience store until it was checked out. Culpepper saw no need to alienate the man with an interrogation if there was proof that he was somewhere else at the time of the killings. Instead he simply chose to sit back and enjoy the moment until he could get confirmation. His attitude and enjoyment would turn out to be short-lived as his entire demeanor changed immediately following a telephone call.

"Walter," Culpepper sighed as he hung up the phone. "Were you down by the docks earlier today? Did you mix it up with any of Jimmy Fang's men after we specifically asked you not to?"

"Negative Captain." Walter replied honestly. "I've been with your detective all day."

"That's correct Captain." Thomas nodded enthusiastically. "I haven't let him out of my sight."

"Then someone, who is comparatively strong, just punched a guy in half and set fire to one of Jimmy's warehouses down by the waterfront." Culpepper revealed. "If you're telling the truth, it looks like your alien friends gave their little toys to somebody else besides you."

"I cannot even begin to speak for a couple of kidnapping aliens who conduct unconsented experiments on people." Walter shrugged, his pixelated face changing to a frown. "I honestly have no idea if I was the only one they did this to or not. I mean, I didn't see anybody else, but that doesn't mean that they didn't."

Culpepper nodded and then began to rub his chin.

"Thomas here mentioned that you have a kind of x-ray vision." He had an interesting idea but wasn't sure that it would work. "If you knew what to look for, do you think you could scan the city for the bombs we are looking for?"

"I could certainly try." Walter nodded. "In order for me to do a decent job of it, I would probably have to go pretty slow. It would take me a couple days to grid it out properly and that's assuming that none of the devices are encased in something I can't see through. Like lead."

"I understand. Thomas could you wait outside a second?" The captain then watched as Thomas nodded and stepped out.

Thomas had just enough time to pour himself a cup of coffee before Walter came out from the office.

"What did the captain want?" He inquired with maybe a hint of nervousness.

"First off he wanted to know if I would keep working with you as a kind of liaison with the department. To which I agreed. We even discussed me being deputized in some capacity. I argued against that. If I were deputized, then some of the rules of gathering evidence would apply to me and quite possibly make the city responsible for some of the damage I caused." Walter then looked a little embarrassed. "He then wanted me to settle a bet he had about a certain officer's tattoo. What it was and where it was located."

"Officer Rodriguez." Thomas nodded, indicating a rather shapely uniformed officer over near the corner. He then looked a little shocked and worried. "We have a pool going. You didn't tell him, did you?"

"I told him it would be unethical." Walter sighed, but something in his voice tipped Thomas off.

"You looked, didn't you!"

"I'm only human, and sometimes the powers work out of reflex without any conscious thought." Walter shrugged.

"So what is the tattoo and where is it?" Thomas pressed.

"It's a duck in a sailor suit, on her right butt cheek." Walter smiled sheepishly.

****

Jimmy Fang was steaming, but he currently lacked a target for his anger. That being the case, his underlings were doing anything they could to make themselves scarce. Several had found out the hard way to be somewhere else when their boss was mad. It was always worse when his anger had no direct outlet.

Mister Koi was not so lucky. He was in his friend's presence when the news came in about his warehouse burning down and the death of his men. He had no choice but to remain where he was and work on getting answers to the myriad of questions that were running around his boss's brain.

"That was our contact within the department." Koi revealed as he hung up the phone. "Officially the authorities are calling this an accident. However, evidence suggests that our facility was attacked."

"By that hero no doubt." Jimmy spat, his desire for vengeance reaching a boil.

"Actually, the indication is that the hero in question was in the police station all night at the request of the major crimes captain." Koi wasn't sure what to make of that bit of information himself. Their contact had yet to steer them wrong, so if he said the man was there it was believable. "He could not be the one responsible. Nor were the local authorities to blame, as their tactical divisions were not engaged at the time."

"Some of Grogon's men?" Jimmy was fishing now. There was no way that Koi could know the answer to that, but he could throw out theories to pursue. "Trying to remain loyal and strike back for their boss."

"It is possible that some of Grogon's survivors have been in touch with contacts back in Russia. It would be logical to assume that some of them are trying to secure backing to take over the very operations that we are attempting to gobble up." Koi then had to put on the qualifier that he knew his boss hated. "There is no way for me to know for sure, but I will put out feelers to see what information I can glean."

"Find out what you can and please hurry." Jimmy grumped. "I would hate to bring down another building only to find out that the authorities had nothing to do with it."

Koi weighed his decision not to inform his boss that several of the devices he had planted had been discovered and again decided against telling him. The letter Jimmy had sent to the mayor was vague enough that he might be able to wiggle out of any guilt if the authorities did close in on him. They also still had the terrorist's body on ice and ready to produce in order to throw blame that way if needed. Koi had taken the liberty of coming up with, what he called, option thirteen. It was one more bomb, the largest of the bunch, planted in a busy downtown building. The terrorist's body was kept close to it so if it was required that it be set off, there would be enough genetic material disbursed to be able to put the blame on him. The police would have a hard time arguing that a lowly mobster was to blame for these terrorist acts when there was ample evidence that this terrorist had set off several bombs in other cities before.

Koi did not enjoy the fact that he would be killing hundreds of innocent people if he set off the thirteenth bomb. But one did strange things for friendship, honor and duty. Besides, saving his employer from the wrath of the feds was also a way of saving himself. Although he had no compunction about running if the situation required it, he would have preferred to remain in the city and enjoy the benefits that his wealth provided him.

"Is there anything else Mister Koi?" Jimmy's question brought Koi out of his ruminations and back to the problems at hand.

"No, I shall go and begin making the necessary inquiries." Koi bowed slightly. "With your permission of course."

"Go on old friend. See what you can dig up."

The two then parted, and a much calmer Jimmy Fang got onto the business of running his expanding mob empire.

****

"How long do you suppose it is going to take to get the plant base up to snuff?" Blikzak inquired as the two sat around trying to work out the logistics of their migration.

"At least a couple of months." Raknid sighed. "We've accelerated the process, but in order to get the amount of seed I want to supply both ships, we need to take our time."

"What about all the scout ships we have in the hanger? We're not going to be able to take them all with."

"We'll fit in what we can." Raknid was not happy with the thought of leaving so much equipment behind himself. "We could possibly come back for some of the others if we find a way to fuel the supply ships once we reach our new home."

"It is going to be so strange to be outside for so long." Blikzak mused wistfully. "And in the daylight as well. I haven't been on Earth in the daylight in eons."

"It will take some getting used to." Raknid agreed. "No doubt about it."

"I will miss this little blue planet. But it will be nice to have a place of our own."

"I agree."

Blikzak suddenly decided to change the subject.

"By the way," He began. "I traced that second nanite program wave. We definitely have another person down there bonded to some nanites, and even possibly a third. The last signal is very faint though."

"Any indication of sentience or free will from the nanites?" Raknid was more than a little concerned now. "Anything like what the records indicate happened back home?"

"Nothing like that." Blikzak put his friend's mind at ease. "They have shown some adaptability and the ability to evolve in a limited fashion, but nothing nearing sentience. Their memory and programming are far too simple for that.

"Everything we have seen them do has been within their basic design. Even jump-starting that human was within the ability of what they had designed into them. We had just never seen it used quite that way before."

"You're talking about the way they can be used to direct electrical energy. Ah, what do the humans call it, the Faraday cage feature the suits have to direct energy and protect the user. The shocking of the human was simply a minor modification of the nanites own ability to direct power among themselves." Raknid had deduced the basics based on the information Blikzak had provided. He just needed to get his mind going on that track, and now that he had it all made sense.

"At least we know that the nanites are not spreading at will." Blikzak finally revealed, which put everyone's mind at ease.

"Then do we know how we got more than one person down there with the nano-suits?" Raknid pressed.

"We do not." The admission was a hard one to make, but it was the truth. "All we know is that there has been ample time for the nanites to have spread from person to person and they haven't. I have to classify this new user as a fluke."

"Well let's hope it's just that." Raknid sighed worriedly. "Unlike the nanites from our home world, these require the electrical impulses from the host body to be powered. They go dormant after a few hours if they end up outside of the body and without power.

"The ones from home could be powered by static electricity in the atmosphere. Also, the ones back home were not programmed to put the host's life first as these on Earth are. An oversight which has caused the destruction of our species I'm afraid."

"Near destruction." Blikzak corrected to which he received a nod from his friend.

"I do not think that we need to worry about the same thing happening on Earth that happened to our home." Raknid sighed, relieved.

"I agree." Blikzak concurred. "But do we leave them active when we move on to Torbid 5?"

"I think that we shall." Raknid decided. "This Walter fellow has proven himself worthy. Not to mention that we can always make some trips back this way to check up on the progress of the experiment."

"Very well." Blikzak approved of his commander's decision. "I'll set up the necessary recording devices and make sure we can get proper downloads."

****

Memory Foam Update: Subject has obtained new contacts within local law enforcement and has received a de facto blessing to continue his pursuits in the name of justice.

Subject is experiencing a great amount of anxiety about the possibility of there being another person with his power. Evidence would suggest that before the introduction of his superpowers, the subject was not well versed nor successful in physical confrontations. It is also doubtful that the subject is aware that he now has access to multiple fighting techniques and styles downloaded to him from the nanites. It is this unit's theory that it will take a direct confrontation for that knowledge to be accessed and become reflexive.

CHAPTER 26

Nikoli had had enough of beating around the bush. His first thought was to torture Jimmy Fang by tearing down his organization around him, making him watch as his empire evaporated, then kill everyone he loved, and for a finale, tear the man in half. To his credit that plan had been working exceedingly well. But after the third business he burned to the ground and the cache of Jimmy's crew he had executed, he became impatient with that plan. In his view, it was time for a more direct approach.

Jimmy had never been one for a strict routine. He believed that any kind of regimented lifestyle was too predictable and left one open to attack. There was, however, one thing in his life that he refused to miss, at least as much as was practical, and that was his weekly massage. The stresses in the man's life were plentiful and his time with a beautiful woman working on his body were his heaven on Earth. His hour and a half of muscle work each week was his sacred time and as such he never missed it.

The masseuse had just finished Jimmy's back and arms and was working down his legs when the phone rang, calling her away. That was only the slightest irritation to Jimmy who, when this happened, would simply request and be given extra time.

Jimmy remained calm, relaxed and dreaming of the day when his son was healed and could take up the reigns of the empire he had built. Perhaps then he could retire, get a nice little house in the mountains and maybe even have a couple of full-time massage girls on hand.

"Hello Jimmy." Came an all too familiar voice. A voice that Jimmy shouldn't be hearing.

He slowly raised his head from the table cut out and turned to see his tormentor.

"Nikoli." Jimmy hissed, more in anger about having his massage interrupted than anything else. "I would say it was good to see you, but that would only be if I were looking at your corpse."

"My, the hatred." Nikoli chuckled. "One would think that you were the betrayed business partner."

"You were never my partner."

"We were supposed to go after the man in black together." Nikoli growled. "Share in the risk and reward. Something that was mutually beneficial to both of us. Instead you held back your best men and when my ranks were depleted you turned on me."

"It was a good business decision." Jimmy shrugged. "One I made after I found out you were planning on selling any technology recovered to DARPA or the DOD, or whoever else you thought you could earn a dollar and perhaps some political capital from. So if you are waiting to hear me say I am sorry, you're going to be waiting a long time."

"Oh Jimmy," Nikoli smiled a wolf's smile at the naked man on the table. "You are going to be sorry. So very sorry."

The tremendous crash brought the masseuse running back into the room only to find Jimmy gone and a huge hole where the outside wall used to be. She then ran back to the waiting room to tell Jimmy's bodyguards that he was gone, only to find that vengeance had already been visited upon them. At that point she had no idea what to do, so she did what most people would do, and called the police.

CHAPTER 27

Nikoli paced around his captive as Jimmy sat on a large rock in the middle of an unfamiliar desert. Of course, all deserts were unfamiliar to Jimmy as he had never been to one. It was not a place that he would have considered beautiful or worthy of his precious vacation time. As he looked around, that viewpoint began to change. The red of the rocks, the strata of the cliffs and even the dusty greenery all had a beauty to it that he would not have thought possible. For a moment he even wondered if his captor, Nikoli, saw any of it.

"Are you going to kill me?" Jimmy inquired as he refused to even look at the man stomping around like a pouty child. "Or are you going to leave me in this heat to sunburn to death?"

Jimmy was wrapped in a towel and had on a loose-fitting white robe. It was the only piece of clothing that Nikoli had grabbed for his kidnap victim. Fortunately, Jimmy's cell phone had been in the pocket of that robe, but he had yet to attempt to use it.

Nikoli's response to Jimmy's question was to punch the man in the face. He had learned to control his power a little better, so he didn't end up decapitating the gangster, but to say it was painful was an understatement.

"Oh you will die at my hand." Nikoli sneered in reply. "There should be no doubt on that front. But first I'm going to grant you the thing you wish to see most. The defeat of the man in black."

"Inconceivable." Jimmy spat blood as he replied. "The man in black is every bit as strong as you are. Maybe even more so. I also have yet to see you display the kind of abilities he possesses. Yes, you ran us out here in minutes at speeds I can't even guess at, but he can fly. Something I would be willing to wager that you cannot do."

"I will defeat him." Nikoli assured his rival. "I am an expert in multiple fighting styles. This hero has never fought anyone as skilled with comparable strength. I will break him in half."

"And just how are you going to get him to fight you?" Jimmy shrugged in question. "I don't think getting him to risk a direct confrontation with another super being to save a major criminal is much motivation."

Nikoli stopped short at that. He hadn't considered how to get this hero out to face him. He didn't even know where he was or how to contact the man. He also had precious little to motivate the man to risk his neck in a confrontation.

"If I may make a suggestion." Jimmy began, earning a glare from Nikoli. "If you'll allow me to make a telephone call I believe I can offer a reason for the hero to come and fight you."

"You'll just call your men?" Nikoli growled.

"In fact, I am planning on calling Mister Koi." Jimmy admitted. "But that is no threat to you. I don't know where we are, and even if I did my men wouldn't stand a chance against you. That was why I needed your help with the man in black in the first place."

Jimmy was playing for time, but in the back of his mind was hopeful that he had nothing to lose by helping Nikoli lure the hero to their location. If Nikoli defeated the hero, then he was in no worse shape than he was at the moment. If the hero defeated Nikoli it would be probable that the hero would stay true to form and return him to the city. He might turn him over to investigators, but he was not currently wanted for anything and they would have to let him go.

Nikoli considered this and reached the conclusion that everything Jimmy was saying was true.

"I did not bring a phone." Nikoli finally confessed.

"Fortunately," Jimmy slowly reached into the pocket of his robe and produced his own phone. "I have one along. Where shall I tell the hero to meet us?"

****

Captain Culpepper had called Thomas and Walter to his office to fill them in on the new developments. Both superhero and cop stopped short when they entered the office and saw who was standing there.

"I believe you are both familiar with Mister Koi." Culpepper indicated Jimmy Fang's second in command who calmly stood there with his hands in front of him.

"Although we have never met, we are certainly aware of his reputation and the implications of his work with Jimmy Fang." Thomas nodded to his captain while Koi simply bowed slightly to the two men.

"What is going on?" Walter inquired as he read the worried look on the Captain's face.

"It would seem that sometime during the night, Nikoli Grogon kidnapped Jimmy Fang." Culpepper explained. "I should probably let Mister Koi explain."

"I received a phone call from my employer who informed me that Nikoli has somehow acquired all of your powers." He looked directly at Walter in an attempt to read him but failed to penetrate the mask façade. "He has now kidnapped Mister Fang and has him held hostage in the desert. He says he will kill him unless you agree to go and meet him head-on."

"And why would I be willing to risk my life to save a known gangster from another known gangster?" Walter asked, as he crossed his arms in front of himself.

"I am certain that you are aware that a terrorist has planted several bombs around the city?" Koi waited until he received nods from everyone and then continued. "In the course of being a concerned citizen, Mister Fang learned the location of all of the devices and is prepared to turn over the information to the proper authorities if he is successfully rescued."

"No dice." Culpepper butted in. "The letter we received stated that there were twelve bombs and we found all twelve. Or to be more accurate our hero here found all twelve devices using his supervision. Jimmy has no leverage there."

"In fact, there were thirteen devices." Mister Koi leveled his gaze at the captain to show he wasn't bluffing. "The last one was encased in lead, which is a material that I wager even our hero here cannot see through."

Koi was lying in a manner of speaking. There was a thirteenth device, encased in lead, planted in a building, just as he claimed. But it had been planted by him, not his employer. It also had the body of the terrorist in question in a freezer right next to it. It was his failsafe to try and get his employer off the hook should the feds come after him as the man who planted the bombs. It had now been activated.

"Where is it?" Walter growled, his emoji-like face turning an angry red.

"I will give you the location after the safe return of my employer." Koi replied calmly. "Also, I should point out that the timer on this device is active. It will detonate in three hours if Mister Fang is not produced."

"And where can I find Nikoli?" Walter demanded.

****

It did not take Walter long to fly out to the desert area where Nikoli was waiting. There, just as promised, were Nikoli and Jimmy Fang, waiting in a box canyon.

Walter landed between Nikoli and Jimmy, as gracefully as he was able, and took up as heroic a pose as he could muster. It felt really tacky, but he wanted to put on a confident front and had no idea how to do it.

"You decided to show up after all." Nikoli shook his head. "I must admit I had some doubts about Jimmy's claims."

"I'll be taking Mister Fang with me." Walter announced in a loud steady voice. "He's needed back in the city."

"I do not think that either one of you will be leaving here." Nikoli returned. "Why do you want to save such a low life anyway?"

"Because that's what heroes do." Walter then cocked his head at Nikoli. "Why do you want to fight me so badly?"

"Because that's what villains do." Nikoli spat back. In truth he had been asking himself that same question. He now had the nanites and could try to work out the technology at his leisure. He could still accomplish the same goals. The problem was that he blamed Walter for the downfall of his organization and the death of his father. It was illogical, and he knew it, but that was the way revenge often was.

Nikoli struck first, throwing a massive stone at Walter. Walter then punched it as it got close, splitting it in two and letting it fly to the sides and behind him.

Nikoli then paused for a moment and then pointed behind Walter.

Walter knew he shouldn't take his eyes off his attacker, but curiosity got the better of him and he looked behind him.

"Oh man!" Walter huffed in a giant defeated sigh as he took in what Nikoli was pointing at.

Behind him, on the ground, lay the stone with Jimmy's limbs protruding out from under it and a large red pool coalescing around it. The rock that Walter had just deflected had continued on to land on top of the Mayor of Chinatown. Thus, ended the reign of one of the city's most notorious mobsters.

"I have to admit, that was funny." Nikoli chuckled. Even Walter managed a pixelated smile at the thought that it couldn't have happened to a nicer gangster.

Nikoli then threw another rock at Walter and shot forward to match speed with it. Walter easily deflected the rock but was sent flying by the punch his adversary landed. Walter's chest felt like it was going to cave in at the impact, but he remained intact and able to fight on.

In midair, while still flying from Nikoli's strike, Walter took off straight up. He then dove down at his opponent and landed a strike straight down on top of him. Nikoli was driven deep underground by the impact.

Walter thought for a moment that he might have just been victorious. That feeling fleeted quickly as the ground began to vibrate under his feet. In a moment, Nikoli erupted from the ground and again stood before him. His thrift store clothing shredded by his activities.

"Why are you wearing those clothes?" Walter inquired as he watched Nikoli breathing hard.

"It's what I could get my hands on after escaping the morgue." Nikoli protested. "I did not have access to my money and so this is what I got."

"But why wear anything at all?" Walter pressed as the two opponents slowly circled each other. "Just configure the suit to what you want it to look like."

"You can do that?" Nikoli was impressed.

"Sure, watch." Walter then changed from all black, to all white, then green, then purple with pink polka dots. "It's easy."

"I can't do that." Nikoli admitted. "At least I don't know how. I can't even fly."

"You know that's a refreshing change." Walter sighed. "I've always hated those movies and books where the villain gets the identical power in the eleventh hour and suddenly he knows how to use them expertly even though the hero has been practicing with them for months or years."

"That kind of thing has always bothered me as well." Nikoli confessed.

"Then I'm sure you won't mind if I throw in a little plot twist in that regard." Walter let an emoji smile crawl across his face.

Nikoli gave Walter a curious look, then was suddenly blinded by a flash of light from his nemesis. For a moment, after the light faded, he stood there not understanding what had just happened. It was not until he attempted to move that he discovered he couldn't. It was as if his body wasn't talking to him anymore. He was still contemplating it when the world spun around him, and he found himself looking along the ground, the side of his face pressing against the ground.

Walter looked on in curiosity as Nikoli stood there. He could see the man moving his eyes in an attempt to ascertain what had just happened. He then watched as his opponent's head fell from his shoulders, decapitated by Walter's heat vision, and bounced against the canyon floor.

Walter strode over to Nikoli, and picked up his severed head, just in time to watch his body finally fall to the ground.

"I'm sorry to rob you of the epic battle you had envisioned." Walter apologized. "But you would probably be better than me at hand to hand combat and I've got a city to try and save."

Nikoli's face seemed to dawn in recognition of what had happened. He was able to give the slightest hint of a smile before the life completely faded from him.

Walter then took no chances. He placed Nikoli's head and body in a shallow trench and used his heat vision to incinerate it. He was careful to make sure that none of the nanites that had been bonded to him survived.

After the completion of that grizzly task he took off into the sky and streaked toward the city. There was still a bomb counting down and no mobster to stop it.

****

Walter arrived at the station and ran straight into the captain's office. He found Koi, the Captain and Thomas all waiting for him.

"Captain Culpepper, Mister Koi." Walter greeted. "Nikoli is dead. Unfortunately, he managed to kill Jimmy Fang before I could stop him." He was tactfully leaving out the assistance he played in the killing of Jimmy Fang. After all, it was an accident.

"I'm very sorry to hear that." Mister Koi announced. "I'm afraid that violates our agreement." Koi was angry that his friend of so many years was now dead. If the bomb wouldn't work to get the police to help him, it might just provide enough of a distraction for him to slip away.

"Agreement or no, you're going to give me the location of that bomb." Walter growled, his face becoming an angry emoji-like character.

"I have no motivation to help you." Koi replied. "My employer had located the explosive devices as a service to the city. He has been repaid with his murder at the hands of a vile gangster. Something you did nothing to prevent. I will now take my leave of you."

Walter was consumed by anger. He reached out and snatched the arrogant man and flew with him out the window, leaving a trail of broken glass in his wake. Koi protested and pounded against the hero to no avail as he was taken higher and higher.

"You know, this flying thing is a difficult ability to master." Walter shouted at the man attempting to wrench himself free. "It took me months to figure it out. Especially the landing part. You have considerably less time than I did."

Walter then released Mister Koi and let him fall.

Koi screamed as he realized he was in freefall. The feeling of wind tearing at him while gravity faded away and then returned. He was not all that fond of heights to begin with and now he was sailing through air without any support at all.

"Tell me where the bomb is." Walter yelled.

"Never." Koi spat back in defiance, but it lacked the conviction it should have carried.

"The ground is coming up awful quickly." Walter pointed out. "As I told you, that landing stuff is pretty tough to master."

"I won't…..I Can't." Koi sputtered.

"I think you have about fifteen seconds before you'll be too close to the ground for me to stop you."

"Alright." Koi yelled. "I'll tell you."

Walter snatched Koi back into his arms and pulled up with all his might. He actually ended up going lower than the tops of some trucks as he arrested his downward momentum. Had there been a bus or something underneath them, it would have been quite painful for Mister Koi.

"It's in the service center." Koi yelled out. "Basement level. Center support. If it goes off the entire building will come down."

Walter flew the man back in through the window he had broken and into the captain's office.

"Service center, basement level. Near the center support." Walter informed Thomas and Culpepper. "All we needed to do was step out for a little fresh air and Mister Koi became quite cooperative."

"My God." Culpepper gasped. "That's right next to Jackson Public School. It's going to be going off at just about the right time to catch all of the kids getting out of classes."

"Any chance of disarming it?" Thomas already knew the answer but had to ask.

"Not a good one." Culpepper sighed. "The feds had experts working hours to dismantle the other devices. We've got twenty minutes on this one. I doubt we can even get the bomb squad fully in place in that time."

"You evacuate the building and the school." Walter announced. "I'll see what I can do about getting the bomb technicians there quickly."

Walter carried the bomb squad trucks one at a time to the building where the bomb was located. It only took him four minutes to get the trucks there with him being able to hop over traffic. It actually took the techs longer to grab their gear. The two people that were going in had decided to forgo the usual suits for a bomb defusing. They reasoned that if they were working on a device capable of bringing down a building the protective suit would be useless.

In the time it took Walter to get the bomb techs there, plenty of street cops and firefighters had arrived and were assisting in the evacuation of the school and service building. It was clear that they were not going to get everyone clear in time.

"We have fifteen minutes." Bomb tech number one announced unnecessarily. Her voice was calm, but her heartrate betrayed her anxiety.

"That's not enough time." Her partner mumbled. Still, they took their dutiful places at the device. "Cameras are up and running. So at least they will be able to see what we did wrong."

"This device is different." Tech one spoke mostly to herself, but loud enough for all to hear. "This device is more complicated. And why is it connected to a refrigerator?"

"There's a body in it." Walter informed her, using his x-ray vision to scan the fridge. "I don't know who or why."

"Patsy." Bomb tech number two surmised.

"We can't do it." Number one mumbled. "I can't even get the casings off in fifteen minutes."

"Fourteen."

"Alright," Walter looked at the two police officers. "You two go and take cover. Get clear. I'll see what I can do to contain this."

"Are you sure?" Number one gasped. "Can you survive a blast like that?"

"We'll find out." Walter patted them both on the shoulder and watched as they ran from the room.

"Oh boy." He sighed to himself as he watched the others get clear. "Why am I even doing this."

****

"Raknid, I mean Senior Commander, I need you to come look at this." Blikzak called out to his friend from his command console.

Raknid came running. It had been a long time since he had heard his cohort sound so agitated. He was eager to find out why.

"What is it?"

"It's our subject on Earth." Blikzak informed him as he called up live news broadcasts and put them on the display. "He's trying to stop a building from being blown up or something."

"Can he survive that kind of blast?" Raknid inquired, fairly sure he already knew the answer.

"Not even close." Blikzak sighed. "He might, might be able to at full power, but at half power, not a chance."

"I guess we can only hope that he gets clear in time."

****

Walter had just made the decision to leave and instead of trying to contain or stop the blast, simply use his superspeed to try and make sure everyone got clear. That was when the call came in over the radio that one of the techs had been left behind.

"The elevators have quit working." Came a panicked voice. "We still have people up there. Some are in wheelchairs and there is no way we can get them down. There's too many of them."

Walter did some quick estimates in his head and came to a sad conclusion. Even using his super speed he would not have time to carefully move people, especially injured or disabled ones. He was going to have to stay.

He looked over the bomb for the hundredth time since getting there and still couldn't make any sense of it. He simply wasn't bomb savvy. He did, however, reach the conclusion that there was no reason for him to actually be in the room when the bomb went off. Instead he decided to go help move people for the next ten minutes or so, and then return for the big show. After the bomb went off, he would do what he could to buy time for anyone that hadn't yet gotten clear.

****

Blikzak had gotten the popcorn and a couple of beers for himself and some of the others of his species. It seemed that this ultimate reality show that they had created had ensnared the attention of most of his compatriots. It seemed that all of the survivors had gathered to watch and see if Earth's greatest superhero could save the day.

Raknid had no shortage of displays to show off their creation. Multiple news agencies were broadcasting the events live and they had tapped into the police feed to watch views not available to the general public.

"What do you think he's going to do?" One of the observers whispered loud enough to be heard by all.

"If he's smart, he'll run away and live to fight another day." Another wagered.

"He'll stay." Raknid sighed, fearing he was about to watch the death of Walter Scrum. "He's that kind of hero."

****

Walter had moved a dozen people and a stalled school bus full of kids before he returned to the location of the bomb. It would go off in seconds and there were still people inside. They had gotten lower and would be clear in minutes, but they didn't have minutes.

Walter hovered just outside the building and slightly above the floor with the bomb, waiting for the device to explode. He didn't have to wait long.

When the shockwave hit him, it felt like the punch from Nikoli all over again. His ears rung, and he could feel his eyes watering. A wave of nausea swept over him, but he controlled himself. He had no time to be sick or incapacitated.

The blast had barely had time to finish and debris was still flying when Walter rushed back inside to the main support beam. He could see it starting to crumble and knew what he needed to do. The problem was that he knew he couldn't do it and it would more than likely mean the ultimate sacrifice.

"AAARRRRGGGG." Walter grunted as he positioned himself under the collapsing beam. He then lifted with all his strength, trying to stabilize the building and halt, or at least slow, its collapse.

One of the police cameras had miraculously survived the explosion and was filming Walter's heroic attempt. Culpepper noticed the feed and switched it to public so that the news could broadcast the hero in action.

Walter could feel the building pressing down. His knees were buckling and his back ached. He knew he couldn't last much longer but he could still hear the screams of those trying to get out. He couldn't abandon his post. He had to keep going.

****

"He's not going to make it." Raknid sighed as he watched the feed on the main monitor. "That building is going to crush him."

"Maybe not." Blikzak handed his superior a reader with Walter's vitals on it. "Look at the suit's power level?"

"Did you do this?" Raknid gasped.

"No." Blikzak shook his head. "The suit is doing it on its own. It's trying to protect him."

"Amazing."

****

Alex Wynn was squinting hard at the hole in the building, when his cameraman handed him a pair of binoculars. He focused quickly and was able to penetrate just enough dust and deep enough into the building to make out the one known as Emoji-man as he heroically attempted to keep the building up long enough for everyone to get out.

Alex could see the strain even without being able to make out any features and could tell that the hero was being taxed beyond his ability. Still he stayed and was successful.

Everyone including the impartial reporter cheered as the announcement came that the building was clear. Those cheers soon turned to screams of horror. Alex was left wondering if he was going to be able to write the best work of his career about the heroic stand of the city's own superhero, or was he going to have to write the greatest obituary in history. Only time would tell.

****

Walter was about spent. The ceiling was beginning to sag and pressing down on him. Sweat poured from his body and every cell seemed to be screaming out in pain. It was then that he felt it. A sudden burst of power flowed through him as his suit reset itself to the highest level. The nanites had recognized the danger to Walter and others and had increased their power themselves.

Walter doubled his efforts and grunted in pain as he pushed again at the ceiling support and raised it back into position. He wasn't sure how long he could hold it. The building was beginning to come apart despite his securing the central support. There was no way he could stop it, he could only hope to slow it down.

"We're clear." Came shouts over the radio. "Everyone is clear. The building check is complete."

Walter could clearly make out cheers from the crowd as the announcement was picked up and circulated.

"Just in time." Walter sighed.

Now came the problem of extricating himself from the mess he was in. He would have to release the central support, maneuver past all of the falling debris and get clear before the building came down on him. He wouldn't make it.

As he was calculating the best route to take out of the structure the main support snapped and separated. Walter was left holding only a fraction of the support and the rest came down around him. Tons of debris rained down on him, dust flew obscuring him from view and his view of the outside world.

At least they got out. Walter thought as the building pressed down on him. He had just enough time to hear the screams of the crowd, as the horror of watching the death of their hero sank in, before his consciousness fled.

CHAPTER 28

Captain Culpepper stood over the site of the demolished building barking orders he had no authority to give, at anyone that would listen. The crime scene was no longer his and rescue efforts had been fruitless so far.

"Dammit people there is still a man down there." He barked for the thousandth time. "A man who might have given his life to save countless others. I want him out of there."

Thomas shook his head in wonder every time he saw his captain there. The man had a serious case of hero worship, but who could blame him? Thomas had been Walter's friend and partner. He knew the man. He had watched a simple, average, white-collar worker become the Earth's first superhero. He had witnessed his transformation into a god-like creature and yet remain humble and capable of great self-sacrifice. The ultimate self-sacrifice as it would appear. It had been three days since the building came down and there had been no signs of life from under the rubble.

****

Blikzak and Raknid had been watching the fracas around the collapsed building for days. Now the search was finally winding down and people were beginning to disperse. At least they had suspended sifting through rubble during the hours of darkness, which gave the aliens a window in which to act.

"Looks like everyone is gone except for a couple of security guards." Blikzak announced as he looked at the scanners on their heavily stealthed recon ship. "This would seem to be the best window that we are going to get."

"Are you still locked onto the nanites energy signature?" Raknid asked, knowing full well that they were.

"Yes. And I have the tractor beam standing by to move the debris."

"We are going to be visible while we are recovering the subject." Raknid sighed. "I guess it can't be helped though. We'll be the subject of another online video and conspiracy theory."

"Happens all the time." Blikzak sighed. "Thank goodness for CGI. Nobody believes the alien evidence anymore."

"Alright, activate the beams." Raknid commanded. "Let's bring our boy home."

The security guards were left breathless as the large alien ship suddenly appeared over the demolished building. One simply ran away while the others got out their phones to record what no one was going to believe.

They then watched as bright beams shot out from the ship and started manipulating the debris. Rubble and beams shifted, furniture fell away, and enough dust flew to eventually obscure the ship from view.

Unseen by all was the lifting of Walter's body and its floating up into the alien ship.

"We've got him." Blikzak announced, slowly shutting down the tractor beams and letting the debris settle back down to the ground.

"Understood." Raknid then punched a number of controls, reactivated the ship's stealth mode and set a fast course for the moon. "ETA back to base fifteen minutes."

"We've got to stop using Earth units of measurement." Blikzak shook his head. "Tens, everything should be based on tens. Math, weight, distance and time. Just like home."

"Guess we've just been here too long." Raknid was a little saddened by the fact that they would soon be leaving their posts for their new home. They had been the longest observers to ever have been left at an outpost and it showed. Now they might just be the last hope for their species.

****

Walter woke up gasping for breath, naked on a familiar white table in an all-white room. Unlike the last time there were no restraints to hold him in place and the aliens he could see no longer frightened him.

"Ah sleeping beauty awakes." Blikzak announced as Walter sat up.

"Really?" Raknid shook his head. "Are you going to say that every time?"

Blikzak just shrugged in response.

"What the hell happened?" Walter groaned, his body still protesting from the treatment he had subjected it to.

"You tried to hold up a building." Raknid informed him. "It didn't work."

"I remember." He then focused on his two benefactors. "I take it I owe you a debt of gratitude for saving me from the rubble?"

"The suit kept you alive, but the rubble was too much for even you to lift." Blikzak joined in. "You simply had no leverage to get it off of you. We removed you from the debris and brought you here, to the moon. We have recharged the nanites, which were draining your body at an alarming rate. Had we been much later they would have run out of power and you would have been crushed."

"Thank you." Walter nodded to each of them. "Thank you very much."

"You are most welcome." Raknid nodded back. "You have been the most entertaining experiment we have conducted in a long time."

"Good to know." Walter grumped. "I would like to believe that I accomplished something better than just being entertaining."

"I believe you have had a positive impact on your planet." Raknid agreed. "The question is, would you like to continue it?"

"I don't understand."

"We are leaving." A statement that made Walter's mouth fall open. Raknid then went on to describe the destruction of his own world and how they were now leaving the moon base to colonize another planet. "The question I have for you is, do you want to continue to have these powers or do you want us to remove the nanites from your body?"

Walter nearly jumped at an answer but stopped himself. This was something he really had to think long and hard about. There were great advantages that came with the nanites but there were also great responsibilities to go along with them. A normal life might just be the very thing he wanted, more than he desired the power and possible isolation that came with the suit.

In the end Walter decided to keep the powers and the risks that came with them.

"Well in that case I will add one more feature to the nanites." Raknid announced. "The ability to maneuver and survive in space. You're going to need it."

"Need it?" Walter repeated in question. "Why?"

"How else are you going to keep an eye on our moon base for us?" Raknid attempted to wink at Walter, but found he wasn't very good at it. "We will be leaving behind a few scout ships and the like, but the ability to fly in space will just simplify things so much."

"You guys want me to keep an eye on your base?" Walter was stunned. "It would be an honor."

"Blikzak will give you a crash course on the necessary systems and how to keep up on the place." Raknid informed him. "There is really not much to it. We'll also leave instructions on recharging the nanites should you run into any problems with fueling them from your own body. Now that they are at full power they will require enormous amounts of energy from you."

"As if I wasn't buying enough groceries already." Walter shook his head. This was going to require flying around to other parts of the country to purchase food as to throw off suspicion about who he was.

"By the way," Blikzak jumped in. "Congratulations on defeating your very first supervillain. It was quite the show. We downloaded the entire event from your mind while you were unconscious. Nice move."

"Thanks." Walter shrugged. "It was kind of a bittersweet moment. On the one hand it was nice to have someone that I had something in common with. On the other hand, it was a necessity that I put down someone that evil, who would only use the powers for crime and profit."

"Yeah," Blikzak looked away for a moment. "About that. You might not be as alone as you think."

****

Thomas rolled out of bed and flipped on the television. He then chuckled as he saw the lead story was about how workers at the collapsed service center had witnessed an alien ship digging through the wreckage. A glimmer of hope flashed in the back of his mind, but he firmly decided not to get his hopes up to high.

He then checked his phone and saw the ambiguous text from Sasha. It was clear by how she had acted on their last date that this wasn't going to be working out. Still it had been nice while it lasted. Three whole dates worth, which he reflected was two more than he usually got.

He stretched and started walking toward the bathroom for the morning rituals decades in the making. After he had relieved himself he stood in front of his mirror and reflected on what he saw. Not old, not young, not wise, not stupid, just a misplaced beat cop trying to figure things out. It made him laugh out loud.

He then grabbed his toothpaste and attempted to squeeze it out onto his toothbrush. His eyes went wide as he effortlessly squashed the tube and ejected the contents all over his bathroom mirror.

As he stood there considering the fluke he had just performed an odd thought struck him. *Why the hell am I so hungry?*

THE END

AUTHOR'S NOTE

As the author I realize that many people will try to point out that Thomas was exposed to the nanites much earlier than Nikoli and he should have exhibited powers much sooner. I point out that the transfer to Thomas happened when his heart was restarted by Walter in the restaurant. The transfer of nanites was much smaller than the transfer to Nikoli. Nikoli was covered with nanite dust when he came into contact with the bare wire from the lamp, which gave him the power boost needed to activate the nanites. So he developed powers much quicker than Thomas did.

I also envisioned the reporter having a much larger part in this story, but it just didn't flow and ended up getting cut. Perhaps if there is a sequel Alex will get a bigger part.

AUTHOR'S EXPLANATION

This story came about as a challenge. Another author, Fleur Lind, decided to challenge me that I couldn't write a story combining aliens, superheroes, and make a pillow a major feature in the story. Thus this story, originally titled MEMORY FOAM was born. Upon completion of the work I decided that the title wouldn't grab an audience the way I originally thought it would, so the name was changed to NOT QUITE SUPER.

It might be of interest to note that this work was never intended to become a novel. It was supposed to be a cute little short story of approximately twenty-thousand-words. It just kept growing and just like Walter, soon got too powerful to control.

Made in the USA
Middletown, DE
29 August 2023